Managing the Matthews

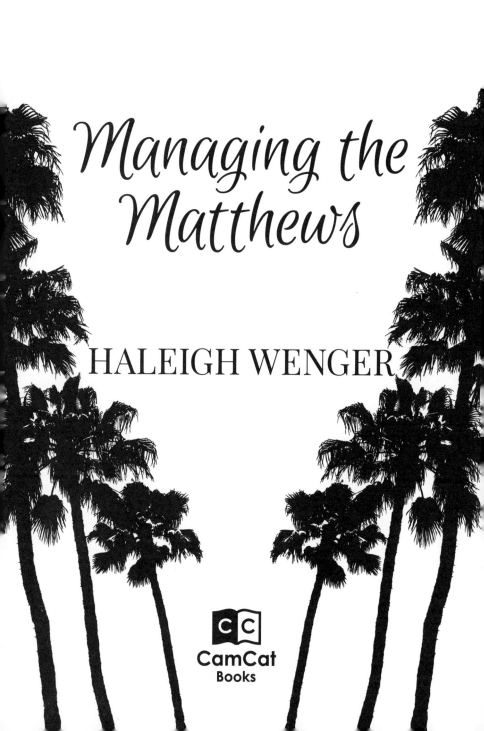

Managing the Matthews

HALEIGH WENGER

CamCat
Books

CamCat Publishing, LLC
Ft. Collins, Colorado 80524
camcatpublishing.com

Paperback ISBN 9780744300116
Large-Print Paperback ISBN 9780744309126
eBook ISBN 9780744310009
Audiobook ISBN 9780744309140

Library of Congress Control Number: 2022950659

Cover design by Laura Duffy
Book design by Maryann Appel

5   3   1   2   4

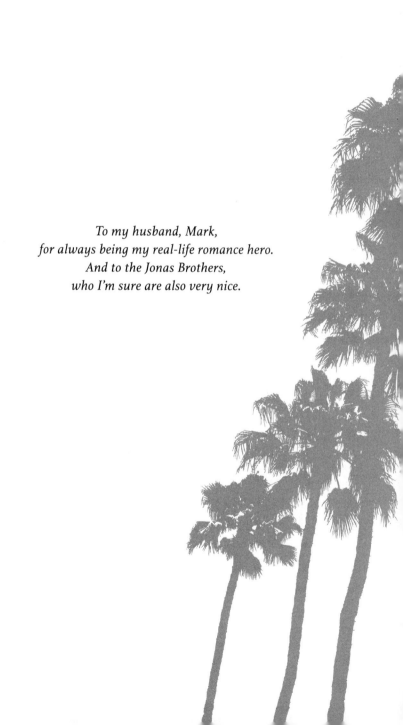

To my husband, Mark,
for always being my real-life romance hero.
And to the Jonas Brothers,
who I'm sure are also very nice.

CHAPTER ONE

❀ ❀ ❀ ❀ ❀

Kell

*B*eing the manager for a trio of hot celebrity brothers sounds amazing until you're the one thing standing in the way of their sleep.

Between the three of them—Ash, Jonah, and Ryan—I don't get days off. Someone always ends up needing to be on set at eight a.m. sharp, no matter the day. Never mind that wake-up calls are most definitely not in my job description.

Today, I have the unparalleled pleasure of knocking loudly on Ash Matthew's bedroom door, waiting outside of it for an appropriate amount of time, and then beating on the door some more. It's a blast. "Ashley! I know you're in there! You have a photoshoot in fifteen! Fifteen min-utes!"

There's not a single sound from inside his room. When yelling doesn't work, I pull my cell phone from my purse and call him over and over and over. He doesn't answer. Instead, a banging sound comes from inside his bedroom and the door swings open.

Ash looks me over through half-open eyes and then flops back onto the enormous California King in the center of his room. I toss my phone back into the bag on my arm and follow him in. "I don't have work today," he says, his words obscured by the pillow he's planted his face into. His dark brown hair splays out to the sides, curling slightly at the ends. I tried to talk him into a haircut a few months ago, but it turns out he was right. Annoying, but right, that the longer hair suits him.

I put a hand on my hip. "You do have work."

Despite the text I received at two a.m. letting me know that he didn't think he'd make it in, I'm not letting Ash off this easily. As his manager, it's my job to keep on top of him about these kinds of things.

He grumbles something else unintelligible into his pillow. I sigh and lower myself to his bed, swaying slightly at the too-soft mattress underneath me. "You're contracted. The movie is almost done. Just promo and then you're off the hook for this one. And, come on, it wasn't that bad. From what I saw of it, there were some really funny scenes."

Ash lifts his head and glares at me, daring me to keep going with the lie. "I want out. I don't want to be the romance guy anymore. Not for movies like this."

"What if I promise to buy you pizza afterward?"

He scoffs. "Bribery doesn't work on me anymore. I can buy my own pizza."

I nudge his foot with my hand, but he swats at me. "It's not gonna happen. I'm not doing the photo shoot."

The dejection in his voice hits me, stalling me for a quick second. It sounds like he needs a vacation. I'll have to check his calendar. Ash and I were friends in college, and when he told me that he was going into acting, it felt like fate: platonic, career-oriented fate. I was nearly done with my public relations degree and had a healthy obsession with Hollywood. He got cast in a handful of quirky indie films, one of them took off, and he's scored half a dozen romantic comedy roles since then. But lately, something has shifted, and more and more often I find myself here, trying to talk him into putting on pants and getting his ass to work.

Things were simpler before fame.

I flip open my phone and scroll through the online calendar while I talk. "I don't know what to tell you, Ash. Ryan does action movies, you do romantic comedies, and Jonah does sports. I can put feelers out for more serious auditions, but for now—you signed the contract. You have to finish this out."

"You'll tell people I'm looking for different stuff?" He arches an eyebrow. He rolls to sitting and leans forward to balance on the edge of the bed. His gray eyes, just the tiniest tinge of blue at the edges, study me.

None of the producers we work with will be very happy with me, but I'll let them know. I'm not going to make him lose himself over movies he hates. When we first decided to work together, we agreed: friendship before business. It may not be a motto that works for everyone, but it's always served us well.

"Fine." He winces. "But I already told them I'm pulling out. I can't go to any more promo for this. It's humiliating."

I'm too late. "You already told them? You're supposed to leave the communicating to me. I could have . . ." I trail off at the look on his face.

Whatever. It's just one more Matthew mess to clean up. "Don't worry about it. I'll deal with it." I fake an unaffected shrug as I smooth one hand over his crumpled bed sheets. I bend to pick up a stray protein bar wrapper on the floor near my feet. There's no point in getting mad when I can get the other thing I came here for: information. "Tell me about last night. How did it go?"

"You should have been there."

I arch an eyebrow, smelling a tragedy. There's something about the way he says it: You *should have* been there because it is my job to know, after all. "What? What happened?"

Ash runs a hand over his face, messing up his hair even further. It only adds to his sex appeal, and I make a mental note to get him a new set of headshots featuring this longer, messier hairstyle. It'll kill with the casting directors, even the new ones he's looking to pursue.

He groans. "It's bad. You shouldn't hear it from me."

I almost stomp my foot with impatience. If it's as bad as his voice makes it sound, I'm surprised I haven't heard it already, no matter the early hour. "I need to hear it, period. I don't care who it comes from at this point. I'm here now, so spill." With every emergency comes a seemingly never-ending cycle of damage control, and if I've learned anything in the past five years of managing the brothers, it's that the sooner I start on fixing their mistakes, the better.

"Talk to Ryan." Ash finally meets my eyes, and I see something there I don't expect. Is that . . . pity?

Ryan's name kicks my chest into double-time, and I slap a palm over my sternum. Great. Just, honestly, great. Sure, I suspected that he was involved the moment Ash said something, but to have it confirmed sets my stomach on edge.

I grit my teeth. "Ash. Please. You're killing me here."

"We were out at the bar last night. After the fan meet and greet, remember?"

I nod. I remember because I was the one who facilitated the entire thing. Except, thanks to a major guilt trip on my parents' part, I couldn't be there. Instead, I spent the day with my GI doctor and the night hosting my visiting-from-out-of-town parents before they caught a late flight. I was forced to listen to Mom bemoan the fact that I work too much for the hundredth time.

"Ryan spent all night with this one fangirl. She was sitting in his lap, and they were all over each other. Out of nowhere, he proposed.

It was bizarre. I've never seen him act like that. I don't even think he'd had that many drinks. It was like he pulled a diamond ring from thin air."

I flinch but cover it as I stand. Maybe we can work out a deal if Ryan agrees to let her keep the ring. I lick my lips and half turn, nodding. "Thanks for the heads up. I'll go find the girl and take care of this. We probably should keep Ryan away from fans for the next few weeks, or they'll all be expecting proposals."

Ryan has done worse, like the bloody bar fight he got into with a fan's husband last month. I'm not supposed to get my feelings hurt about him going out and doing things like this. Still, as his manager, it's a nuisance.

But as just me, Kell, it feels like a betrayal.

Ash doesn't laugh at my dumb attempt at humor. The space between his eyebrows furrows, forming a sharp V. "I doubt they will. Now that, you know, he's engaged and all."

The room freezes around us. "What do you mean?"

Ash gives his head a slow shake. "I told you. He proposed to this girl at the thing last night. Which means . . . Ryan is engaged. He says they're getting married. Having an actual wedding. The whole big thing. He seems serious for once."

"Serious about some woman? Who even is she?" My body flushes hot and then cold as a mixture of emotions hits me at once. I stutter but nothing comes out. I'm completely out of words.

"Just some fan who he's been out with a few times. I don't think anyone saw this coming."

A hysterical laugh nearly chokes out of me. "This is ridiculous. Ryan wouldn't . . . Ryan's not . . ."

"I'm sorry, Kell." Ash's voice is soft but out of focus. "I don't know what he's thinking. But yeah, it seems real."

"How could it be real?" Somehow, I find the doorknob, and I prop myself up on it with one hand. I thought that this was another one of Ryan's stunts. He does over-the-top public displays and then sends me in to clean up the ensuing chaos. None of the tabloid-worthy escapades are real, though. Not wedding-planning real.

The floor spins beneath me as I try to gather my thoughts because this can't be happening. Ryan getting engaged without so much as a heads up is a PR nightmare, but I will deal with it because I have no other choice.

Normally, I can deal with anything. But with Ryan, things are different, and there's no way I'm letting him do this without having a serious conversation for once. Given our history, it's way overdue.

CHAPTER TWO

❁ ❁ ❁ ❁ ❁

Ash

*A*fter Kell leaves, I crawl from bed and look at my phone. It really sucked having to be the one to tell her about Ryan. Especially since I don't think I'm supposed to know, but—I know.

Kell isn't exactly subtle. Not about the way she gapes at my brother. I knew even before I walked in on them getting hot and heavy a few weeks back. Unfortunately, I've known for years. Never worried about it because I thought we had an unspoken agreement that Kell was off-limits. She's our manager, for crying out loud. But my brother wouldn't understand that. Nothing is off-limits to Ryan.

Seeing them together was something. Believe me, I *still* wish I could purge it from my mind. We'd just gotten back from going out to dinner. It was all of us, which is rare. Jonah took a call and started spouting football stats into the phone. I took a shower to scrub off the makeup they caked on me during filming. And Ryan and Kell stayed behind in the living room. Not out of the ordinary since Kell is the one we all go to when we need someone to talk to. Just how it's always been. I figured that Ryan wanted to whine about his latest career drama. I came back to them sucking each other's faces off. I'd never wanted to un-see something so badly.

And now he's engaged to some fan he's met a handful of times. I could see right away that it hit Kell. But it's also none of my business.

I get out of bed and practically sleepwalk into the kitchen. Hunger wins out, or else I'd stay in my room all day since I don't have work. Might never work again after the way I blew off movie promo. I'm just about to open the fridge and stare at the contents when someone dashes past me. I turn just in time to see a flash of Kell's light brown hair swinging behind her. Her head is ducked and her face not visible, but I can tell from the sounds that she's crying. The back door bangs shut.

Damn it.

I slap a palm against the cool stainless steel of the fridge door. And then I go find Ryan. He's lounging on our leather couch, his legs outstretched and spread wide. He's not wearing a shirt.

"What did you say to her?"

He turns his head slowly to face me, his eyes wide. Oh yeah, here comes Ryan Matthew's famous innocent act. "What are you talking about? You mean Kell? I think she's stressed out, man. I didn't do anything. I didn't say a word."

He's serious. The three competing brain cells he's got left wouldn't see anything wrong with that, would they? Kell would though. Him ignoring her is the whole issue.

I glare at him until he scowls back and asks, "You got a problem, bro?"

Yeah, I have a problem. "The problem is you. You messed things up with Kell. Now you need to go fix it." I point to the door she rushed through seconds ago. She's most likely still outside trying not to cry. I've only seen her cry a handful of times in the years I've known her.

She's tough. Too tough to care about my boneheaded brother, but here we are.

Ryan gives me a cool look. "Lay off, man. Kell's a grown-up. She knew what the deal was. I never promised her anything."

My finger is still outstretched so I step closer and jab it into his chest. "Go. Talk. To. Her. Now." I'm dangerously close to doing more than poking him. Maybe he can sense it because for once Ryan gives in. If I had to guess, I'd say it's the guilt. He knows what he did.

He holds up his hands. "Okay. We'll talk. Calm down, Hulk." Ryan laughs, knowing his use of my childhood nickname is the perfect revenge. I was a chubby kid with a propensity for temper tantrums. Call yourself the Hulk once and your older brother will never let you live it down.

I follow him to the back door. Slam it shut behind him before walking to the kitchen. On the counter I find a paper bag. The outside is labeled *muffins* in curly handwriting. Kell. I open it and am hit by the smell of warm blueberries.

Exhibit A in my reasoning of why she is too good for us. There's no polite way to tell her that she has to stop taking care of everyone in this house. No way that won't hurt her feelings. I reach for a muffin and stuff it into my mouth, sighing around the warm, buttery goodness. I'm going to kill my brother.

The back door swings open and Kell bursts in followed by Ryan. Her face is the shade of a tomato.

"Kell—"

Ryan reaches for her like he might try to hug her. But he stops short and pats her shoulder instead.

I should disappear or give them some space. Can't bring myself to do either, so I just stand here as an unwitting witness to their drama once again.

She sniffs and looks up at him with watery eyes. "Please just tell me that this is some kind of stupid prank."

Ryan winces. His head ducks down. "You'd really like Samantha. I've already told her all about you."

"Samantha." Her mouth forms silently around the name. "I don't understand how this happened. When did you even meet her?"

It can't have been very long. They kissed sometime last month. Or maybe it was more than a kiss. I left as soon as I saw them on the couch. Whatever it was clearly led Kell to think something was happening.

Ryan glances at me like I'm supposed to help him. No way in hell am I getting involved in this. I have my brother's back, but I draw the line at relationships. Especially when we both know he's in the wrong.

"I don't know. A few weeks." He scratches his chin. "I think it was a month ago."

The look on Kell's face says it all. She makes a small choking noise and shakes her head. "I—I can't do this right now."

She pivots and turns down the hall, where the front door slams shut seconds later.

Ryan sighs. "You happy?"

I set down the last bite of my muffin and resist the urge to throw it at him. "No."

"Are you jealous or something? If you wanted to go for Kell you should have told me." He cracks a half smile. "All those romantic movies are turning you soft."

I grit my teeth so hard Ryan can probably hear the sound of bone on bone. Exactly the reaction he wants from me. "And you're a jerk. Maybe all *your* movies are messing with your head. No one thinks you're James Bond in real life. It's not cool to play with people's feelings like this." If Dad were still alive, he'd lay into Ryan. But maybe he'd do the same to me. I haven't been doing so hot lately either.

Ryan scoffs and reaches around me for a muffin. "Relax. Kell will get over it. It's not like we were actually dating." He stalks back to his spot on the couch with his muffin. "Blueberry. My fave."

Ryan is either oblivious or heartless. Not sure which would be better. It makes hanging out with him that much harder when he's like this. What I should do is go find Kell and talk her down myself. But if I were her, I wouldn't want to see a Matthew brother face for at least a few good hours. Instead, I take a shower and get ready for the day. Then I wander down the long hall to Jonah's side of the house. As often as we piss each other off, I guess it says something that we all choose to live together.

Those movies I've grown sick of making pay well enough that I could have my own house far away from Ryan's exploits. Hell, I could probably have my own street. But there's something about living with both of my brothers that grounds me. I feel more like Ashley Matthew, middle child, than Ash Matthew, movie star. Not exactly great for my ego, but that's the point.

I knock once on his closed bedroom door. "It's Ash."

He's wearing gray sweatpants and a UCLA hoodie, but his muscles still show through. All the hours Ryan and I spend sleeping in, our youngest brother uses at the home gym set up in his spare bedroom. "Hey." He notices me looking around. "Jessie's at work."

I nod. His live-in girlfriend is often either gone at work or gone because they're in a fight. "So Ryan is going through with the engagement thing, apparently. Kell's upset." I don't say any more because I haven't told anyone, not even Jonah, about seeing Kell and Ryan together.

"I thought she might be," Jonah says thoughtfully. His phone buzzes and he picks it up. While he looks at the notification on his screen, my phone buzzes too.

A group text from Kell.

Kell: *Emergency meeting tonight at your place, seven. Someone order pizza.*

This has to be about Ryan. And based on how upset she was, it can only mean one thing. One thing I'm worried about anyway.

"You don't think she'd quit on us?" Jonah's eyes match the worry I'm starting to feel.

I know I'm always saying that we don't deserve her, but that doesn't mean I think I can make it for a second without her.

❀ ❀ ❀ ❀ ❀

While we wait for Kell's meeting, Jonah, Ryan, and I are in the home gym watching as Jonah goes for his personal record on the weight machine. He grunts out each rep and Jessie, who's just gotten back, cheers him on after each one.

Ryan is holding an ice pack to each side of his face. He's puffy and dotted with multicolored bruises from needles. Dermal fillers. Apparently, he spent half the day letting a plastic surgeon experiment on him with the newest technique for a toned facial structure.

Meanwhile, I'm trying to make sure we're all on track for convincing Kell not to leave us high and dry at this surprise meeting she's set up.

"Why are you so worried about this?" Ryan slaps me on the back and then winces with the movement. "You think Kell would ever leave us? She loves us, man."

"Kell does love us," Jonah agrees, but he's only half listening. Half concentrating. He prefers to walk the thin line in between our disagreements. Likes waiting it out until things blow over. This time I wish he'd tell Ryan he's being a dick. Coming from Jonah it might be harder to ignore. The way I see it, Kell's love for us is the problem.

I shake my head at my brother. "If she does quit, it's your fault. You know that, right? We'd lose all the connections she's made for us. We'd be back at square one without Kell."

Ryan shrugs and changes the subject. "We're making her good money. I don't see her complaining about that."

I almost flick one of Jessie's resistance bands at his head. "Money isn't the problem."

Ryan rolls his eyes. "I'm going to call Judith and grab a fresh ice pack. I have auditions to prep for tomorrow."

Jonah grunts and sets down his barbell. "We ordered pizza. It's already on the way."

"I'll be quick." Ryan wanders off and Jonah gives me a look but goes back to his reps.

"Jonah. You've got to talk to him. Tell him to stay away from Kell until she cools off at least."

My younger brother doesn't look back as he focuses on the weights. "I tried last week," he says around heavy breaths. "Not about Kell. But his whole . . . thing. His attitude lately. Didn't listen.

"He's obsessed with taking on more projects," Jonah adds.

"Yeah, I've noticed." Last week when I tried to ask him how he had the time to star in a commercial for a brand deal and shoot two movies back to back, he almost bit my head off.

"He told me that he's not going to stop auditioning for stuff until he's the most recognizable name across the board. Not just movies. I don't know what set this off."

"Well, no one can control Ryan, but Kell deserves to be heard," Jessie says, looking at me. She keeps one eye on Jonah as he lifts. "Why don't you talk to her before the meeting? You're closest with her and it sounds like she might need someone to talk to."

"We don't talk about relationships," I say, exhaling. Our friendship has always been solid. No point in ruining things by bringing either of our love lives into it.

"Maybe you should start." Jessie raises her eyebrows at me pointedly.

She might be right.

I'm capable of talking if that's what Kell needs to stay. Like I said, leaving might be what's best for her, but I'm going to have to be selfish. I can't do my job without her. Especially not the new projects I'm pursuing. Yeah, we need to talk about it. Maybe I'll be the one to convince her that Ryan isn't worth her time. I hope so.

"I'll go call her before she gets here. Your girlfriend is smart," I tell Jonah. He looks up at her and they both smile. It's a private moment and I've disappeared to them. My gut twists and I don't even know why. Maybe because no one has ever looked at me like that. And all of this drama is messing with my head. I'm going to go ahead and blame that on Ryan too.

CHAPTER THREE

✿ ✿ ✿ ✿ ✿

Kell

A lizard scurries past my feet, eliciting a silent screech from me that only adds to the hellish morning I'm having. The lizard crawls to the other side of the stone privacy wall separating us from the house next door where Kelly Clarkson lives, at least for part of the year. I lean carefully against the white stone and resist the urge to bang my head on the wall.

Ryan. Is. Engaged.

It's only a matter of time—half an hour maybe—until I'll have to field calls from reporters salivating over this story. Which means no matter what level of humiliation I'm experiencing, I have to be a grown-up about this. I can't avoid my clients forever, no matter how tempting it sounds right now. I squeeze my eyes shut and replay the last several minutes after Ryan followed me outside.

I really can't believe I let him do this to me.

The problem is that when it comes to Ryan, I throw all my rules out the window. Rule number one in the industry: never date your clients. Ryan Freaking Matthew. My weakness and clearly—clearly!—my downfall. There's no greater low than this. I walk to the driveway and sit in my car outside of the Matthews' stupidly charming mansion and beat my fists against the steering wheel. I can't drive like this, but I also can't sit here and risk one of them seeing me. My chest pangs right under my skin, and I almost look down to see if the crack I feel in my heart is visible. I raise a hand to my eyes and swipe at the wetness accumulating on my lashes. At least I have my life together enough that I'm wearing waterproof mascara.

One. I suck in a gasping breath. *Two.* I close my eyes and focus on anything other than Ryan. *Three.* I blink open and sniffle. Everything still hurts, but I'm pulled together enough to leave. If I'm going to fall apart, it has to be in the privacy of my own apartment.

The drive home is a blur of more threatened tears and the blaring radio despite the traffic. The music is supposed to drown out my thoughts, but it isn't enough to distract me from replaying the conversation with Ryan over and over. I catch my usual glimpse of the Hollywood sign as I turn past Sunset Boulevard, but it does nothing for my mood. Usually, it's a daily reminder that I'm making it in an industry that's supposed to be impossible. That despite the headaches and the stress, I have something to celebrate. Today the sign is a gut punch. My only three clients are collectively a mess, and I can't measure success by this.

Instead, at the red light I watch the hills behind me in my rearview mirror, dotted with mansions just like the Matthews'. And along the freeways are the tent cities, filled with unhoused people trying desperately to get by day-to-day. The two realities of one of America's most famous cities and a sinking reminder that Hollywood is rarely all it's cracked up to be.

Inside my apartment, I let myself deflate. My shoes slip off and go into the little cubby next to my front door. And then my feet carry me over to the couch, where I pull my favorite yellow throw blanket over my body like a cocoon. I can handle a lot. I've had a chronic illness since I was in high school, so I'm no stranger to physical pain thanks to Crohn's disease. Emotional pain though? That's a different story. A whimper escapes my throat. This was supposed to be the year that Ryan fell in love with me. I wished it on my twenty-fifth birthday candle and everything like an obsessive creep. College is when my crush really started, and I've been hooked on him ever since, dreaming of the eventual relationship we'd have when the timing was just right. And then, after our amazing night together last month, everything was falling into place.

Except, apparently not.

That night, we'd all gone out together, and then Ash had wandered off somewhere and Jonah and Jessie were sequestered on the other side of the house. Ryan and I were on the couch, sitting close and talking about work. The conversation shifted to other things, college and friends, and then to us. He'd leaned close and taken hold of my hand, the most simple of gestures, but it meant so much. As many women as I've seen him with over the years, I'd never seen him touchy-feely like that. Never tender or sweet.

It felt like a token of faith, like he wanted to touch me even if one of his brothers walked in and saw us. And then our eyes met, and everything else didn't matter. He'd kissed me, pulling me on top of him on the couch, held me so close. I was convinced it was the big turning point for us, and I went home that night sure that a real relationship was the next step.

We've both been busy with work since then, and I was naïve enough to think that was all that kept him from kissing me again.

Oh, how very, very wrong I was about *everything*. The weight of my blanket and the warmth of my small apartment swell over me. Maybe if I close my eyes for a second, I can pretend none of this really happened.

Bzz. Bzz. Bzz.

I wake up to my phone buzzing against my leg and drool staining my shirt. "Hello?" I croak into the phone, hoping it's no one I need to impress.

"Our boys are having quite the week, aren't they?"

The sardonic voice snaps me straight up and suddenly I'm wide awake. Judith Holmes is the last person I want to sound like a sleep-deprived troll on the phone to.

Honestly, she's the last person I want to have any conversation with, despite finding myself in that exact spot almost weekly. She has the tendency to make me feel like I'm crap at my job. And say what you want about me—because I know I still have my flaws—but I'm amazing at my job.

Even if the Matthews make it one million times harder than it needs to be. I've never met a contract I couldn't swing in my clients' favor or a bad deal that I couldn't spin a compromise for. Judith may be an extremely sought-after agent who works almost as hard for the guys as I do, but she's also an obnoxious cow.

"We're not discussing that at the moment." I pause, wondering if I heard her correctly or I'm still half asleep. "Did you—did you say boys, as in plural?" It's been pushed aside because of all the other things happening, but Jonah is also being fined thirty thousand dollars for profanity on live television. There's Ash's change of heart, and then of course Ryan's engagement, which I thought hadn't hit news sites quite yet. I can't lie—if Judith knew about it before me, it would only make me feel worse. Between the four of us, our whole little team is a little bit of a disaster right now, and I can't think of a worse time for any of it to be advertised.

I can feel the weight of her satisfied smirk over the phone. "Oh yes. Of course you know about Ryan's exciting public engagement. And then there's a rumor about Ash. I hear he's not showing up to work and might lose a few contracts. Not if I have anything to do with it, of course, but still, he's awfully close to making enemies of some good names. And Jonah . . ."

She sighs. "I'm sure you know all about his fine. But really," Judith continues, "I'm interested in the photos of you and Ryan that are popping up everywhere. Care to comment on that?"

My stomach sinks.

Photos? What photos? I flip open my laptop from where it's charging on the coffee table beside the couch. I angle my phone away from my hands and try to type as quietly as possible. Article after article pops up, along with a particularly unflattering picture of me and Ryan leaning against the sidewall of his home, our heads close in serious conversation. Holy crap, this was taken this morning. The story is being run in conjunction with his engagement announcement, like the two events are somehow linked. This morning I woke up full of hope for a romantic future with Ryan, and now, just hours later, I'm the other woman.

Me, the other woman when I've been there for Ryan longer than anyone else. Some profanity of my own slips out. This day could not get worse.

"Exactly my thoughts," comes Judith's voice. I'll bet she was waiting for my reaction, savoring it. How lovely. I'm waiting for her to get to her point, unless the point of her calling really is to taunt me.

"But sometimes," she continues, "these little indiscretions have an advantage. We have three very visible clients right now. That's rare. And something you might consider capitalizing on."

So this is a business call after all. Despite my abject humiliation, I roll my shoulders, happy to dive into something that I'm good at. "Do you have an offer for one of them? What are you working on lately?"

Her tinkly laugh is more unsettling than anything. "Oh, I have an offer for them. All of them, and it's straight from a highly sought-after producer." She pauses, and I swear it's for dramatic effect more than anything else. "Ryan and I have been keeping a little secret, but I think we can convince him to welcome more cast members. How do you feel about a reality show starring the three Matthew brothers?"

❅ ❅ ❅ ❅ ❅

A few hours later, I find myself driving through the gates of the Matthews' private neighborhood, trying to ignore the black cars parked nearby, their windows down and cameras poised. They must have already gotten all they need from me because I pass by without a fuss.

Once I park, I draw in a long, slow breath and get out of my car. I can handle myself with professionalism and class because the alternative is I quit my job and move back in with my parents. And as much as I love my parents, that is no real option because I've already made too big a point about how much I *love* Hollywood. Admitting I was wrong about my dream career just might be the thing that kills me.

I'm not sure who to be angrier with. Judith is supposed to work with me, and she's supposed to keep me solidly in the loop so that I can better everyone's careers. Withholding information about a signed contract that's already in preproduction is all shades of unforgivable. But at least it's the kind of underhanded move I'd expect from Judith.

Ryan, on the other hand, is my client. My entire function is to help him through auditions and the casting process, to make everything go smoothly so that he doesn't have to worry about the small things. For that to work, there needs to be a level of trust between us. Trust that he shattered the moment Judith filled me in on their little secret.

But I can't afford to mope around about any of it. Shoulders back, head held high, I march to the back door and knock lightly. No one answers, so I use my key and let myself in. Their cars are here, so reason follows the guys are around somewhere since they all assured me they'd be here to talk.

As soon as I hung up with Judith, I did my research and weighed my personal pros and cons. Pro? More work for my clients equals more money for me. Con? Reality shows are as far from classy as you can get. Do I really want my name or the guys' names associated with something like this? It comes down to what they say in the meeting, which is why it's so important to do it right away while Judith's offer is still fresh.

I walk through the kitchen but stop cold as a deep voice, devastatingly familiar, calls from only a few feet away, "Hi, beautiful. I was hoping I'd get you alone before the meeting."

My heart absolutely sinks.

CHAPTER FOUR

✿ ✿ ✿ ✿ ✿

Ash

*W*hen I round the hallway to my room, Ryan's standing in the kitchen walking toward someone. And unfortunately for me, I'm only a few seconds behind him. I recognize Kell's profile right away. She must have gotten here early. I've seen her hundreds of times in dozens of different scenarios. I couldn't miss her small, upturned nose. Or the S-shaped curve of her hair around her face. As familiar to me as the back of my hand.

I can't miss Kell's familiar look. Ryan can though. He calls her *beautiful* and I'm half a second from landing a punch in his gut when I realize. He thinks Kell is someone else. When I scan her face next, she looks like she's the one who's been punched. She steps into the light, and her throat moves as she swallows her disappointment. Now she really is going to ditch us.

As soon as the light hits her, Ryan flinches. He takes one big step backward and laughs. "Whoa. Not who I thought you were, Kell. Samantha texted me that she was on her way, so I . . ."

Some semblance of tact hits him way too late. Ryan runs his hands over his close-cropped hair. "You're here for the meeting."

"Yes, the meeting." She looks at a space just past Ryan's actual face. Won't even look at him. "And it's a client-only meeting, so you'll have to tell your fiancée to wait somewhere else when she gets here."

"That's cool. She can hang out in my room since that's where we're going to be for a while anyway." Ryan shrugs. Yeah. He actually just said that.

Kell produces a glare made of pure steel and brushes past him. For a minute it looks like she wants to keep arguing. Then she spots me and her eyes darken. Great. Now I'm in trouble too. Not my fault that I heard the whole exchange. I never should have listened to Jessie about talking to Kell. I wouldn't be stuck between her and Ryan right now if I'd minded my own business.

She moves toward me. "Is Jonah here?"

I nod. Kind of afraid to talk to her now. The last thing I want is to end up on her bad side too.

"I guess he's working out?"

Nod again. I'm feeling like a real genius. Something about the way she's spitting questions makes this feel more like an interview than a conversation. An interview I'm failing.

"What's this meeting about, anyway?" Ryan interjects. Because of course he just has to ask. It's not that he doesn't get the hint that Kell's not speaking to him. Dude just doesn't care.

Kell's jaw twitches. "You already *know* what it's about Ryan. That's part of the problem." She doesn't turn to him, just acts like he's the most inconsequential thing in the room. Lower than the toaster oven we've never used once.

"I—" Ryan starts but stops just as quickly. My interest is officially piqued. I want to know what he's going to say, because whatever it is has Kell more worked up than ever before. He can't seriously have done something worse than getting engaged without telling her.

Ryan's voice is a lowered pleading. "Can we talk before the meeting? I wanna make sure we're on the same page."

"No." Kell shoots him down with one curt word. To his credit, he stops talking and shifts on his feet sullenly.

"I do want to talk to you," Kell adds to me. It's hard not to let that make me smug. No matter what kind of crap my brother might put her through, at least Kell knows she can count on me.

"You can go. You've done enough." She gestures at Ryan, who is still standing in the kitchen looking lost. I don't feel bad for him at all, but it's awkward as hell. Facing off against a disapproving Kell is a lot like getting called to the principal's office. Ryan was never a straight A student, but we were raised right. None of us likes getting scolded.

He shuffles away, shaking his head like Kell is the most confusing thing in the world. I can tell it only makes her madder. Her face pinks up again. Eyebrows scrunch while she stares after him.

I put out my arm to form a kind of barrier between them. We don't need any more words exchanged. Not tonight. "Hey, ignore him, he's an idiot to pass you up . . ."

"It's so not about that anymore." Kell grabs me and pulls me with her to the side of the kitchen. I stumble after her until she stops at our walk-in pantry. She points. "Get in."

I blink but do as she says. She shuts the door behind us and steps closer. My entire freakin' body hits high alert. I don't know what's happening but I'm not about to complain. Not when she already looks murderous.

CHAPTER FIVE

✷ ✷ ✷ ✷ ✷

Kell

*A*sh's brows shoot up into his hairline, widening his eyes. "The light switch," I mutter. The switch is just above his head in the cramped pantry. "It's super dark in here." I reach for it, but this only pulls our heads closer, caging us together until we're nearly nose to nose.

Ash's throat moves slowly as he swallows. His gaze flicks to my mouth. Neither of us says a word.

My heart hammers in my chest in the dark, quiet space, and even without the light my eyes are glued to Ash's as we watch each other. His lips part slightly, and my pulse picks up further in response. No one knows we're in here. The rest of the house is otherwise occupied, and there's no one to see—or not see.

His face is shadowed, his lashes sweeping darkly over his cheekbones as he blinks. He's ridiculously attractive. Shaking myself out of it—this is Ash, my friend and client, who I'm looking at after all—I flick the switch, illuminating the pantry. The light breaks the silence.

"I needed to talk to you. Alone." I try for another explanation and watch as his features shift in understanding.

"Oh," he says. "I was actually on my way to call you. I thought you might want to talk. Or something." Ash steps to the side, putting some much-needed space between us.

Still, a stab of disappointment courses through me. Was I hoping that Ash would actually kiss me? It wouldn't be the worst idea considering the day I've had, but it's Ash, so then again, it would be a terrible idea. Our friendship is the only thing saving me from declaring all Matthews a no-go at the moment.

He's right that I do need someone to talk to about this entire fiasco. But I'm not entirely sure if he's the best person to vent to, not in this situation. As much of a mess as I've made by letting my feelings for Ryan get the better of me, I have to try to be professional. And Ryan is still my client—for now—as is Ash. "I'm okay. But I do have something I want to run by you." I take in a breath and tell him about Judith's proposal, leaving out a few key details.

"How in the hell is reality TV going to land me more serious roles?" Ash crosses his arms over his chest, and I try not to stare at his arms. I know he's been hitting the gym a lot more lately to keep up with Jonah, but *wow*. I guess I didn't realize how much. The muscles under his skin ripple as he moves.

"I know it sounds counterintuitive, but trust me. Okay?" I tear my eyes from his muscles.

He wrinkles his nose but relaxes his arms.

"The producer does reality shows and dramas. Like exclusively. Get in with him and you're golden. I'm working on getting a movie written into your contract. We can leverage the show as free promo for whatever project you get next." I try to angle the offer in a way he'll understand. As much as I hate what Judith and Ryan did, Judith is too smart at what she does to discount her. A reality show featuring the brothers is an offer that demands serious consideration.

It might temporarily cheapen the Matthews' brand, but it also offers unparalleled visibility—and on their own terms.

Ash nods thoughtfully. "Why do this, though? I've heard you talking trash about *Keeping Up with the Kardashians*. You don't want to be known as a reality TV show manager, do you?" I can tell that his interest is there, but he's still wary. Honestly, I'd be worried more if he weren't a little hesitant. I know the risks, and I don't love them either, but the precedent is there. Stars have managed to juggle big roles and reality TV at the same time and emerged unscathed with well-respected successful careers. The Matthews can do it too.

I don't think his question is meant to be insulting, but it stings all the same. "I'm already known as manager to you three, so I can't imagine tacking on a reality show is going to do any extra damage," I retort.

Then I sober because I haven't even told him the worst part of it. "I didn't put this in motion. Judith did, and apparently it's been in the works for the better part of a year. But I hadn't heard a word of it until today when we spoke on the phone."

Ash widens his eyes. "How is that possible? She can't sign us up for a show without talking to us. Or to you. Right?"

This was my exact reaction too. Until I twisted the full truth from her and immediately regretted what I was hearing. "Ryan signed for the show six months ago. A solo show."

I try not to let the anger boil up again, but it's tough to ignore the utter betrayal. "It was supposed to be a show about him, and Judith claims he was going to talk to you and Jonah about it at some point, but shooting starts soon."

Ash stares at me before letting out a few choice words that echo the ones I said after hanging up with Judith.

"I know."

"So, if it's Ryan's solo thing, why is Judith asking about it now? I don't know about Jonah, but I'm not interested in jumping on board some pity project. If Ryan wanted us in on this, he would have said something before now." Ash is annoyed, and maybe a little hurt, which I get. Oh, do I get it.

I let my eyes fall closed for a second and then blink them back open. What I'm supposed to do in this situation is stay neutral and come up with a solution that makes everyone happy. "The producer has been following yours and Jonah's careers, probably for this exact reason. You're both hot right now for different reasons, and now they're asking if you'll sign on so they can shift the show to focus on all of you."

"You really think this is a good idea?"

"Yes. I know it's unorthodox and it's out of the blue, but I do think we can make this work in your favor. If you're up for it, that is."

Ash holds his hands out in defeat. "Okay. I'll do it because I trust you. I don't want personal drama, though. Tell them to keep the focus on Ryan."

"I think that can be arranged."

"He's got enough shit to keep people entertained all on his own." Ash stretches. "In this case, I'm more than happy to be a side character in Ryan's world."

The sad thing is I'm pretty sure that's exactly how Ryan sees us.

"So, I guess we should go talk to Jonah and Ryan?"

Ash opens the pantry door and leads the way out of the kitchen. My hands start to sweat for some reason, and I stop outside of the living room hallway. He turns back, waiting for me. "You okay?"

"Yeah, I'm . . ." It's hard to lie to Ash. For some terrible reason I find it much easier to lie to myself. I can say that I'm not that bothered by what feels like an epic betrayal and I'll force myself to believe it.

I don't want to walk into the room and see Ryan. I'm not prepared, not near ready enough for it not to hurt. But I made a decision earlier, and that was to keep doing my job as normal. I swallow. "I just need a minute."

I don't have to finish the sentence. Instead, Ash walks back and puts an arm around my shoulder, easing my head against his chest. I don't cry. After earlier, I genuinely don't think there is enough moisture left in my body to make that happen. But I do suck in a breath and get a whiff of cinnamon.

I asked Ash about it once and he showed me the unbelievably expensive deodorant he buys. Apparently, it's infused with cinnamon cloves, which doesn't sound that nice, but the smell is worth it if I'm being honest.

"You smell good," I mutter against the fabric of his shirt.

He shrugs. "I've picked up a few basic hygiene habits since college."

Ash never smelled bad in college, but he likes to pretend he was somehow undesirable back then and not still a huge hottie. "Oh, well, thank goodness," I say, wiping at my eyes just in case tears start to leak out.

"You don't have to talk to Ryan, okay? Just get in and get out. That's more than he deserves," Ash says quietly.

I groan. "Stop making it sound like we're in one of his stupid spy movies."

Ash wrinkles his nose in disgust. "Spies are *so* last year," he says in a falsetto Valley girl accent.

A smile slides into place without warning. Ash can always make me laugh. "Do I even want to know what Ryan did to his face?" It was a purplish-blue when I glimpsed it in the kitchen, not exactly his best look.

"Oh, you definitely do." Ash raises his brows. "Cheek filler. To go with the new jawline he got done last month."

I groan. There's nothing wrong with plastic surgery. But I've seen enough of LA's addiction to it to be scared straight and hoped my clients were the same. I'll argue that point some other time, though.

For now, I straighten. "Okay. I'm ready." I need to face everyone sooner or later, and at least I know Ash has my back.

He gestures for me to go first, and we walk in to where everyone is waiting.

CHAPTER SIX

✿ ✿ ✿ ✿ ✿

Ash

"When were you going to tell us about this?" I can't help the edge that slips into my voice when I turn to face Ryan. There's the fact that he didn't tell anyone about this show, but mostly it's about how he screwed over Kell. It's not right.

Kell gives me a look that says *let me handle this*. I step aside but I hate it. She moves close to Ryan and somehow manages to look intimidating even though he's almost a foot taller than her. "If you ever pull something like this again, we're through. I'm not kidding, Ryan. I won't work with you, and we won't speak. You'll be dead to me." Her hands are balled by her sides. Maybe I'm imagining it, but I think they're shaking.

Ryan swallows. "Got it. I apologize, Kell. You know I'm trying to keep my schedule full."

"There's such a thing as it being too full," Kell says. "If you keep up this pace, you won't have enough hours in the day to attend all your shoots."

He goes to rub the side of his jaw, then stops like he's just remembered his bruises. "I'll keep that in mind."

Silence falls and then Jonah speaks up. I've been watching for his reaction. And he looks—well, he looks resigned.

"I think the show could be good. I figure I owe this to you all," he says a bit sheepishly. His mess-up on-air has been bugging him, and I know he's been dreading Kell finding out. Kind of why I let her find out on her own. It's not his fault that he has a dirty mouth, and his network is family-friendly. Anyway, Jonah has the sense to feel remorse for causing Kell grief. Unlike some Matthews. "I'm in as long as Ash is," Jonah says.

"This isn't about me," Kell insists. "It's a good business decision for all three of you individually. So, if you're all on board . . ." She looks at us in turn and I nod resolutely. My decision has nothing to do with anyone's career except for hers. Without Kell, I wouldn't get half the jobs I've gotten. I wouldn't even know where to start looking for the new roles I want. I'm keeping her around, and I don't want to be selfish about it. Means I need to play ball and do what makes Kell happy. She may not think highly of reality shows, but this seems like a move she wants us to make. And in this case, I want whatever Kell wants.

Brown eyes wide, Kell nods. "Okay. I'll make the necessary phone calls and stop by later this week to go over the paperwork. We're in new territory here, guys." Her smile is not wholly convincing. I'm glad we feel the same about this reality show business. I can't remember a time we *weren't* on the same page, but it's still nice to know.

"I'm pumped! The three bros, all together. I love it." Ryan throws an arm around Kell's waist and brings her in close for a bear hug. I step to her half a second before she's already pushing him away. Unfurling herself like Ryan's a piece of garbage clinging to her shirt.

Ryan, completely unfazed, claps me on the shoulder with a resounding *whack*. I narrow my eyes at him and turn to Kell, but her face is already a mask of professionalism. Not an ounce of hurt stitched on there. This is why she's the best.

"I'm glad we're all happy." She turns and gives us a sort of half wave-salute.

The door closes, leaving a draft of her flowery perfume with it. I want to smack the audacity out of Ryan, but he's already moving toward the door. "Ryan. Give Kell some space, all right? She's upset."

He puts a hand to his forehead and mock salutes me. "Yes sir, little brother." He pauses. "Going out. Samantha wants to go somewhere for dinner."

Jonah frowns. "The pizza is almost here." He nudges me to say something, but I shrug. More pizza to go around and no Ryan? Sounds like a win.

"We'll save him some," I assure him. The baby of the family and he cares more about keeping the peace than any of us. But this time neither of us can stop what Ryan started. That's going to have to be between him and Kell.

Jonah wanders to the back of the house, presumably to find Jessie, and I crash onto the huge sofa in our living room. A cool-white leather number, something that kind of screams rock star, in my opinion. I don't even know if I like it anymore, to be honest. When we first bought our place together, Ryan brought in this designer for the stars, a woman with strong opinions on house decorations. She bought everything for us, even the pictures on the walls. Said it made us look legit. I thought it was cool at first. I don't know anymore.

I was happy to be invited back when we first started. I didn't care if the movies I was in were good or not. Didn't even care if they were movies actual people were going to see. Hell, I probably would have jumped at the chance for a reality show like this one. But I've soured to it all over the years. Everything feels shallow, and I can't imagine doing this for the next five, ten, twenty years. Not unless something changes.

I want to be known as more than my last name or my looks. Acting is my first love. I've been chasing the thrill of delivering the perfect, heartfelt line ever since I played the Tin Man in my middle school production of *The Wizard of Oz*.

Kell is the only person I can talk to about it. Ryan couldn't give a shit, and Jonah is still waiting for his big break—sportscasting is a different animal. But Kell sees how hard I've worked, how most of it has come back and bit me in the ass. Like last awards season when everyone else in my summer blockbuster hit was nominated for something. I wasn't. I was just eye candy and it sucked to finally realize. Not one person took me seriously. I was supposed to stand there and look pretty, delivering dumbed down lines for two hours straight.

Even my own girlfriend treated me like an accessory, something to be seen but not heard. The closest I've ever come to a serious relationship since college is Celeste, the model I dated for six months one year ago. She broke up with me once she found a newer, shinier model who didn't question the way this industry works. The whole relationship was a wake-up call, triggering my need to take acting more seriously.

The doorbell rings, and I see on the camera that it's the pizza guy. I text Jonah and Jessie and then scroll over to Kell's name.

Ash: *You should have stayed for pizza.*

I see her typing immediately and laugh to myself. Pizza is practically her siren song. We lived off of the stuff in college after we became friends, spending every late night we could planning our Hollywood futures. Amazing that some of those dreams have actually come true.

Kell: *I had some work left. You owe me pizza next time I'm over.*

Ash: *Deal. I'm sorry about today. I'm here if you want to vent.*

She types for a moment and then the three dots disappear. I wait a few more minutes before she responds.

Kell: *I'll let you know when I need signatures. Talk later.*

I sigh as Jonah and Jessie get to the living room. They're both smiley and in love, and I suddenly feel like the dark shadow hanging over their night. "Gonna take some slices to my room," I mutter, scooping up a drink and a plate piled high with pepperoni pizza.

Behind me I can hear them convincing me to stay, but I wave them off. I wouldn't be any fun. Instead, I skulk to my room and devour too much cheese while I queue an episode of *Keeping Up with the Kardashians*. Time to see what I'm in for, I guess.

CHAPTER SEVEN

✿ ✿ ✿ ✿ ✿

Kell

*O*kay, so this is happening.

Part of me was hoping they would say a big, resounding no, and that the whole idea of a reality show would be off the table. We could all tell Ryan to stick it where the sun doesn't shine and move on with our lives.

But maybe Jonah and Ash are smart enough to realize the opportunity in front of them. Maybe it's easy to forgive Ryan because they know him so well already. Technically, he didn't do anything to his brothers, just to me.

And speaking of wrongdoing, I should set up a time to talk to Judith, but I'm dreading it. I was too shocked on the phone to say much of what I really felt. She doesn't owe me anything, but it sure would make my life easier if she treated me as an equal when it comes to our clients' career choices.

After leaving the Matthews' last night, I ordered Chinese food and fell asleep in front of my work laptop before momentarily waking up and dragging myself to bed. Now I'm up before the sun has fully cracked over the trees and swallowing a pair of Tylenol. Mug of herbal tea in one hand and my computer in the other, I perch on the edge of my sofa and click to my emails. There's a reminder from my GI doctor about my upcoming appointment, and I click over to add it to my calendar before moving on to work.

I purposefully avoid any news sites because I know my own name and picture will be there to haunt me. My parents have already sent half a dozen unread texts, I'm sure demanding to know why I haven't told them anything about a relationship with Ryan. And the texts are unanswered because I already know that they will not accept the truth—there's absolutely nothing to tell. The relationship never existed.

I just wish the pictures didn't exist either.

When I open my email account, I groan. What used to be a dozen emails about my three clients has turned into hundreds of messages, each of them marked urgent. I'm living what *used* to be my dream, and I'm desperately trying to figure out how to keep that dream alive. But it has to be worth it because I've put in too much work to stop now. Sure, it was better in the beginning when we really had to fight for a spot among the other hopefuls, but that's the natural evolution of the job. We're in a different, busier phase now. My parents don't get it. Neither does my best friend, Claudette.

Claudette works out of her loft apartment downtown making and selling these amazing flowy dresses online. She was even recognized earlier this year as one of the top independent Black designers. Claudette's job makes her unbelievably happy, and she seems to think that there's something out there that will do the same for me. I'm convinced that working for the Matthews is as close as I will get.

Was it easier when Ryan, Ash, Jonah, and I were all on equal footing, just starting out? Of course it was. Are things a bit more complicated now that it feels like everyone wants something different? Well, yeah. But the fact remains that I started college hoping and praying to one day be a successful manager. And here I am, manager to three well-known names with more than enough work between them to keep me perpetually busy. That should be enough.

And the truth is that this thing with Ryan has been a long time coming. I don't know how many times I've replayed little moments together, holding on to them like wildflower promises. Like on my twenty-first birthday, when Ash threw me a party at our favorite pizza restaurant just off campus.

My eyes scan the glass front doors as I laugh at a joke Ash made to his girlfriend of the month—I think her name is Indie, but it could be Ivy. The pizza is getting cold, but I saved half a box for Ryan anyway. He promised to be here, but he's probably just running late.

Ash swats my arm. "You okay? Ready for cake and another round at the bar?"

I lift a shoulder, looking one last time at the doors, but it's already dark outside. "I'm ready. I want cake before Jonah eats it all."

Ash's younger brother is in town visiting, and he has the appetite of a powerlifter. He grins sheepishly. Ash makes a big show of lighting a candle and forcing everyone to sing for me. I lean forward to blow it out, eyes half closed to make a wish, and then there he is. Ryan staring back at me with heart-squeezing familiarity.

I don't need a birthday wish anymore.

Ryan finds me right after, leaning into my neck to whisper, "I have a surprise for you. Come here."

He tugs on my hand, leading me outside to the dimly lit parking lot in front of the restaurant. We stop at his car, where he opens the passenger door and hands me a single red rose wrapped in green cellophane. "I saw this and thought of you," he says.

Roses aren't my favorite flower, but that doesn't matter. Ryan isn't treating me like a friend of his brother's right now—that's what matters.

"It's beautiful! Thank you." I stand on tiptoes and wrap my arms around his neck. The stubble on his cheek scrapes my skin until he pulls back, flicking his eyes down to my mouth.

His lips melt into mine. It's not soft or sweet but hurried and hungry. I'm all at once floating and on fire, a combination of so many things that I feel like I'm going to burst. The pressure of his hands on my lower back, sliding across the sliver of exposed skin on my waist—it's all perfect.

When he pulls back, I gasp softly, bringing my hand to my lips.

"Happy birthday, Kell," he says. "I'm going to head out, but I'll see you soon."

"You're leaving? Do you want to go somewhere together?"

He stops and turns back to look at me. He moves close, dragging me into his orbit once again. "You know how much I like you, but when the timing is right, we'll know." He lifts a hand to my face and brushes my hair back, letting his hand linger there at the top of my ear. It feels so intimate that I forget to say anything for a second.

"Yeah, we'll both know when it's right," I agree. I look up at him, mesmerized by his body so close to mine, at the way he touches me so tenderly. I can wait for the right timing. It's not like I don't have goals of my own to work on meanwhile.

He flashes a blinding smile. "I figure it's only a matter of time until we, I don't know, give in to the universe's demands. Don't you think?"

I remember thinking that was so romantic. What's wild is that I even thought it was romantic the next three times he said it, all years apart. He said he thought we were destined for each other, like soul mates. Except soul mates usually end up in a mutual relationship. Not one where just one partner comes and goes as they please, never making any sort of commitment beyond *let's make out tonight and maybe someday we can do it more often.*

How ridiculous am I for falling for this?

So ridiculous that I can't even bring myself to think about it any longer. My email refreshes and a new message from Judith sits at the top of my inbox. I almost spill my tea in my rush to click on it. She's included paperwork for me and signature pages for the guys. Plus, a film-start date of September 22. Two freaking weeks away. I clasp a hand to my mouth, aghast. Nothing moves that quickly in film or TV. There's no way it's possible to get everything ready by then, and Judith has to know that.

So either she's banking on chaos and disorganization reigning supreme to make me look bad, or she has some secret formula to whip it all into shape real quick. It better be the second option or else she's dealing with one irate manager.

I know I'm supposed to email her back and sit patiently for a response, but to hell with that. I call her phone while chewing on the inside of my cheek, nibbling the skin raw. After several rings she answers with a bemused, "Hello?"

"We aren't starting in two weeks. That's impossible."

"Kell," she starts with a little laugh that makes me grind my teeth together. "That's the start date. I'm sure you can work it out. It's reality, all right? You don't have to do a thing. Just let those boys of ours be themselves. Besides, it's been in the works for quite a while and most of the preproduction work is wrapping up already."

Yeah freaking right, I don't have to do a thing. She'd like that, wouldn't she? The Matthews' house needs to be set up for filming.

The guys need coaching on an agreed-upon list of subjects that are and are not up for discussion. It's too much. But I don't say any of that to Judith because I don't want her mocking me again.

"I'm not okay with you pushing me around like this. Don't take this the wrong way, Judith. I'm playing along here because Jonah and Ash want the show to happen. But I'm not happy with the way you shut me out of the initial deal. Ryan is my client too, and I've more than earned my spot in the industry."

"Of course you have." Her voice jumps an octave and borders on condescending. "I apologize that you didn't know about the show until late in the game, but I thought that Ryan was going to fill you in on the details. That's the impression I was under."

Really, I don't know who, or what, to believe anymore. I've said my piece and just the act of sticking up for myself makes me feel better. I square my shoulders. "Well, we're all in agreement now. I will be in touch today and tomorrow with my clients' needs. Look out for my email."

She sounds more than pleased with herself when we end the call. Stupid Judith. It's bad enough that I'm in reality shows now, but working with Judith always gives me a headache. She's great at what she does. The problem is that part of her job entails making *my* job harder than it has to be. She forgets to cc me on emails weekly. She name-drops other managers to the Matthews right in front of me. And now this.

I work furiously on a list of demands for the guys, including a house cleaning team personally provided by Judith. Sure, the Matthew brothers have their own cleaners, but if I can make Judith foot the bill as their agent, you bet I'm going to do it. I take a break midway through working on the guys' riders to scroll social media. It's never a true break for me, though, because I'm always on the lookout for damage control, and I can't resist peeking at Ryan's page. Jonah exclusively posts sports updates or pictures of him and Jessie.

Ash has social media because I set up his profiles, but he never posts. But Ryan, true to form, is unpredictable online.

He's gone through phases of DMing random fans and chatting them up, sometimes even sending them pictures that really shouldn't make their rounds on the internet. And other phases of posting a daily morning selfie, usually shirtless, accompanied by quotes from his own movies. I never know quite what to expect when I scroll through his pages, and I find myself holding my breath, hoping for something harmless.

The first few things I see are just that. A picture of him eating a bowl of cereal this morning. His buzzed hair perfectly shows off his bluer than blue eyes, and his plain gray T-shirt makes him look effortlessly cool and relatable. He has reposted a few articles that mention his latest movie project, and obviously I always approve of self-promotion. Love to see it, in fact.

What I don't love is the next picture, posted late last night. A gorgeous redhead with very convincing hair extensions is perched on his lap. Ryan's arms are around her, pulling her in close. Both their eyes are closed as they lean in for a kiss. The caption reads, "Thought it was time I introduce the future Mrs. Ryan Matthew to the world."

My face steams as I click away as fast as I can. It's funny how a perfectly decent morning can be ruined so easily. Samantha. I should have done this immediately after finding out about her, but I couldn't stomach it at the time. I'm still not sure I can. Resolutely, I scroll back to Ryan's page and click on Samantha's name.

Her page is barer than I expected. Other than her age—four and a half years younger than Ryan and two years younger than me—there's not much information to dig through. I thought she'd have a whole timeline dedicated to pictures of her and Ryan. That's the typical fan behavior. If I didn't know better, I'd be inclined to think she was a perfectly normal woman.

But it's much more likely that someone else on Ryan's team, maybe Judith, advised him to have her clean up her profile, just in case. Usually image is more my expertise, but I get why Ryan may not have come to me, given my obvious feelings.

My joints ache in that very specific way they do when I haven't gotten enough sleep and my medication schedule is too far off track. I push myself away from my computer and stand to gingerly stretch. I'll see about my medicine later. For now, we have a lot to discuss if filming is going to happen at the end of the month.

CHAPTER EIGHT

✾ ✾ ✾ ✾ ✾

Ash

By the time I'm showered, dressed, and standing in the kitchen, an entire film crew has congregated by the fridge. I'm used to being on camera by now. But not at home. Not in my own space.

They're still setting up for a test shoot, virtually ignoring Jonah and me as we skirt around them looking for breakfast. Even though no cameras are rolling yet, I feel the need to lean across the table and lower my voice. "Where's Kell?"

"I don't think she's coming. When I talked to her the other day, she said she'd see me at the photo shoot." Jonah shovels cereal in his mouth while looking unconcerned.

The promo photo shoot isn't until the end of the week. Kell doesn't come to all of our workdays, but I thought she'd show up for this. I push my spoon around my yogurt, suddenly annoyed.

It only gets worse when Ryan walks into the kitchen wearing just his boxers. He's leading his fiancée by the hand, and she's looking at him like he's some sort of prize. Jonah and I both cover our eyes.

"Dude," Jonah protests, gagging into his cereal bowl.

But Samantha giggles and nods. "I know, right? I told him to put on some clothes first. But you know Ry, he never listens."

I watch as her eyes widen at the sight of the half dozen people wielding camera equipment a few feet away. Ryan doesn't look surprised at all. He squeezes an arm around her waist and goes for a full-on kiss. Samantha's pale cheeks darken, and she laughs again. Either she's a decent aspiring actress or she is in way over her head with my brother. I glimpse the sparkly rock on her left hand and inwardly wince. What was he thinking?

Samantha moves to the table and pulls up a chair across from Jonah. Always the nice one, he smiles at her. He pushes the box of cereal he's working on toward her. She takes it and drums her fingers on the side. Ryan sidles up to one of the cameramen and starts asking a ton of stupid questions. Trying to get on their good side before filming even starts. Then we all fall into an awkward silence.

That night that Ryan proposed to Samantha is such a blur. I wish I could remember it better. As far as I know, it was my first time meeting her, and she didn't make a very distinct impression. It was only later on, when I saw Ryan spending hours tucked away in a corner with her, that I thought something might be going on. Nothing significant though.

She's a pale redhead with a light smattering of matching red freckles. Ryan is tall—slightly taller than my six feet last time we measured up—but Samantha is nearly as tall when they're standing next to each other. At first glance I'd assume she's a model. But with a deeper, quiet voice and a habit of observing more than talking. I'd guess she's not a part of this world my brothers and I are in.

"I don't know if I ever heard how you and Ryan met," I finally say.

Samantha's eyes widen and she lets out a little breath. "Oh, well, we met at work. My work, I mean. I'm a shift manager at Brenna's

Beans, the coffee shop?" She pushes away the cereal box and blinks at me. "I'm in grad school, and it pays the bills."

I've been to the same coffee shop with Ryan a dozen times over the years. I don't remember ever seeing Samantha. Seeing as she's my future sister-in-law, I don't admit that. "Oh, right." I nod.

"What do you study?" Jonah asks.

Samantha lights up. "Social work. I got my first degree in teaching, but after one year in the classroom I realized it wasn't for me." She wrinkles her nose. "One of my past professors emailed me to suggest I check out this program, and I don't know, something just clicked. I graduate next spring, and then I'll be looking for jobs again." She's passionate about her work and it shows. I can respect that a whole hell of lot more than her being in love with Ryan.

"That's really cool," I admit. "I wish I had some leads for you on jobs, but unfortunately, I don't know much about social work." Feels a little embarrassing to admit since philanthropy probably should be higher on my list.

"You're always welcome to find out more," she says, a teasing look in her eye. "I volunteer with some of the other people in my track at the shelter downtown. We're there every other Sunday."

This woman is either fake or confused about what she's gotten herself into in this family. We're decent people, but we're not the type to volunteer multiple times a year. "I'd like that," I say. It feels like another reminder that I'm not as grounded as I'd like to believe. I'd ask Kell if she wants to go with me sometime and see what the volunteering is about, but probably not a great idea. She and Samantha might like each other in some alternate universe. Not this one though.

Probably best they don't run in the same circles.

Ryan finishes sucking up to the film crew and stands behind Samantha's chair. "Getting to know each other? Watch out, Sammy, Ash here has a mean temper. You don't want to make him mad."

She casts me an apologetic look. "Oh, no, we were just talking about how we met and school . . ."

Ryan laughs and slides into the seat next to her. I stand up with my uneaten yogurt. I give Samantha my version of an *I'm sorry* smile. If she's going to spend a lifetime with my brother, she'll learn it fast. I know and love the douchebag, but it's no secret that he's a hard pill to swallow. "I'm going for a run."

Upstairs I put on my running clothes. But a minute later when I've laced up my shoes, I'm not in the mood. Jonah's voice in the back of my head is the only thing getting me out the door. Gotta be faster than Ryan. Gotta be stronger than Jonah.

Does it make me a petty middle sibling to be so motivated by outdoing my brothers? Yep. Doesn't matter because it works. I slip out the back door and wind around to the sidewalk in front. My feet hit the pavement and I suck in a breath of warm humid air. The palm trees lining the sidewalk don't give much cover, if any, from the sun. LA doesn't care that fall is supposed to start soon. LA will be hot as long as it damn well pleases. Sweat trickles down the small of my back, but I ignore it.

I'm not the kind of guy who gets any innate sense of joy from exercising. That's Jonah. But I do like the way I'm able to focus better. Running is a good time for thinking, and there's something I've been trying to untangle all morning.

When Kell dragged me into the pantry, I thought something completely un-Kell-like was about to happen. Yeah, she looked mad as hell right before that, but I don't know. She's a complicated woman. One I've never looked at in that way. Not really. Not lately.

Knowing she was in love with my brother should be a turnoff.

Hell, her being my manager should be my first clue to stay away.

Then there's the fact that she's my friend. Has been for a long time. She's seen me through some tough times. And vice versa, I'd like to think.

But ever since that stupid pantry conversation, I can't stop myself from thinking about Kell in a different way from before. She even infiltrated my dreams last night. You're not supposed to think about your friend naked.

Not supposed to wonder what it would be like to touch her. There's only been one moment in our entire history when things have slipped across that invisible line. The month after we first met, we ran into each other at a party.

I'd just broken up with one of my college girlfriends, and when I saw Kell I almost lost my mind. It was like I was seeing her through clear eyes for the first time. This cute girl with long poofy hair and huge brown eyes. She waved at me, smiling so big it looked like her face was going to crack. Cured my heartbreak then and there.

Somehow I convinced her to leave with me and get pizza. I couldn't stop staring at her while we talked about everything. I've never talked about so much of myself. Not even in the years since then. I told her about my dad who'd died the year before and how distant Mom was since then. Kell told me about getting diagnosed with Crohn's disease and spending her sixteenth birthday in the hospital.

Sounds stupid, but that's what did it for me. The fact she trusted me, and I found myself trusting her with things I wouldn't tell anyone else.

Definitely not the girl I'd broken up with that same day.

And then she'd leaned in close in that flirty way, her hair tossed back and one hand lightly touching my knee. My heart was pounding a mile a minute, I was so nervous. It wasn't like kissing some girl I'd met at a party. It was Kell, and already that meant something more.

My hand cupped the back of her head, easing us closer. The brush of her skin was silky soft, and she smelled like soap and flowers. I ducked my head to kiss her just as she cringed.

Actually cringed.

"Sorry, I don't think we should . . . uh . . . yeah, sorry." She slid out of the booth and walked outside, leaving me to puzzle over what I'd done wrong.

As much as I hate that memory, Kell stopping me probably saved our friendship. Otherwise I would have kissed her and then avoided her the rest of the year. Sucks, but it's kind of who I was.

Anyway, we laughed about it the next time we hung out and we've been fine ever since. Now I'm losing it though. I shake my head to clear it and pick up the pace. I run past a little black Honda that looks just like hers and almost trip over my feet. I crane my neck but catch a flash of gray hair in the front seat. Not Kell.

I run a hand through my sweaty hair and curse. I can't do this. I turn up the hill in our neighborhood and start running up it. My knees lift higher, and my breath comes faster. All I have to do is outrun any thoughts of Kell and I'm golden. Somehow, it's harder than it should be.

CHAPTER NINE

❁ ❁ ❁ ❁ ❁

Kell

Claudette frowns up at me from where she's hunched over a pile of bright green fabric. "You look like you could use a girl's day." Her black hair is pulled into a bun on top of her head, curls peeking out on the sides.

I sag in her doorway, wishing it wasn't so evident. I cringed at my own reflection this morning, at the bags under my eyes and the fine line creasing between my brows. Between Ryan's surprise engagement and the new show, I feel like I'm being pulled in one million emotional directions. The past week has flown by. I've been knee-deep in contract negotiations and trying my best to expedite any loose ends. Despite Judith assuring me that everything was "basically done," it's been near circus levels of chaos. I sigh and sit on the ground next to Claudette's desk, tucking my knees against my chest. "I'm okay," I tell her, even though the lie barely convinces even me. There's no time for anything but another workday crammed full to the brim.

She gives me an all-knowing look. "You're not okay. You're way too busy, and on top of that you're heartbroken. It's okay to admit it." When I say nothing, she jabs a sewing needle in the air in front of me. "What did he say when you confronted him?"

I twirl a strand of hair around my finger, feeling caught. "It's messy. I can't stop working for Ryan without it being weird for everyone else. They all live together. Right now they're working together. And besides, I only have the three clients. Bumping that down to two cuts my income by more than a third." I could still make do without Ryan, but I don't say it. I think Claudette knows it anyway.

"So you didn't confront him?"

"I attempted to confront him. It just didn't work so well." I squeeze my eyes closed, trying not to let my mind wander to the painful conversation.

"And then there's this reality show, which you know is so not my thing." I open my eyes and breathe deeply. Watching reality shows is fine. We all do it. But having my name attached to one via the guys? It kind of feels like a blow to my ego.

Claudette gives me a sad smile. "I've been telling you for months. As much as you care about the Matthews, you need a break from them. You are too invested in their lives. It's not healthy, Kell."

It's an old conversation we've rehashed one too many times. Between Claudette and my parents, it feels like a broken record. "It's a healthy balance. I promise," is what I say now and always.

"Okay." Claudette, to her credit, doesn't argue. "When I finish, let's go to dinner. What else do you have going on today?"

"Nothing. The film crew is scouting at the guys' house, but they don't need me there." I don't want to be there either. From what Judith explained of the setup, I would just be in the way. The crew needs room to move around the house, tracing the paths that they'll use to follow each of the Matthews as they pretend to go about their days completely normally. Besides, I'm sure I'll hear all about it later from Ash. He's the one I can count on to fill me in on the days I'm not there.

While Claudette finishes a dress, I take my laptop from my bag and go over my clients' schedules for the week, making sure I'm not forgetting anything. The tab with Samantha's profile is still open, even days later, and I linger over it. I stop myself from pressing the little X. I might need to look her up again, so it's better that I leave the page open for now. "Can you believe that Ryan's girlfriend is almost five years younger than him?"

Claudette turns to gape at me.

"What?" I shrug. "I just think it's pushing the boundaries of what's appropriate—don't you?"

"You've got to be kidding me." Before I can react, Claudette reaches over and snatches my laptop away. She gasps. "You're stalking her online? Kell, you have to stop obsessing over Ryan. It's never going to happen."

She meets my eyes, and I look away. I slip my computer from her hands. "It's my job to check up on people who spend time with my clients," I say, ice in my voice.

"Don't be mad. I'm worried about you, that's all." She reaches for my arm, but I turn and move away from her reach.

Claudette means well. I know she does. "It's fine. I'm not mad."

I feel like the world's crappiest friend as we sit in silence. I'm not lying about being upset with her, because the truth is the only person I have to blame in this situation is myself.

To Ryan, I was nothing more than a convenient fun time.

So, yes, my best friend is absolutely right. I may not be delusional about Ryan anymore, but I am heartbroken, and in order to keep my job functioning normally, it's important for me to pretend the opposite. I have more pressing matters at hand, like the ache in my stomach that most likely means I'm pushing myself too hard. No amount of morning Tylenol seems to help.

"I'm sorry," I say, nudging Claudette gently. "Let me buy dinner tonight."

"I want dinner *and* dessert. Fancy pastries, Kell. And I want you to swear to me that you will stop wasting your time on guys who don't deserve you." Claudette aims a finger at me like a sword.

My tongue catches in my throat. "I swear. I know the stalking is weird, but it really is for work."

She laughs under her breath, shaking her head at me. "You're ridiculous, you know that, right?" She stands. "Forget dinner. Let's get those pastries now. I'm starving. I feel like we earned them already, right? Who says dessert has to wait until after dinner?"

I follow her to the door and wrap my arms around her. "Thank you for always looking out for me."

Claudette scoffs. "I figure I'm stuck with you anyway, so . . ."

I make a fake hurt face and she tilts her head back and laughs, pulling away from me and leading the way out the door. And just like that our argument is settled.

CHAPTER TEN

❀ ❀ ❀ ❀ ❀

Ash

*A*nticipation over filming has me up early pacing my room. Watching other reality shows hasn't helped much. If anything, it's gotten worse the more I've seen. A lot of what's shown is a mixture of improv and reenactment. I don't have much experience with either. Yesterday, what was supposed to be our first day turned into a lot of set up and stalling. Not much actual filming happened due to a series of events. First a whole new set of forms needed to be signed, and then the crew needed a tour of the house. Somehow staging the grounds took several hours. Two weeks of waiting and then a full day of hurry up and wait some more. Typical show business.

I know I'll be fine once the cameras start and we get into the rhythm. The problem is with the actual episodes. Once they air—if they air—how will I be portrayed? I've seen enough to put together that reality stars are characters more than they are real people. And the drama. Like I said, that's not my thing, it's Ryan's. The reality stars

I've watched—they're only half-selves while the cameras are rolling. The whole thing has me analyzing all of it. The way I talk and dress. It's new for me, overthinking people's perceptions of my life. I've never given it much thought. I have to suck it up and get it done, so I try to push the worry out of my head.

Ash: *First day of filming. Wish me luck.*

Kell: *Luck! Don't get into too many catfights!*

I frown at the phone. Kell thinks she's being funny. The one thing I won't do with this show is let it tear us apart. My brothers can be insensitive and shortsighted. But they're my brothers and we're not going full Kardashian on this show. Not if I can help it. Not that I think she's serious, but still.

Pocketing my phone, I head to the living room where they're setting up. Jonah is there talking about basketball with the lighting crew. Ryan is leaned up against the front door with his hands in his pockets. He acts like every day is a modeling gig. Freaking ridiculous.

Jonah goes outside to be interviewed. It's a small segment where they plan on introducing each of us individually in the first episode. Kind of a "Meet the Matthews" thing. From the window, I watch him sit down in a booth. He talks for a while and comes back in. From the sounds of it, he goes right back to talking sports.

My turn is next. Outside, I sit down in what they've deemed the confessional booth. Really, it's what looks like a photo booth that you rent out for events. The curtain has been removed and the bench faces the outside to where a single-manned camera focuses on me. It's kind of cramped in here. My legs stretch in front of me as I try to position myself comfortably. I clear my throat and nod to the cameraman. He tells me to give a quick rundown on myself, so I jump right in. "My name is Ash Matthew. I'm twenty-six-years old. I started acting straight out of college, and I live with my two brothers who are also in the acting business."

Easy enough.

"Ash, tell us, how did you get into acting?"

Damn, such a simple question. Not sure I have a good answer. I sit up straighter and scratch the back of my head. "It happened kind of fast, to be honest with you. Kell, that's my manager, got me an audition here in LA for a minor role in an indie film. She basically email bombed the assistant casting director, who turned out to be one of her dad's past students." I lean back and crack a smile at that. Remembering the head rush of those early days with constant updates from Kell. And then came the eventual triumphant call that she'd gotten through to a real person, and I had a real audition.

"The only problem was," I pause for greater effect because I'm enjoying this trip down memory lane far too much. It's been a minute since I told this story. "I was still in school. And the audition she'd booked was the exact same time as my last final." I shake my head. "My public speaking final."

The camera guy blinks at me. "What did you do?"

A smarter man would have leveled with the professor. It wasn't like it was a secret that I was desperate for a career in acting. She was a cool professor and would have most likely let me make it up somehow. Never said I was smart in school. I smirk. "I had Kell come with me to the audition. She recorded the whole thing and then I sent it to my professor and asked her to consider it as my version of the final."

I can look back and see how cocky that was, but at the time it felt ingenious.

"And?" Camera guy prompts. "Did that work?"

Shrugging, I hold up my hands. "I passed the class. She gave me a C. But to be fair, I think she was fine with it as long as it meant getting me out of her classroom."

None of the scheduling had been a problem for Kell, who took her finals a week early and aced every single one. She came in at the top of her class and made the dean's list each year.

Kell was all of her professors' favorite student.

"Why do you live with your brothers?"

That's an obvious question, but one I'm sure viewers will be wondering. Fair enough. Moving back in with your parents, sure. I've seen it done pretty often. But three successful men living together in a giant house is kind of weird. Jonah used to rent an apartment near UCLA. Really nice place, too, but Ryan and I brought him around here enough that he gave in.

"Rent control," I say with a straight face. When the camera guy doesn't laugh, I give my honest answer. "This job can get lonely. I may not always see eye to eye with my brothers, but I know they have my back. I'd say we live together because it's good for us."

He nods. The rest of the questions are much simpler, things like my hobbies and small talk about my past films. The time goes quickly. When we're done, he lowers his camera and gives me a thumbs up. "Great job. If you see Ryan, can you send him this way?"

Interviews aren't my favorite way to spend an hour, but that wasn't so bad. I head inside but the living room has mostly emptied. Jonah still has one guy cornered and is scrolling through his fantasy basketball league on his phone.

I can't find anyone else inside, so I check out back. A crew is loosely set up around the basketball court where Ryan plays by himself. I walk across the full-sized court and hold my hands out for the ball.

Ryan dribbles without passing. He raises his brows in challenge and that's all it takes. I shake off Interview Ash and move into position. Stealing the ball from my older brother is as natural as breathing. Or at least it should be after so many years of this. Ryan can't even just play a friendly game. Always has to make it a competition. I'd be kidding myself if I said I wanted it any other way though. I quick step next to him and reach for the ball. Ryan spins and takes a shot. We both groan when it bounces off the rim. Before he can rebound, I elbow past him and snake the ball. Bouncing on my toes, I go for a three-pointer. It swooshes into the net and Ryan shakes his head while I pump my fist. Nothing feels better than scoring on him.

Ryan takes the ball back and points a cocky finger at me. "Watch and learn." I'm right on him but he fakes left and goes for the shot. The ball sinks in.

When I get the ball next, I don't waste my time trash talking. I dribble steady and low, keeping the ball out of his reach. Ryan crouches low to match me and tries to take it anyway. I move right but so does he. Out of options, I point the ball at the hoop and go for a Hail Mary.

We both freeze as we watch the ball arc and fall just barely too short. Ryan picks it up and has the decency to appreciate how close I was. He clicks his tongue. "I thought it was going in for sure."

Hands on my knees, I curse my bad luck. "Your turn for the interview."

"Nice." Ryan lets the ball drop. It bounces off the court and rolls into the grass along the side of the house. "Good game, bro," he calls behind his back.

The cameras still focus on me standing there alone, but I can almost pretend they're not there. I hustle over to scoop up the basketball and dribble it between my legs. I take a few shots and make almost all of them. Even after losing to Ryan, I'm feeling pretty good.

CHAPTER ELEVEN

❁ ❁ ❁ ❁ ❁

Kell

J've never been camera shy, but I've also never had the desire to be the one in front of a camera. Judith called this morning to relay that I was needed for a scene—urgently. Her tone of voice said all I needed to know about whether her idea of urgent matched up with mine. It doesn't really matter in the end, though, because in order to keep everyone happy and make contracts happen, I have to be flexible.

The guys are great at this because it comes naturally to them. Standing under the hot lights with all these strangers staring at me feels like one of those terrible nightmares I had the summer before I started high school. The ones where I was always inexplicably naked or running late and put in front of a test I'd never studied for. Somehow this is the adult version of that.

Ash is being dusted down with powder by a team of two makeup ladies while Jonah is in the corner talking softly with Jessie, both of them laughing. And Ryan hasn't even come downstairs yet. Under normal circumstances, I would march to his room and drag him out here, but I can't bring myself to do it. Samantha is in his room with him, most likely in his bed.

If this is going to work, if I'm going to keep working for Ryan, I have to keep some distance. Especially when it comes to what goes on in his bedroom.

"You okay?" Ash is done with his makeup and standing by my side, his eyes searching my face.

I fold my arms over myself and turn. "I'm hot and hungry, but I'm fine. I just want to get this over with."

"You're cute when you're nervous." Ash's lips spread into a smirk.

"I'm not nervous," I say, but my voice sounds strained even to my own ears. "I'm just . . ."

Ash gives a full grin. Great. I'm so glad that I can provide some much-needed entertainment. My nostrils flare as I open my mouth to cut him down, but my mouth sags at the sight of Ryan and Samantha floating down the stairs. Her hair is a graceful mess and her lips are red and puffy. Ryan looks like an Olympic god with the morning sun hitting one half of his face just right and making it shine a golden hue.

I turn away, but not quite in time. "Babe, you have to meet Kell." Ryan makes a beeline toward me, dragging his fiancée by two hands. My stomach roils. I can't do this.

Samantha's eyes shift between Ryan and me, and honestly, she looks a bit lost. I almost feel bad for her for being pulled into this. Almost, but not quite. "It's so nice to meet you," she says, her voice deeper and more even than I expected. "Ryan's told me before that he owes his career to you."

That feels like a very un-Ryan thing to say. Especially coming from the man who carelessly cut me out of a deal for this very TV show. I cock an eyebrow and nod back. Professional. Remember, Kell, be a professional. "It's nice to meet you. I'm glad you could make it for shooting today."

"Ryan insisted I come," she says, lowering her voice conspiratorially. "But I think he just wanted to show off how fun his job is."

I force a smile.

"I haven't started my career yet," she continues, "but once I finish school, I hope to be as excited about it as Ryan is. It's got to be nice doing something that you love so much it doesn't even feel like work."

"That's true." Ash catches my eye and waves me over to where he's moved by the back door. I clear my throat. "Excuse me. I'll be right back."

I wait until I'm following Ash out the back door to audibly exhale. Leaning back against the wall, I let my body sag. "Thank you," I breathe. The fresh air outside wafts over me, combatting the sweat accumulating at the back of my blouse.

Ash shakes his head. "You were actually sweating. Are you going to be okay?"

We have never fully talked about my feelings for his brother. Because of the nature of our friendship slash working relationship, most of the things we talk about are Ash things. Like his fling of the moment, his career moves, and even his future goals. Most of my more personal venting happens in front of Claudette, for better or for worse. I hadn't wanted to acknowledge whatever I had going on with Ryan because for me and Ash, it was out of our comfort zone.

Now, however, there isn't really a point in pretending he doesn't know. "I'm fine. It's not an ideal situation," I admit.

Ash snorts. "You being in love with my brother, or him being too dense to appreciate it?"

I laugh despite how crappy I feel. Ash has a way of making things seem not so bad. "I'm not in love with him." Not anymore. "It's kind of hard to love someone who treats me like he has lately."

He nods thoughtfully. "I support you getting over him. Want me to list all his worst traits? It might speed up the process. But I will warn you that it could take a while. The list is long."

"No, thank you." I wrinkle my nose and instead sidestep the subject of feelings. "Samantha is different than I expected."

"She's cool, actually. I'm starting to wonder what she's doing slumming it with my brother." Ash tilts his head. "Are you okay to go back in? Or are you hiding from the cameras now?"

He's found me out and I wish he hadn't. And he's right about Samantha. She's not what I expected—she's normal and *nice*. But I'd still be fine hiding outside with Ash until the entire day is over. I could avoid Samantha and Ryan and avoid looking ridiculous when the cameras come around. More than anything, I don't think I can handle another front-page moment forcing me into a form of spotlight I never asked for.

But Ash is leaning close, his eyes searching mine thoughtfully, so I lie and say I'm fine, and we go inside. There's no point in making Ash worry over me.

The second we do get inside, a lady with an enormous camera and a man following her with a hanging mic swarm us. Behind them, another woman waves her arms and mouths silently, "We're rolling."

My skin prickles as I freeze up with nerves. In the briefing email I received, some of the tips were to act natural and to start in the middle of a conversation. Above all, pretend like everything is normal and there aren't cameras and people staring at you. It's easy enough in theory. Something tells me that my execution might not be so hot.

"So what did the director say when you pitched me for the new movie?" Ash moves to the kitchen and grabs a loaf of bread, a jar of peanut butter, and a knife. He spreads his piece of bread with peanut butter, folds it in half, and scoots the knife and peanut butter across the counter to me. He stuffs the half sandwich in his mouth.

Confused, I pick up the butter knife and dip it into the peanut butter jar just for something to do with my hands. "Um." I shake my head. My peripheral vision shows the camera crew inching closer, panning in on my face. We've already talked about this. The director for Ash's current rom-com said he thought he would be a great fit for the more serious period piece he has his eye on. And on top of that, Judith has recommended him for an upcoming role with the producer on set today. Ash was so excited, I thought he'd put a hole through his wall with all the victory punches he was doing.

"He said you'd be a perfect fit. I'll send over the details later." I catch Ash's eye and he nods.

"I know you want to move in a different direction with your career," I say, getting into the flow of this fake conversation. "It's looking really promising with a few other directors, too."

Ash chews his sandwich thoughtfully. Then he lifts an arm and pulls it around me, crushing my piece of bread in the process. "Hey, it's all thanks to my amazing manager. You're the best."

I toss my head in what I hope is a saucy way. "I am, aren't I? Anyway, I've been wanting to talk to you about something."

"Okay. What's up?"

"The paparazzi photos," I say, lifting my shoulders. This is something that I would have loved to address in private, but Judith insisted it would make good TV when she overheard me bringing it up. So here it goes for the world to see.

"They were totally misconstrued by the press. I'm really happy for Samantha and Ryan, and this isn't the first time that paparazzi have managed to get on the property and take photos. I think that we should look into some higher-level security around the house."

Ash squeezes my shoulder. "You're right. That shouldn't happen. I'll take care of it."

We watch each other, and I try to silently thank him for being so good about the whole thing. He called a security company and had them here this morning before filming even started.

I see the camera moving away from us out of the corner of my vision. I made it through an entire scene.

"That wasn't so bad," I whisper, but my throat is dry as I speak. The crew says something about going on a hunt for Jonah and Jessie, probably hoping for juicier content.

"I don't know what you were so worried about." Ash snatches the partially made sandwich out of my hands and nibbles a corner. "We should go out. Celebrate the first week of filming."

Judith is talking to one of the cameramen when Ash and I wander into the living room. I offer a tight-lipped smile, still less than thrilled to see her. It's going to take me a while to forget about this whole fiasco. She lights up, waving the cameraman away and sweeping over to us. "Just the two I was hoping to see this morning," she chirps.

I tense and make myself put down my phone even though notifications come in at a steady stream. Judith smiling at me is suspiciously like the time a squirrel at Lake Balboa Park spent an hour eyeing down my picnic lunch. She wants something. Though, I don't know what else she could want from me, since I'm already here at her request.

"Aaron and I were chatting last night about show trends. Relationships are a very big selling point in this type of market."

"Okay. That makes sense, I guess."

I can't tell if Ash is oblivious or just refusing to take the bait. I, however, see exactly where Judith is going with this line of thinking. I'm guessing that Aaron, the show's producer, is used to getting his way, just like Judith. "If you're suggesting we set Ash up with someone solely for the show, that's not going to happen."

Manufactured relationships between stars really do exist, no matter how ridiculous it sounds. They usually come about when one higher profile name is in a PR crisis. By pairing up with a lesser-known actor, both parties benefit and then, when the contract ends, they go their separate ways with no one the wiser. That's how it's supposed to work, at least, but I've seen some huge disasters come about due to these kinds of relationships. Taylor Swift and Tom Hiddleston, for one. The only good thing to come out of that pairing was the inspiration for "Getaway Car."

Judith manages to look appalled at my suggestion. "I wasn't insinuating that at all, Kell. I was merely passing along what the producer had to say. Relationships are profitable, and Ash is the only brother currently single. That's simply a fact. And since you're his manager, I thought you might want to be included in the conversation. I know you've been sensitive about that in the past."

I let out a short huff and press my lips together. I look to Ash, who frowns at Judith just like I knew he would. "I'm not going to pay some random woman to be my girlfriend." He gives a dry laugh. "I'm not that desperate."

"Of course not." Judith laughs along with him but forges on anyway. "It could be anyone. And they wouldn't have to be your girlfriend, it could just appear that way for the cameras. We'd let the audience think what they want. But it could be an ex-girlfriend, a friend, anyone. Even Kell."

Both of their heads swivel to me, Judith's glance nothing short of predatory. She just crossed the line from a nuisance to insufferable. Seriously, where does she get the nerve? Before I can say anything, Ash puts a hand on my back. "I'll let my brothers handle the relationships. We're headed out to lunch."

When we break away from Judith, Ash drives us to our favorite lunch spot, a Thai restaurant nestled in between a health spa advertising fifty percent off Botox and a brand-new green smoothie store. We found it one day after driving around getting hangrier by the minute. Ash had turned into the parking lot and dragged me from the car, insisting that the best restaurants don't look like anything special from the outside.

With its basic gray stucco and crumbling sign, I was a skeptic, but it turns out that Ash was right. I won't get pad thai from anywhere else now. The drive is quiet, and I take the chance to scroll through my emails on my phone on the way over.

"I texted Jonah to come meet us," Ash says when we pull up. "He got all mad last time we came here without him."

"Good idea," I say. I shift in the passenger seat and turn to look at him. "So, are we going to talk about what Judith said? It doesn't matter what the producer wants, because if it's not in the contract, you don't have to do it."

Ash looks out at the parking lot, where the empty building next to the restaurant is decorated in spray paint. The streetlamp next to us is splattered in colorful flyers advertising for sketchy casting calls and missing pets. He lets out a heavy breath. "I told you before, I'm down for whatever it takes. If it's a sticking point for the show to move forward, I'll figure it out, I guess."

"Figure it out? What does that mean?" I narrow my eyes. "Do you want me to find you a willing TV girlfriend?"

Ash eyes me with exasperation. "You're ridiculous. Let's just go eat."

He doesn't want to talk more about it, so I stay quiet and follow him to the restaurant, but if Judith brings it up again, Ash will have to say something.

Maybe what Ash *won't* say is that he wants more than a fake partner. Maybe watching Jonah and Ryan throw their happiness around so casually is hard for him. I'm not sure what to make of his avoidance, but I do know that Ash could do better than a contractual relationship, if that's what he really wants.

CHAPTER TWELVE

❂ ❂ ❂ ❂ ❂

Ash

My day off is dedicated to audition prep. When I started acting, I adapted Ryan's routine and I'm too superstitious to change it now. It's worked well enough so far. The gist of it is vocal rest, liquid diet, and research while staying in character as much as possible.

This time around, vocal rest is out due to filming for the show tomorrow, and liquid diet may as well be out too. At least the role doesn't call for anything other than shirt-off scenes. Could be leaner, but I think I'm okay.

That leaves my focus on research and character. Judith sent over a feeler for the movie. There are other roles, but I want the lead and I don't see the point in going after anything else. Not at this point in my career.

It's a period movie set during the Great Depression, but really it's about a big family. The main character spends the whole script trying to work hard enough to save his family and their farm. I might not be a struggling farmer, but I do know something about working with family.

Acting is interesting like that. You can take an emotion you've felt for something ordinary and transfer it. People think of good actors as good liars. Like it's a bad thing. To me it's more that actors are good at empathizing. Not to get cheesy, but it's all about the universal human experience. More so than standing around while a team mists you down with a spray bottle and you stare dumbly into the distance.

Time to get to it. I open my computer and sit back on my bed. Best place to start is by studying my own projects. It sounds stupid, but it works. I try to start all my character research by watching myself act. Sure, sometimes it's hard to get through. Some actors I know can't watch themselves without cringing over their mistakes. Little things will always be there. Things I want to change or wish I'd done or said differently. But that's why this works for me.

I'll start this time with my latest movie. The movie itself is fine but the whole aftermath still stings. Awards season was a beast. Mostly, I've tried to push it all out of my mind. But, for the sake of preparation, I drag myself back.

For the first part of the movie, I get lost in the story. My character starts off funny. Kind of awkwardly charming until he spirals into this silent, scowling caricature. The whole last half of the movie is me bare-chested wearing the tightest pants wardrobe could fit me in. I don't have one line worth noting.

I remember a group of women coming by and touching my bare stomach at the end of one long day at work. They cornered me, and it didn't feel like I could say anything. Probably was supposed to be a compliment. But all it did was make me feel dirty the rest of the week. I can almost see the misery on my face on screen.

Maybe it wasn't just the character arc that ruined things for me.

I toggle away from the movie and lean back. Best takeaway here is not to let myself sign on for another disaster like this one.

To balance it out, I'm gonna throw myself a bone and watch something I know will cheer me up. There's a fine line between critique and inspiration. If I go too far, I'll never be ready for another role. Scrolling through the options, I stop at the last movie Judith's producer worked on, a movie set around the Vietnam War.

Watching something I'm not in switches up my mood immediately. This producer is known for being part of award-winning films, and I can see why. The dialogue is gritty and real. The characters feel dimensional. And the shots are all clear and pack a punch.

Halfway through, I pause the movie, feeling more optimistic already. I stretch and grab my wallet. It's not necessarily part of the routine, but I always buy juice when I'm prepping. Not green juice or any other health stuff, just sugary juice. My official reason is that it's good for my voice. The science probably doesn't add up there, but I don't care much as long as it gets me results.

I drive to the gas station a few blocks from our neighborhood, a notorious spot for celebrities because we all seem to live in the same bubble. But it's also close by, so I take my chances. The billboard next to the highway flashes between an image of Ryan's latest spy thriller and an advertisement for the latest diet pill. I snort at the juxtaposition. The store is small, so the juice is easy to find and they always have my favorite. I grab it and get in line, ready to get in and out. Still a ton of audition stuff to focus on. After I pay, a rush of long blond hair fills my side vision. I turn to look and curse under my breath.

Celeste.

The odds of running into my ex should be low. I'm not going to run out of the store, but I'm sure as hell going to pretend I don't see her. She's with a friend who looks eerily similar to her—same bleached hair, fake nails, eyelashes, and plastic surgery. The cashier hands me my receipt and I'm almost out when a voice behind me hums in my ear. "Oh, juice. I'm guessing you have an audition coming up."

I breathe out a quiet sigh and bite the inside of my cheek. So close to getting out of here. Turning around to give her a half nod, I start to push the door open.

"What? No small talk, Ash?" Celeste laughs, putting her hand on my bicep. It stays there until I take another step back.

"Hey, Celeste." I sigh again. "How are you?"

She tilts her head to look at me. "I'm really good. Gah, I haven't seen you in forever. But I heard about your new show! Congratulations." Her friend looks me up and down with muted interest.

Of course she's heard about the show. When we were together, Celeste made it a point to know all the gossip. Half the time, she didn't care if it was real or not. If she's thinking my show will give her a leg up, she's wrong. "Thank you," I say and leave it at that.

"Come on. You don't want to tell me all about it? I'll even let you buy me dinner." She bats her outrageously large false lashes.

"There's nothing to tell right now."

She looks at me for another second before tossing her hair over one shoulder. "Well, I hope it goes well. Reality TV is such a big risk, and I'd hate to see your career tank. Especially after all the drama last awards season," she says in a whisper that the whole gas station can hear. Celeste's friend smirks but says nothing. My heartbeat speeds up, but I don't give her the satisfaction of a comeback. I learned not to engage.

Celeste shrugs. "It was so good to see you, Ash. Really. Text me the next time you're out at the clubs, okay? I'd love to get drinks or something."

No way in hell am I going on anything resembling a date with her. I grip my drink and back out of there. It was exactly like when we dated. Nothing she said was wrong. It's *how* she says things. I'd walk away from every interaction feeling like shit about myself. Took me way too long to realize I wasn't the problem in the relationship.

In the car I untwist the cap on my juice and chug half the bottle. Cold and sweet, it glides down my throat. I wipe my mouth with the back of my hand and shake my head. That part of my life, who I was when I dated Celeste, that's when I was unhappiest. I didn't start out wanting to be some shallow clone of a dozen other men in Hollywood. What I wanted—what I still want—is to *act*. Really act.

More determined than ever, I drive home. I grit my teeth and do vocal exercises. I finish off my juice. Then I watch the rest of the movie and try to match my style to the lead's. No more wishing my career was different. I'm making it happen, no matter what. I think over filming, how Judith said relationships were hot. That's what I need to be doing, going after whatever will make me big enough to get the big jobs. If a fake relationship makes the show a big hit, that's more eyes on me. More fans who will bring viewing power to the table. That kind of thing is important to movie people.

With this in mind, I send Kell a text and pray she doesn't laugh me out of the state.

CHAPTER THIRTEEN

❀ ❀ ❀ ❀ ❀

Kell

*C*laudette drives and I sit in the passenger seat and stare at the text Ash sent me late last night. I keep rereading it, wondering if I'm missing the punch line here, because it has to be a joke.

Ash: *Starting to think Judith is right about faking a relationship for the show. I'm in if you are.*

Claudette and I pull up to the Matthews' house and walk inside. I haven't told her about Ash's text because I wouldn't even know where to begin. Ash can't mean that he wants me to pretend to be the woman he's dating. There are so many things wrong with that, starting with the fact that I'm his manager and ending with my past with his brother.

I guess that would fill the drama quota for a reality show pretty well.

My mind spins with all the reasons it's a terrible idea, but a tiny voice in the back of my head won't shut up. The lingering tabloid rumor of me trying to ruin Ryan's engagement thanks to the pap photos would be squashed and hopefully forever put to rest. And in the meantime, the producer would be happy, and the show would have its fill of money-making romance with all three guys loved-up. Everyone wins in that scenario, right? Even me.

I turn my attention back to the present, knowing I have to text Ash back at some point and make a decision. Claudette shakes her hair, letting her braids bounce in a halo around her head. The front rooms in the house are empty and suspiciously quiet. "Where is everyone?" she asks me.

The first time I brought her over to meet the guys, I was sure it would be a disaster. The Matthews are just a bunch of regular, albeit extremely good-looking guys, to me. But I'm still well aware that they're much more than that to the rest of the world. Seeing someone face-to-face who you've only ever seen on a movie or TV screen can be bizarre. I know this because I practically went into anaphylactic shock when I spotted Keanu Reeves across the room last year at a schmoozy fundraiser.

It's not like that at all for Claudette, and it shouldn't surprise me. But even if I knew she wouldn't care about their fame, it was still something else to see her march in and put them in their places so quickly that first meeting. Ryan stood there looking like the poster boy for sexy action hero. I was just waiting for him to say something bad, and he went right for it, eyeing Claudette up and down and taking on a deeper, sultry voice. "It's okay if you're nervous to meet me."

She'd looked at him with absolute steel in her eyes. "I don't see what the fuss is about, honestly," she'd said, before walking out of the room and asking me to show her around the backyard. Ever since then, when Claudette comes over with me, Ryan gets a kick out of poking the bear.

Now, we move through the house and finally find them hanging out in the kitchen wearing tuxedos and making sandwiches. Ryan makes a beeline for Claudette, grinning like a little boy caught making trouble. Behind him, Ash and Jonah watch with half-amused, half-concerned hesitancy.

"Did you bring me anything nice to wear today, Claude? What do I have to do to get one of your special outfits?"

She doesn't crack so much as a smile. She also doesn't comment on the fact that they're pigging out on lunch meat when they're supposed to be out the door to a fancy banquet dinner. "Buy one like everyone else, asshole. We all know you have enough money."

Jonah guffaws, choking into his sandwich. Ash looks at me like he's gauging my reaction and getting ready to step in. I shake my head minutely because I'm confident that Ryan and Claudette can handle each other just fine.

Ryan shakes his head, unfazed. "One of these days I'm going to do it."

"You know where to find me until then," Claudette tells him.

Turning back to me, she smiles. "Kell, let's go find Jessie."

I follow, failing desperately at holding in the laughter trying to escape from my throat. I only wish I were half as fearless in the face of Ryan's ego. If I had the ability to shoot him down so easily, I probably never would have given him the power to break my heart in the first place.

Claudette must read the emotions on my face because she loops her arm with mine as we round the corner. "You deserve so much better than him," she says.

We find Jessie curled up in a corner of her and Jonah's bedroom, sitting in a plush armchair with a book. She looks up to see us and grins. "Hey, you two. Claudette, did you come to terrorize Ryan?"

"I have no idea what you're talking about." Claudette's smile hides nothing. "We came to see if you wanted to hang out with us while Jonah goes to the banquet. It looked like they were about to leave."

Jessie sets down her book, marking the page with a bright red bookmark. "Are we going to use the theater room? I made Jonah buy more butter for the popcorn machine so we don't get stuck with the gross stuff like last time."

"Sounds perfect," I say. We don't get to do this very often, hanging out without the guys and their drama.

The theater room is impressive and one of the only other communal spaces in the big house, aside from the kitchen and the main living room. It's stocked with movie posters from both Ash and Ryan's projects and, obviously, houses every single one of their projects.

Jonah has a little shrine in one corner with some of his sportscasting awards and a football from the game he helped his team win his senior year at UCLA. The game that happened right before the one that permanently messed up his leg and changed his career goals from NFL to television.

All three of us cuddle onto the oversized sectional with bowls of popcorn. Jessie puts on a movie we've all seen before, the perfect background to a night of catching up. "How is work going?" I ask, shoveling a handful of buttery popcorn into my mouth.

Jessie shrugs. "It's okay. The school is losing funding every year and of course my department takes the most hits. We're scrambling for supplies, and I give as much as I can out of my own paycheck. But my students deserve better." She wrinkles her nose. "Education is everyone's last thought, and it sucks sometimes."

Claudette shakes her head. "My mom says the same thing. Her school had to have a fundraiser last month just to buy pencils and paper and other basic stuff. It's ridiculous."

Jessie has been a special education teacher as long as I've known her, and I've never met anyone as passionate about teaching kids. I hate that the system is so screwed up. "I've seen their accounts recently, and I have it on good authority that the guys can afford a few hundred thousand more in donations this year. Want me to make sure some of it goes to your school?"

She laughs. "Oh, they've already written checks. Sadly, it only goes so far. Generous donations are great, but what we really need is actual support from the administration and up." She blows out a breath. "Anyway, that's me at work. What about you two?"

Claudette pulls up pictures on her phone of some of the latest models wearing her designs. We drool over the gorgeous outfits together while the characters in the movie have their first kiss.

"Kell?" Jessie asks, "What about you? I mean, I know some of what you've been doing, but anything else exciting?"

"Just the reality show," I say with as much enthusiasm as I can muster. Obviously, it's not just the show, but I'm not ready to share about Ash's proposition or what it could mean for the group dynamic. I'm also not ready to confess how stressed my job has made me lately.

Neither of them is fooled. Claudette puts an arm around my shoulders. "I feel stupid complaining about work when it only affects me," I admit. Jessie has real problems and Claudette has real, hard-earned success. I have stuck-up LA issues because I'm too good for reality television.

"It's a valid concern," Jessie says. "I honestly never pictured the TV show working out, but it's been great. Jonah likes spending more time with his brothers, and I think it makes him feel like he's part of what they're doing, you know?"

I nod. That makes a lot of sense, actually, since Jonah is usually part of a different, less intense world of filming. And I know that Ryan and Ash have liked the show, too, both for their own reasons. I'm the only one who still has reservations, and that weighs heavy on me because it shouldn't matter to me. A good manager is only as happy as her clients are, but my clients are content, and that used to be enough for me. Lately, I'm not so sure it is.

"Okay, no more work talk," Claudette says, tossing a popcorn kernel at me. It bounces off my forehead and rolls off the sectional, and I laugh, stunned.

We watch the movie while talking about the Matthews' banquet and taking bets on whether or not they'll do something embarrassing there. Jessie says yes, one hundred percent, and Claudette agrees. I swear up and down that they will be model citizens because it's my job to have faith in them. Secretly, I'm pretty sure they'll create some new mess for me to clean up.

❀ ❀ ❀ ❀ ❀

I'm not sure how much time has passed, but the movie room is dark and empty. I blink my eyes as Ash sits down next to me on the couch. His voice is soft, almost a whisper. "You fell asleep," he tells me. "Jessie's with Jonah, and Claudette told me to tell you that she had to do a last-minute call with a client in the UK. She took over the living room."

I yawn, rolling my shoulders as I try to fully wake up. "Okay. How was the banquet?"

Ash shrugs. "Fine. We won Hottest Related Celebrities and Ryan almost got into a fight with the Hemsworths. But then we all donated a ton of money to the Make-a-Wish Foundation, and Jonah smoothed it over for him."

I cock an eyebrow because, knowing Ryan and Jonah, there has to be more to the story. But Ash says, "I'll tell you all the details tomorrow, but for now, can we talk about my text?"

I should have expected that lead-in. I drop my head onto his shoulder. He smells like cinnamon and new clothes, and the combination really works for me. I suck in a breath. "Let's do it. I think it could be good for the show, for you . . ."

I trail off and Ash supplies, "For you too?"

"Well, yeah. When you're successful, I'm successful. That's how this works."

If he suspects there's more to my motivations, he doesn't push.

He just reaches up and brushes away the piece of hair that's fallen in front of my face. He tucks it behind my ear. "Okay, then. How exactly do we do this?"

The movie room is dark except for the warm glow of the blank screen opposite the wall. I watch our shadows curled together like this, one black unit that's almost indistinguishable. "I don't think we have to do anything different from what we normally do. It's like Judith said; all that matters is that the audience assumes we're together."

Ash grabs a handful of what's left of the popcorn and chews thoughtfully. After a moment, he reaches for my hands, which are folded in my lap, and squeezes gently. "Should be pretty easy then. We've always made a good team."

I don't know why this sends a flush over my skin, but I'm warm and presumably red when I nod. I try not to look at his lips as Ash's tongue darts out to catch another handful of popcorn. This is going to be fine. We are absolutely capable of pretending to be more than longtime friends. Just like Ash said, we make a good team—always have. Why, then, does the whole idea suddenly make my heart race?

CHAPTER FOURTEEN

✿ ✿ ✿ ✿ ✿

Ash

*K*ell's index finger touches my cheek. The softest brush of skin on skin. My breath catches. My chest feels swollen with wanting.

Like she knows what she's doing to me, Kell smiles. She traces that finger farther across my skin, ending at my lips. I can't keep still any longer. Her eyes widen as I part my mouth and suck on the tip of her finger. Every inch of her tastes so good.

My hand finds its way to her stomach. The smooth feel of her bare skin nearly takes me out. Kell brushes against me, pressing closer, and . . .

My eyes break open. A cold sweat flushes my skin. What the hell was that? The last thing I need to do right now is to start panting over Kell. She's the only one holding things together. I sit up and run a hand through my unruly bedhead. One dream about your hot friend is fine. It's bound to happen. Two dreams in the same month makes it weird. I can't keep having these dreams.

Kell and I agreed to fake a relationship for the show, but my subconscious doesn't seem to be buying it. I need to figure some things out. Clearly.

I run the shower and stand in front of the steam while the water heats up. I've always felt protective over Kell. She's this driven, smart, objectively gorgeous woman. Guys line up to take advantage of that. It's not my place to protect her, but it's hard to stop the urge to. Yeah, it's gotten more intense since the whole drama with Ryan went down. But that's because I feel partly responsible. I never should have let him cross that line with her. I should have made sure Ryan knew that he was supposed to stay away from Kell. I never should have let her get hurt.

My shower is short because we have another early day of work. Today is the day that we're shooting promo video and photos. Kell will probably be here by the time I'm downstairs. I wouldn't be surprised if she's here already.

I dry my hair with the towel and get dressed, then hurry to the kitchen. Ryan is the only one there. He's at the table scrolling on his phone with one hand while he eats oatmeal with the other. I grab one of Jonah's yogurts from the fridge and sit down across from Ryan. He nods at me. "Hey. Ready for the photo shoot, little brother?"

I spoon enough yogurt in my mouth that all I can do is shrug.

"You're not wearing that, are you?" He looks at my gray T-shirt and dark jeans and laughs.

I'm not in the mood for this. I ignore him and keep eating my yogurt, but Ryan taps his fingers on the table between us. "Hey, what's your problem?"

My spoon falls to the table with a loud clatter. "No problem, bro. I'm eating. And yeah, this is what I'm wearing. The brief said keep it simple. This is simple."

Ryan shakes his head. "No, you've had a problem with me for weeks. What is it? You're supposed to be happy for me. I'm getting married. And we're finally working together. But you're ruining everything by skulking around the house like you're too cool to be a Matthew anymore."

My head feels like it's going to explode. Ryan has no idea what he's talking about. "I'm too cool? Oh, that's hilarious." I jab a finger in his direction. "You're the one trying to get big at the cost of everyone else. You're the one ruining things for Kell."

Ryan's eyes narrow, and he leans back in his seat. He tips his head back. "You serious? That's what this is about? You still have a crush on our manager? I thought we were past that, Ash. Kell wouldn't still be here if she didn't want to be. If you have an issue with that, it sounds like you're the problem."

My hands ball into fists in my lap. I grit my teeth and struggle to keep my voice calm. There are cameras on the other side of the house. It would technically be fair game for them to pick up on this argument and run with it. "Kell is my friend." I swallow. "And you did wrong by her."

"You sure she's just a friend?"

I stand up and throw away my half-eaten yogurt. "Yeah, I'm sure. Just do me a favor and stay away from her, okay?"

Instead of doubling down, Ryan cracks a smile and steps back. "You got it. Can we play nice now?"

He's my brother and as much as I think he's an idiot, I don't want to hate him. Maybe Ryan is right. If Kell is fine with him, then I should be too. She's got her life together more than anyone else in this house. It's only fair that I acknowledge that and let her handle her own business. "Okay," I agree, still mad but trying not to hold on to it. "But seriously, what's wrong with my clothes?"

Ryan laughs. "You're hilarious. Come and see what I had my wardrobe people send over."

His wardrobe people turn out to be Gucci. He volunteered to wear their clothes on our show as promo. He volunteered Jonah and me too. The fitting people help me into a blue plaid suit, which I have to admit looks pretty sharp. The only thing I'm not too sure about is the dainty blue bowtie. But apparently it's fashionable.

Kell is here and she's dressed up too. She's wearing a sleeveless green gown with a slit up one of her legs. Her hair is long and loose with little waves that brush over the top of her chest. My own legs go unsteady. Damn.

She sees me and does a spin with her arms out. "I know I'm only technically a guest star, but they want me in some of the cast pictures. I kind of look great, right?"

"You look great," I confirm. "Really great." I gesture to the dress. The fabric looks silky. "Do they have you in designer too?"

"Yep." Kell grins. "Should I accidentally spill on the dress so they have to let me take it home?"

If she doesn't, I will. The dress was made for her. I laugh but it sounds strange in my own head. Like the laugh of a nervous stranger. Kell tilts her head, her eyes tracking mine. Then she drags her gaze down to my shiny leather shoes and up over my suit. "Wow." Her lips pucker into a perfect red circle. "They should let you keep yours too. You clean up nice."

My throat is dry. I want to run my hands over Kell's dress and see if it feels as soft as it looks. "Thanks."

Judith stands next to the director and starts waving everyone over. They've cleared everything out of our living room except for the couch. Lights are staged behind it and a set of assistants direct us where to arrange ourselves. Ryan, Jonah, and me front and center. My brothers are wearing suits similar to mine but in different patterns and colors. Jonah's has little golden basketballs dotted everywhere. Nice touch.

Once they've taken an hour's worth of photos of us, they bring in our guest stars. Samantha, Jessie, and Kell are the main ones, but they also include our housekeeper slash cook, Ava, who we would never survive without, and Jonah's trainer, Mike. The group pictures feel a tad ridiculous because none of these people are ever in the same room together in real life. But it's not real life. So, there you go.

Things go fine until Judith whispers something to the director before he clears the room again except for my brothers and me and the three women. From where I'm standing against the doorway, I can see the panic in Kell's wide eyes. "Let's create a bit of drama, shall we?" Judith rubs her hands together like a Disney villain. I swear she cackles too.

"Our lovey-dovey couple." She hooks an arm through Samantha's and drags her to the couch. Ryan follows obediently. Judith positions them so that Samantha is perched on Ryan's lap. Pretty similar to how they were the night he proposed. Judith is either an evil genius or just evil.

Jessie isn't one to take orders. She cocks a hand on her hip and tells Judith how she and Jonah will be standing—behind the couch, back-to-back like the power couple they are. Judith looks pissed, but she's smart not to argue.

"You." She crooks a finger. "Have a seat here by your brother."

I sit on the couch next to Ryan and Samantha, my legs spread. Judith tells me to put my chin in my hand and lean forward. I do it. Better to go along with this and get it done.

Judith turns to the producer. She cocks her head and frowns. "I thought this might happen. The balance is all thrown off. Don't you think, Aaron?" He shrugs. Something tells me he's getting sick of Judith following him around on his own set.

"Exactly." Judith clucks her tongue. "Kell. Why don't we fit you in this one too? You'll even out the numbers.

"Right here." Judith points to the spot directly between Ryan and me. To Kell's credit she takes it all in stride, sliding in between us and sitting on the edge of the sofa with her knees angled toward mine. This is what we signed up for, so it shouldn't come as a shock that we're already being paired off and displayed as a couple. The moment we let Judith know what we'd decided on, all of this became fair game.

Kell's leg brushes against mine. Even in these suit pants, the warmth of her bare skin traces mine. Knocks me off balance for a second, and I forget to pose for the photo. I probably look as goofy as I feel. Being close to Kell like this does that to me. As hard as I try, I can't get the dream of us together out of my head. Not ideal when we're sitting so close that every part of our bodies sits flush against each other.

Next, they split us up to do solo couple photos. We watch Ryan and Samantha wrap up in each other with their tongues down each other's throats, but Kell handles it like a champ and doesn't flinch. Jessie and Jonah, always casual, hold hands and lean in close. It hits me that we're supposed to do something like that just as Kell and I are called over for our turn.

"Just pose like normal," the photographer instructs. "Pretend I'm not here."

Kell's mouth twitches. She's got to be thinking the same thing I am. If the photographer weren't here, our normal wouldn't be posing like a couple. She's frozen a good six inches from me, so I take the lead. I step behind her and wrap my arms around Kell's shoulders. She tenses right away.

"Hey, we've got this," I say low into her ear. "First lesson in acting: No one is going to believe it if you don't believe it yourself. Pretend it's just us."

Her chest moves as she takes in a breath. I feel her relax under my arms. Kell's hands reach up to rest on mine. The photographer points at us. "Love it. Lean in more. Ash, kiss the top of her head and hold it."

Taking direction like this is almost second nature. For Kell, it's much less so. But if she's still uncomfortable, she hides it well. She shimmies closer, bringing her head to nestle right under my chin. I bend down and plant a kiss on the top of her hair. I stay like that while the camera flashes. My gut tightens, and even though it's just a picture, I want to hold her to me like this for hours. None of this is doing much for that invisible friendship line between us.

We're waved away to wait for more direction, and I sit on the sofa with my hands behind my head. Kell follows and lays her head in my lap. This is good for optics, and I know that. But it's feeding the inner battle I've been fighting for weeks. I swallow.

I touch Kell's arm lightly. "Good job today."

She laughs, and I can feel it more than hear it. She shakes softly against me. "It's so weird because it's me and you and we've been friends forever, but at the same time it's so easy. You know?"

I know.

"Yeah. I think we were pretty convincing."

We fall into silence, and I watch Jonah and Jessie across the room trying to hide the fact that they're fighting about something. Jonah's jaw is tight as he stares at the floor. Jessie talks in a low voice. Everything about her screams annoyed.

I'm not really sure how my brothers feel about the show so far. For me, it feels good doing something different for work.

I know Kell isn't too happy about this new show. And I feel for her. I most likely wouldn't be for it if I were in her position. It's okay with me, though. It's the last thing in the world I thought I'd enjoy, but reality show filming has been cool. I wouldn't mind more of it. Especially if it opens the doors Kell thinks it will. If it takes branching out to get a foot in the door for more serious projects, then so be it.

CHAPTER FIFTEEN

❀ ❀ ❀ ❀ ❀

Kell

*A*fter an incredibly long day of standing around and smiling for cameras, my bed sounds like the best thing in the world. Unfortunately, Judith lingers at the Matthews' house after the rest of the crew has left. She finds me while I'm waiting on the front porch, hoping for my chance to end the workday and drive home.

"Our boys are gorgeous, aren't they? I could have them standing around in their underwear saying nothing at all, and the show would still get viewers."

I hate the way she talks about the Matthews. The gleam in her eyes makes her words worse. No wonder Ash feels objectified on most sets, if he's being treated like this. People like Judith are everywhere in LA, and especially in film and TV, and it's always bothered me how prevalent the wolfish attitude is.

"They're so talented," I counter. "And passionate. This has been the perfect thing to get them out of a rough spot. Ash is really excited about working on some new things. And Jonah could use the experience in something other than sportscasting. It's been good for them."

Judith gives me an amused look. "One project at a time, right? I'm hoping to put together something for Ash like we talked about, if the show does well. But the other two are a little flighty. There's something to say for loyalty in Hollywood, am I right?"

I shake my head. Either I'm more tired than I thought, or Judith isn't making any sense. "I can assure you that there's nothing to worry about there. They've all been loyal to me for over five years." Ryan is on thin ice, yes, but how many more secrets could he really be hiding? "They've always stuck it out with projects, even when things didn't go as planned." I can't keep the sharp sting out of my voice. The Matthews may be oblivious morons part of the time, but they're my oblivious morons, thank you very much. Judith is one to talk about loyalty, speaking about her clients like they're completely dispensable.

"That's the problem with being too friendly with your clients, Kell. You're a smart girl, but you have trouble seeing them clearly." Judith's lips pinch into something haughty, her expression hiding something I wouldn't even know to guess at. She's enjoying this far too much.

Blinking back at her, I can't think of what to say to that. It sounds like she's insinuating something secretive with one of the Matthews. Ryan has been known to keep a secret or two—hello, surprise fiancée and reality show—but I trust all three of them to let me in on the important things from now on. I've made it clear where I stand.

Judith's mouth is still set in a smug pout, full of fake sympathy for a fake weight she feels like she has over me. "Oh, I meant to say, good for you for going for the relationship angle with Ash. Aaron was pushing hard for it, so it was definitely the right choice. Pass that along, will you?"

"Sure. It was nice chatting," I say as shortly as I can, making sure that she knows it wasn't nice at all. I feel just fine about my decision to get cozy on screen with Ash all on my own. I don't need Judith's, or anyone else's, validation. To be fair, Ash probably does care about that stuff since it's the whole reason he's putting his all into this show. He wants to level up his career at any cost, and I can't say it's not admirable.

I watch Judith drive away, the picture of cold, calculated professionalism. Is that what I risk turning into, given a few more years in the industry? Sharp, quick, and successful but dead inside is a fate I don't want to be dealt. I can already feel some of the hardening. Things that would have bothered me at the beginning roll right off my back now. For better or worse. Judith insinuating I don't know how to handle my clients might have broken me a few years ago. Certainly it would have left me in tears.

The door opens and Ash joins me on the front porch, a cold drink in hand. "Looked like a fun conversation."

Despite the tension rolling off my body, I laugh. "It was something. I knew that working on a big project like this with Judith would be difficult. But honestly, I don't know if I prepared myself well enough."

"If anyone can handle her, it's you." Ash offers me his drink, and I take the frosty can and put it to my lips. "Did you mention finding any more auditions? She was supposed to talk to Aaron and let me know."

The drink slides down my throat easily, and I sigh after swallowing. It's never fun not being able to give your clients the answers they want. Ash wants more serious work. He deserves it, but when I brought it up, all Judith could do was talk in circles and give nonanswers. "She only had time to talk about the shoot today. I'll make sure to get with her soon to iron out the details."

Ash doesn't let on if he can tell I'm bluffing a little. "Okay, that's fine. And hey, sorry you had to be in front of the camera so much today. I know that's not your thing."

"It is not." I meet Ash's eyes. He's watching me, always watching me like he sees too much. Knows too much. It can be unnerving at best. Neither of us says anything else for a moment. Ash is one of the only people in my life, aside from Claudette, whom I can have these prolonged silences with. It's never weird and there's never any pressure to fill empty space with meaningless small talk. It makes for a good friendship, but it also has led us here, to this space where we're able to pretend so well at being much more than friends. It's tenuous ground, really, touching and flirting for the cameras but switching back to something purely platonic the rest of the day. Someone could get confused really easily.

Ash's unfairly dark lashes flutter over his lids, squinting at me. He waves a hand in front of my face, gesturing to the way I'm silently studying him. "Are you plotting my murder or just zoning out?"

I stick my tongue out at him. "I'm going inside to raid your fridge before I go home to crash." My stomach gurgles dangerously, but I can't tell anymore whether it's upset or hungry. I'm too busy to think about it too hard.

Ash follows me inside, which is much quieter now that it's just the Matthews left. I scan the kitchen and see that Ryan is alone.

Samantha left after the crew did, and Ryan's been sitting at the table scrolling on his phone ever since. I've been working up the nerve to talk to him, and I guess now is as good a time as any other.

I poke Ash. "I'm going to talk to Ryan about next week's filming. Make sure he knows the schedule."

Ash gives me a look, another one of those disappointed frowns, and I hate it. I don't deserve to be on the receiving end of one of these looks. I put a hand on my hip and frown right back. "What? This is literally my job."

"You know what." Ash touches my arm, letting his thumb brush over my skin. "Hey, I'm trying to look out for you. I don't want to see you hurt again."

My laugh is stale. "Hurt? From what? I'm going over there to have a sixty-second conversation. I'll survive."

Ash opens his mouth but pauses like he's rethinking what he's going to say. Then he plunges on anyway. "Last time you and Ryan disappeared together after work it didn't end well for you. That's all I'm saying."

The blow lands straight to my heart. I stagger back, shaking my head at Ash. I can't believe he went there. I grind my teeth and hiss back, "You have no business trying to tell me who to date or not date. It's actually completely inappropriate for you to even bring it up."

"Inappropriate?" he scoffs. "How about dry humping my brother in our living room? Or is it only inappropriate when I say something *true* that you don't like?"

I turn away from his touch and his frowny face and move to Ryan. I run a hand through my hair and pull my tongue along my teeth to check for runaway lipstick. My eyes sting with unshed tears, but I swipe them away. Ash is a dick.

Ryan puts his phone face down on the table as soon as he sees me. His face lights up with a big, welcoming smile. To say that things have been tense between us lately is a massive understatement. It's important that I work to repair some of that. We need to rebuild trust, or I don't know how we'll keep working together. *That's* what this is about, and Ash can go to hell if he wants to insinuate it's anything more.

"Kell. I feel like I've barely seen you lately," Ryan says by way of greeting. He doesn't mention the reasons for why we've been avoiding each other, but I guess he doesn't have to. They're obvious enough to the both of us.

I pull out the chair across from him and sit. "It's been a busy time. And today—who knew that photo shoots took so long? I thought I'd be out of this dress in a few hours, max." I run my hands over the front of the shimmery dress that feels like velvet.

Ryan's eyes catch the movement and I stop, wrapping my arms around my front. What am I doing? For a brief, sick moment, it was like none of this mess happened and I *wanted* him to look at me, to admire me, and that was not my intention in coming over here. Or was it? Screw Ash for getting in my head and making everything weird. Or weirder than it was.

"Everything okay?" Ryan still watches me closely. "Do you want to go outside and talk? Take a walk or something? I know things with us are still, uh, funky, but—"

"Oh. No. We're good here." Straightening, I move my hands from my dress and clear my throat, composing myself. "I wanted to make sure you saw the schedule changes for next week. Some of the times moved around a bit."

"I saw it." Ryan nods. "Samantha, uh, actually pointed out all the changes. She's really good with stuff like that."

"That's perfect." I stand and give him a little wave. "I'll see you soon, then. Great job today. You guys all looked really good."

Ryan's eyes shift, like he isn't quite sure what to make of our professional, concise but friendly conversation. I don't know that I am either. I still walk away and wait until I'm out of sight to let out the biggest sigh ever. My body sags against the hallway wall, and I let it because no one else is around.

Great. Now my stomachache has doubled in intensity, and I have no one to blame but myself.

CHAPTER SIXTEEN

✤ ✤ ✤ ✤ ✤

Ash

*D*on't know what it says about me, but I'm starting to forget the cameras even exist. Aaron told us that when the camera crew can't be following us, we should film on our own cameras twenty percent of the time. It's filler footage, obviously. He's got to know we're not about to film ourselves being idiots and willingly hand it over.

Ryan is taking it to overkill though. He bought a nanny cam type thing and set one up in every main room. Swear he'd put them in our bedrooms if we let him. Ryan wants more shows like this one, more everything. I don't know what will be enough for him. He would do anything to get one, apparently, even film himself eating every meal and pretending to work out with Jonah. I don't mind the show, but I want this to be a stepping stone to something more.

By the time I wake up on Friday morning, the sounds of filming carry down the hall. I wash my face and throw on sweatpants. Then I sit next to Jonah and eat breakfast. We make small talk while we eat eggs made by Ava. It's like any other normal day, except for the five other people crammed in our kitchen.

I shovel in a forkful of cheesy eggs over medium. "I haven't seen Jessie in a few days."

Jonah doesn't look up from his plate. "Yeah. She's busy, man. She's got work."

I've seen them like this before, and it usually means they're in another fight. Before I can ask any more, Ryan comes in spreading his arms wide like a benevolent grandfather. "My bros!"

We nod at him and continue eating our eggs. He's always been like this. Waking up at the crack of dawn with alien energy. It's annoying.

He looks around. "Jones, where's your girlfriend? Trouble in paradise?"

I kind of want to know the same. I'm not about to make Jonah talk about it on camera after the way he reacted. I playfully slap Ryan on the back, but hard enough that he knows I could take him if I need to. "We could ask you the same thing. I don't see Samantha here."

"My fiancée." Ryan's smirk grows. "I thought I'd be a gentleman and let her sleep in. We had a late night." He waggles his eyebrows and Jonah and I groan. Really glad our house is big enough that I didn't have to hear the dirty details of their late night.

I haven't seen Samantha since the photo shoot last week, but I haven't been on Ryan's side of the house much. Haven't seen Jessie either, and what I've seen of Kell has been scant.

When we don't react past that, Ryan grabs some eggs and pours a big glass of orange juice. He smacks his lips after a huge gulp of it. "Have either of you talked to Kell? She was so weird at the photo thing last week and she usually texts me about work, but it's been radio silence."

I pick up my fork and poke at the remaining eggs on my plate. I shrug. I'd rather hear more about Samantha and Ryan's late night than talk about Kell. She's barely talked to me since the photo shoot either. On the one hand, I'm proud of her for resisting what she might feel like are my brother's charms. We didn't leave things on the best terms.

What I said might have been true, but now she's pissed. We've kept up the relationship ruse when the cameras are around, but after a quick scene here and there, she's hurried off saying she has to work. I probably should have apologized already.

"Maybe she finally got sick of us." Jonah casts me a nervous glance. With his second most recent violation, he's not in the best position to look for new representation. Kell wouldn't do that to him. If she's leaving anyone, it's Ryan. After our fight, maybe me too.

I shake my head. "I'll call her later and feel her out." Kell might be sick of us, but she wouldn't screw us over.

When the camera crew is outside following Jonah and Ryan doing who-knows-what, I go to my room and text Kell.

I stretch on my bed on my back. I don't want Kell thinking I'm only asking to hang out because of the fight. It's kind of true, but she hates when we aren't up-front about stuff. We're both stubborn, and sometimes it stretches on before one of us breaks and talks to the other person.

But usually that's me.

Ash: *I'll buy you pizza tomorrow if you promise to stop throwing darts at my picture.*

She responds right away. Knew she would. Kell is predictable as hell and always on her phone.

Part of the job.

Kell: *The darts are really fun, so I'm not promising anything, but I am free for lunch.*

A second later she texts again, and I can't help feeling hopeful that she's on her way to forgiving me.

Kell: *Good luck at your audition later. You're going to do great.*

❄ ❄ ❄ ❄ ❄

"My name is Ash Matthew. I'm reading for the part of Eric."

The casting director smiles at me. She gestures to start the audition. The small room they've put me in is enough to get my nerves up. Then there are the three big names staring at me from a table near the door. Aaron is producing the movie, and he got me the audition per the terms of Kell's contract for the reality show. That's a foot in the door, but I need to nail this audition if I want more than that.

Right now they're all looking at me like I'm vaguely familiar. That guy from the summer movie who spent the whole two hours with his shirt off. I would kill to be known as more than that. They stare at me expectantly.

I clear my throat and deliver the lines. Pretend I'm Eric, a farmer living in Iowa in 1931. The Great Depression hit my family hard, and I'm worked to the bone. I don't know when I'll see another penny. Or scrap of food, for that matter.

Twelve hours. That's how long I spent this weekend studying for this part. I checked out a stack of books from the library about this era. I researched other movies done in the past. Watched actors who I want to emulate. Haven't told anyone how badly I want this one. Not even Kell.

The audition ends and they ask me about myself. The lady at the end of the table tilts her head. "I like your voice. I felt like you empathized with the character. Very nice." She cracks a small smile. "I bet you're better with romance. Am I right? You've certainly got the face for it."

The woman sitting next to her grins, catlike. "He might be too pretty for this movie. But not too pretty to look at." The look they share borders on the edge of uncomfortable. I'm used to being leered at, but not in auditions. Not to my face like this.

Celeste used to say the same sort of shit. She'd argue that there was nothing wrong with giving a compliment. But it doesn't feel like a compliment when it's all they have to say about me. I force a laugh for the room. "Thank you," I say, waiting for more feedback. None comes.

This audition was a mistake.

The guy at the end of the table gives me a bored stare. "Why this role? Why the switch from romance?" He gestures to his colleagues. "Clearly the ladies love you, and I wouldn't give it up if I were you."

Yeah, I'm only going to answer his first question. The others don't seem necessary. I angle my head toward the storyboard behind them. The board is tacked to the wall like a low-budget classroom. It's set up with a list of the cast and the basic rundown for the script. "This is the kind of movie I loved watching with my dad. He was a Marine, so it was historical films, war or not. He watched them all." I swallow. "I've been fortunate to do some well-received movies, but doing movies like this one is the goal. I'm ready. I know I am."

The first woman looks at me like she's maybe seeing me for the first time. Her friend is still smirking. The man stands to shake my hand. "Well good," he says. "We'll be in touch."

CHAPTER SEVENTEEN

❊ ❊ ❊ ❊ ❊

Kell

*A*sh laces his fingers through mine as we walk along damp sand, edging close to the evening tide. He stretches out his free hand and points to the ocean where waves lap gently, rising and falling in a rhythm all their own. The sun is out and warm even though it's officially fall. A steady ocean breeze ruffles my hair. "Do you see the dolphin?" he asks.

I squint at the water. "No, I don't see anything. Where—" I stop suddenly as a gray-blue fin glides through the waves. "I see it!" Giddiness hits me, pulling me up on my tiptoes as I strain to get a better look.

When I turn back to Ash, he's grinning. "I think that's supposed to be good luck, seeing a dolphin by itself."

"Luck is good. I'll take extra luck."

I stare back out at the ocean. We've both been on our best behavior since our argument about Ryan and subsequent makeup over pizza at DeSano's last week. It's new territory, us getting into it and having to make up. Add in filming for the reality show where we're meant to look like a couple, and it's a very different vibe.

But it's nice, walking together like this and enjoying the nearly empty beach. If I close my eyes, I can almost pretend like that's what we're doing.

Almost.

This is as good a time as any, so I clear my throat and say, "Oh, well, speaking of good luck, I have some news about your audition…"

Aaron's voice cuts through the comfortable silence, shrill and impatient. A crew with boom mics and cameras follows us and stops on Aaron's command. "Stop, stop. This isn't working. Ash, Kell, let's have you two come back to the pier and start walking again. Take it from the top of your conversation."

Aaron shoots me a tired look. "Give us a little more energy, sweetheart. That's all I'm asking."

Funny, that's all I'm asking of myself, too. If only I had energy to spare like everyone seems to assume I do. Living with chronic illness means that what I do have is limited, and honestly, I prefer to use my resources to get actual work done. Not to rehash a conversation that never even happened in real life.

I manage to keep my annoyance hidden and take my place next to Ash. The setting sun glints across the ocean waves, reflecting on the white sand underfoot. It would be a perfect Malibu beach day if not for the cameras.

"So," I start again, already sick of this. I don't know how the Matthews repeat the same lines over and over again while on set for productions. I feel like a broken record, and I know that each time I start, I sound more robotic than the last. "I have news about your audition!" I try for an upbeat singsong melody, and I know instantly that I sound as ridiculous as I feel by the way Ash tightens his hand on mine. "You've made it to the next round, and they want to have you come in and read again."

Ash stops walking, catching even me by surprise. "That's amazing." His eyes light up, dancing and mimicking the exact shade of the sea. I hold my breath while I look at him, a little mesmerized at how convincing he is. And, also, maybe a little mesmerized at how beautiful he is to look at. The Hollister ads of my youth have nothing on Ash in sandals and a pair of striped board shorts slung low over his hips.

"Got it," Aaron pronounces, and it should break the spell because we have the shot and it's done, but I don't move my hand from Ash's. We don't stop watching each other, our eyes locked. My breath hitches at the slide of his thumb over mine, such a simple thing.

"Lovebirds! Over here." Ryan's voice booms toward us, and he catches my eye with a questioning glance between Ash and me.

Without another word, Ash steps away, and we turn toward where the rest of the group waits at the end of the pier. We have chemistry, there's no denying it, which is I guess why Judith thought this whole deal would work out so well. But chemistry does not equal anything more than two people who get along well. It's not worth it to try to explain this to everyone who sees us together, but I'm finding it increasingly important to remind myself of this concept. I've been fooled by chemistry with a Matthew brother before, and look how well that ended up.

The pier and our little section of the beach has been taped off and guarded against a small crowd of fans who have been tipped off about filming. Judith is undoubtedly the culprit there, but it's a public beach, so I can't get too upset with her. Some of the signs they're waving I can read from here, half a dozen variations of *Ryan is sexy!* and *Notice me Ash!* plus a few for Jonah too.

I find a bench on the pier and sit down to watch the three of them laughing together as Ash joins his brothers. They don't do that very often anymore, and it makes me sad to see the subtle ways fame has changed them. But right now, in this sun-soaked beach moment,

Jonah and Ryan are each grabbing one of Ash's legs and pretending to swing him over the edge of the pier out into the water. It's exactly the kind of juvenile, weird brother bonding stuff they'd do in the past, and right now it feels really good to see. The cameras are off, and aside from the few dozen fans screaming their names, it just feels so *real* and *normal*.

On the drive home, it's just Ash and me again, and my eyes are heavy from the wind and sun. I lean my head back against the headrest. I can't turn off thoughts about the show and the falsity of it all, and some of it spills out of my mouth before I can stop myself. "Do you think that doing this show is ruining us?"

"Ruining us how? What do you mean?

"I don't know exactly. The show makes me feel dishonest with all the pretending and posturing, and it's weird with Ryan and Samantha and with us . . ."

Ash's brows go up. His hand lands on my knee. The pressure is warm, firm. "No, hey, no. The show is just a show. I think you're reading too much into it. We are friends first. Always. That's the deal, remember?"

My heart steadies a little. "Yeah," I agree. "That's the deal." *The deal* feels much more complicated now with the two of us on screen instead of me safely on my own end of the business.

Ash lifts his hand and runs it through his hair. It musses the front perfectly.

I let out a long breathy sigh. "It's just that so much has happened. I feel like we're stuck in this new show. I don't hate it, but you're right. It's not for me, and I'm struggling with what that means for me, for my job. Jonah keeps getting these ridiculous fines. I don't know who I am or what I want anymore, Ash. And it scares the hell out of me."

The silence in the car is thick. I should not have said all of that. Not to Ash, who is yes, my friend first, but also my client as a close second.

These are the kinds of thoughts I'm supposed to keep to myself. Or at the very least spew unfiltered to Claudette. Ash parks in front of my apartment building and keeps the car running, the hum of the engine mimicking my own internal rushing thoughts.

I drop my head back again and groan. "I'm sorry. That didn't come out right. Thanks for dropping me off. We're okay, right?"

Ash's jaw ticks. "Don't do that. Don't apologize for saying how you feel." His gray-blue eyes stare into mine. It's not hard to see why he's such a popular romantic lead. If he weren't Ash and we didn't have the history that we do, I could see myself falling for him. But he is Ash Matthew, and we would never, ever work in a romantic way. Not without a camera to coax us into the act.

Instead of saying any of that, I stick with work conversation because it never seems to fail us. "Why not do more romance work, Ash? You could do serious films and some romance at the same time. It doesn't have to be all comedy."

He shifts and he's the one to turn away from me now. His hands brace the steering wheel. "You're right about the pretending. It kind of sucks."

I blink at him. "Isn't that what acting is? Pretending?"

Ash shakes his head. "Pretending to be in love. The movies I've done, the ones I've been typecast into, that's how it is. By the end of the movie, the lead always has to be all-consumed with the girl."

"And you haven't experienced that in real life?" Ash has had his fair share of girlfriends. He had a pretty serious girlfriend, Celeste, in the last few years. She was this gorgeous, untouchable model. It surprises me to hear Ash talk about pretending to be in love.

"No, that's the easy part. I'm not some cynic, Kell." His voice goes soft. "I believe in love. I have nothing against romance. I want all of it someday. It's just that it never works out for me." He spreads his hands. "I don't know how to act like I'm happy in love because I've never had that. Never had a successful relationship."

I tilt my head, processing. My chest hurts for Ash. He deserves love. He's one of the best men I know. "You'll get that. There's some extremely lucky woman out there waiting for you. And as for movies, you only have to take the jobs that will make you happy. We're working on it, right? Judith said that your audition went well." She called to update me on it a few days after, and it hurt that Ash didn't let me know himself, but at least I got to pretend for the cameras that I was the one to give him the good news.

Ash gives me a funny look. "Do you really think that? That there's someone out there?"

"Of course I do."

Ash gives me a full smile, and I get the vague feeling that we've been talking in circles and I'm not in on the secret. It's not lost on me that he's also being forced to pretend to be in love with me. I hope it's less awful of an experience than his other projects.

When I get out of the car and walk to my apartment door, what I really can't stop thinking about is Ash's face when he said he'd never had a successful love. It was wistful and sad all at once. I guess it just goes to show that being a Hollywood heartthrob does not equal a happy love life. Which probably also means if someone as great as Ash can't find someone, I'm officially doomed.

CHAPTER EIGHTEEN

✾ ✾ ✾ ✾ ✾

Ash

*J*onah is sitting on the sofa alone when I get home. Phone out, he looks lost in it until he sees me. "Did you get a chance to talk to Kell?"

I shake my head. Jonah and I are closer than Ryan and I, but we don't really talk about personal stuff. Not that feelings are a no-go. More so that relationships aren't a common conversational topic. I give him a hard time about hurrying up and proposing to Jessie, and he occasionally asks me about dating. That's about it.

My head is all messed up over Kell. Part of me doesn't want to bring it up to Jonah. It might make it real. I sit on the other end of the sofa. "Kell isn't going to leave us. She's fine." Not one hundred percent true, but what Jonah doesn't know can't hurt him. I do know that Kell wouldn't do anything without good reason. She hasn't said anything about quitting, exactly. Jonah refuses to stop worrying that his growing stack of fines is going to push Kell over the edge. I doubt it. But I'm not going to be the one to put the idea in her head.

"That's good news." Some of the tension seems to roll from his shoulders. Jonah sets his phone on his lap. "Thanks for talking to her. You're her favorite and you know her the best. You were my only chance."

"I don't know, man." Do I know Kell better than anyone else? Yeah, I like to think I do. But some of the things she said today caught me by surprise. Some of the things I said surprised me too.

"You've been with Jessie a long time," I say, tapping my fingers on the sofa cushion.

Jonah laughs. "Not this again. We've talked marriage but we're not in a rush."

"No, I mean, you've been together a long time. How do you make that work? Are you happy?"

Jonah's eyes light up. He gets me. "I'm happy. Being with Jessie…" Jonah's not sappy, but he's not afraid to say it how it is. "Nothing is more important. I just got off the phone with her actually. We always figure things out, that's what I love about her. She puts up with me, I guess, and I try not to make it too miserable for her." Jessie is head-over-heels for Jonah, and vice versa, and everyone knows it.

He grins. "Why? You dating someone I don't know about?"

"No. The only woman I see regularly is Kell, and I—"

"You what? What does Kell have to do with dating?" Jonah's face shifts. He points at me. "Oh shit."

My jaw goes tight. "Don't be an idiot."

"You like Kell." Jonah's voice is ten levels higher than it should be. Might as well rent a megaphone and stand on the roof. "You're in love with Kell."

I glare. All I can do is glare.

"You're actually into Kell? I thought it was just for the show." Jonah shakes his head. "Man. So does she know?"

No. No way Kell knows what I've been feeling. I barely know it myself. I rub the back of my neck. "Nothing to know. She's beautiful.

She's funny. Smart. I don't have a chance in hell with her, so there's no point."

"Now who's the idiot?" Jonah laughs. "It's perfect because you're already friends. That's how it was with Jessie and me. We already knew everything about each other. When we decided to make our relationship official, it was the easiest thing. We take breaks occasionally." He points to his phone. "But we work it out."

I don't need to hear this. No use getting stuck on an idea that won't pan out. "She's in love with Ryan." My voice comes out rough. I stand up and shrug. "Or she was. I don't know. Besides, like I said, she doesn't see me like that. So don't make it a thing, okay?"

"I won't if you won't." Jonah frowns after me and turns back to his phone. I'd bet a dollar he's texting our whole conversation to Jessie right now. "You should have come to me sooner about this. I don't want to brag, but I know some things about being in a long-term relationship."

I scoff, but he's right. "I've been in a long relationship," I say. What I had with Celeste wasn't the same as Jonah and Jessie. We both know that. We never lived together, and we barely saw each other except for events. We were essentially really convenient PR. Not that I realized that until much later. I screw up my mouth and let a breath go. "Fine. What's your relationship advice?"

Jonah leans back onto the couch. He steeples his fingers. "I thought you'd never ask, bro. Have a seat."

He pats the couch cushion, and I sit again. I don't know why I'm wasting my time.

"Remember my first date with Jessie?"

This is already not going well. I shake my head. "No."

Jonah smacks his hands together. "Exactly! That's because there was no first date. We were friends, all our friends were friends, and we just hung out a ton. But one night, this, like, random concert was happening down in San Diego. I can't even remember the bands that played. But I remember the night because me and Jessie were the only ones from our group who actually showed up. We ended the night in a hotel room together and never looked back."

I give him a blank look. Still not getting how this is supposed to help me. If getting Kell alone in a hotel was the solution, we would be married by now.

Jonah leans forward again. "Look, what I'm saying is, you have to find that moment with Kell. You already have the groundwork, this cool friendship, right? But put it out there that you are open to more relationship-type stuff happening and then wait for the perfect moment to come. You know?" He raises his eyebrows.

"I love you, little brother," I say, slapping him on the back as I stand. "But no, I don't think that applies to me. Sounds like you just got lucky."

Jonah laughs. He yells after me, "Love you too!"

Back in my room I sit on my bed. Think about what Kell said in the car. She didn't sound against the idea of her and me. Didn't say anything for it either, but maybe that's just Kell. She liked Ryan for years in mostly silence. Could be that's how she operates in love.

As long as I've known her, there haven't been many relationships. Guys are always trying, but Kell either goes on first dates and finds something wrong or gets too busy with work to even try. Not that I'm complaining that she's not dating more. I know she could if she wanted to. Hell, she could have a line of men if she so much as hinted she'd be receptive.

I go shower. After I'm dressed, I check my phone. My damn heart jumps in my throat when I see a text from Kell. Guess she could sense I was thinking about her.

Kell: *Can you do me a huge favor? Lunch with my parents tomorrow and I need backup.*

Kell's parents love me. Her parents aren't big on the idea of Kell spending her life stuck with my brothers and me. From what Kell's said, they want her in a less high-stress job. Stress is the driving force in Hollywood, and Kell has always been good at handling it.

But luckily, we were friends before that, and I've never done anything to make them hate me personally. Wonder if Ryan can say the same. Given how loyal her parents are, Kell might not have told them about the whole thing. It says a lot that I'm the one she invites to lunch. And I probably should still give it more than a second's thought before texting back that I'll be there. I don't.

Kell: *You're the best. Dad wants seafood. Can you get us a table at that place we went last year?*

Kell coincidentally loves seafood too. Prawn is a hipster seafood place downtown that has a waiting list a mile long. I did a movie with one of the owner's sons last year, and he insists on getting me a table whenever I want. Least I can do is share the perks of the job.

Ash: *Got it. I'll make the reservations for noon.*

Jonah thinks I should tell Kell what I'm feeling. I'm not going to go that far until I know for sure myself. But this could be a start.

CHAPTER NINETEEN

❁ ❁ ❁ ❁ ❁

Kell

*M*om and Dad insist on picking me up at my apartment so that we can drive to the restaurant together. It doesn't matter to them that traffic runs in the opposite direction from their hotel and they're adding a good half hour to their trip. What I really think appeals to them is the chance to trap me in the car where I can't escape their endless questions. They definitely begrudge the fact that my apartment is too teeny for them to stay in, forcing them to stay in a nearby hotel when they visit, as if the three of us squishing into my one-bedroom would make their trip that much better somehow.

My parents are great. They both work full time and have busy careers in education, and they still make time to drive to California from Washington every few months. They take me out to eat and trail me around while I work. It's just that I get the sense that they want more for me than the career I've chosen. And when I say I get the sense they want more, it's because they explicitly tell me that's the case.

My dad turns completely around in his seat even though he's supposed to be the driver. He's fearless, even, apparently, in LA rush-hour traffic. "Kell, your mother tells me that you're doing some acting nowadays."

I snort. "No, Dad. I told Mom on the phone that I got dragged into this project for my clients. It's a reality show and they wanted to film them talking to their manager." I wave my hands in front of my body, like *ta-da, that's me*. The part where I pretend to be dating Ash, I conveniently leave out.

Dad gives me a frustrated frown. "But it's for TV?"

"It is. It's a reality TV show," Mom says, swatting his arm. "Like on MTV.

"Do you think acting is something you'd like to do more of? Maybe it's the next big step for you. I've always thought you'd be much cuter in the movies than half of those girls." Mom turns to where I sit cramped in the back seat. She grins at me.

I smile back and fight the urge to put my head between my knees. I haven't gotten hit by a wave of carsickness since I was a kid, but this feels close to it. The stress of being trapped with so many *loving* opinions about my life is enough to make me very nauseous.

"She's got a good movie face, but you know Kell is too shy," my dad says. For the record, he's not wrong.

I may have gotten over my adolescent shyness for the most part, but I definitely do not belong in front of the camera full time. I've seen the actors who do belong; I manage their careers. They have a natural charisma, an ease that translates so well to movies and TV. And I—I have great managerial skills.

I decide to set them straight before the conversation gets further out of hand. "Don't worry, no more acting. This is a one-time thing. I'm still really enjoying managerial work." Not to mention that my appearance in the show with Ash as of late has cemented my belief that I belong behind the scenes only.

Mom nods, resigned to her daughter forever living a dull, non-celebrity life. I can picture her at her book clubs every month trying to come up with a new and increasingly creative way to spin my job. Every time I go home to visit and see someone I used to know, they always reference my "Hollywood gig" or how great it is that I "rub shoulders with the stars." Mom's doing, of course. I can spot her words from miles away. For all her worry about overworking myself and ending up a lonely spinster here in LA, that's how I know she's proud of me. We park and give Ash's name at the front of the restaurant while Mom spitballs new career ideas all the way to our seat.

"Is Ash meeting us for lunch?" Dad changes the subject, and I'm glad for it because no matter how many times Mom suggests I follow in their footsteps and go into teaching, I'm not going for it. I've heard enough of their horror stories about the profession.

"He is. He's the one who got us a table." I sit to the left of my parents, leaving a seat for Ash so he doesn't get trapped right next to them but can still run interference. It's probably a little mean of me since he went out of his way to get us the reservations, but he still owes me a little bit for what he said about me and Ryan after the photo shoot last week. I don't hold a grudge, but I do keep a petty score occasionally.

Mom unrolls the cloth napkin in front of her and tucks it gracefully over her lap. "His girlfriend doesn't mind that he spends so much time with another pretty woman?"

I bust out laughing, which prompts Mom to scowl. "Sorry, Mom. He doesn't have a girlfriend right now, but when he has in the past, they've never minded. We don't see each other like that, so it's not weird."

Mom huffs. "See each other like what? He doesn't appreciate you for all the work you put into his career? Or your fun personality?"

I grip my water glass and take a long sip to avoid answering. She's completely indignant over . . . nothing. It should probably be touching that she goes to such lengths to defend me from any perceived slight, but honestly, I wish my parents would give it up. They didn't even get this upset when I told them the abridged, cleaned-up version of what happened between Ryan and me. They wouldn't stop asking once the pictures surfaced and I figured the truth was better in the long run. But all Mom said after I told her was that she was happy Ryan was getting married to someone else because she never pictured him as a very good son-in-law.

But Ash, oh he's always been special. Ever since the first time I mentioned my friendship with Ash in college, they've been hoping it would blossom into a romantic relationship. It only made matters worse once they actually met Ash and he turned on the charm. I tried to tell them that he's an actor and turning on charm and wooing strangers is literally what he does for a living. My dad said that he'd seen a few of Ash's movies and he wasn't *that* good of an actor. Mostly, I try to remind myself that my parents want to see me happy. They just don't seem to understand that strong-arming two unwilling people into a relationship doesn't equal happiness. Maybe inviting Ash here was a flawed idea.

"Here he comes," Dad says, gesturing over my shoulder. "Why don't we ask the man himself what he thinks of Kell's brilliant personality?"

Water spews from the sides of my mouth as I choke on my drink. If I don't pull myself together people are going to start thinking I don't know how to drink water. Okay, inviting Ash to lunch with my parents was definitely a *deeply* flawed idea. I can't believe I failed to predict this unpleasant turn of events and stop it from happening. "No, please no. Leave Ash alone," I hiss, but they aren't listening.

My parents stand and Mom wraps him in a hug while Dad thumps him on the back a few times. Maybe if I take charge of the conversation, I can steer them away from further embarrassment. I turn to Ash the second he sits so that they don't get a chance to bombard him with questions about all things Kell. *Quick, distract us,* I think, but don't dare say it out loud in such definitive words, and instead I use my eyes to beg him to save me. "Tell us about filming! I'm sure my parents want to hear all about the new show."

Ash raises one eyebrow. "Okay, sure." He nods slowly, confirming my suspicions that I'm coming off like a lunatic. "Filming on the new show is going great. I was unsure about the idea at first, but that's why we pay Kell. She knows her stuff. I'm already getting offers for new projects just based on promo."

A predatory smile spreads along Mom's face. *Please, for the love of all that is holy in the land of helicopter parents*, I silently beg, *leave it alone.*

"It's interesting that you would bring up how good Kell is at her job, Ash." Mom glances at my father like they're in on some sort of secret mission. "We were just wondering about something. Maybe you can help us."

CHAPTER TWENTY

✿ ✿ ✿ ✿ ✿

Ash

*L*unch with Kell and her parents is always fun and easy. They're a close-knit family, and as much as Kell likes to whine about her parents smothering her, I know she loves them. She invites me because she can count on me to behave around her folks. You couldn't pay me to mess that up. Really, it comes easy because they like me and treat me like a son for the most part.

We get started talking about filming for the new show. I can tell that Kell's a little jittery, so I try to take the lead talking. She's so hell-bent on being teacher's pet that I've noticed she even gets like that around her parents sometimes. I don't mind taking the heat off her. It's the kind of thing we do for each other.

So when Kell's mom leans forward, her eyes all big and innocent, I know I'm in for it. She looks a lot like Kell when she stares at me like that. I can count too many times the shady shit I've been talked into when it was Kell and me in exactly this position. "We were just wondering about something. Maybe you could help us."

I nod. "Sure. I'll do my best. What is it you were wondering?"

The gleam in her eye grows. Kell's dad isn't staring at me like he wants to order my bones for an entrée, but he's not embarrassed either. In my peripheral vision I see Kell ducking down in her seat. Looks like she wants to crawl under the table. Why do I get the feeling I just walked into some sort of trap?

"You and Kell have been friends for a long time now. Your mom has met her, and we've met you and we think you're a great man."

I smile appreciatively as both her parents grin across the table at me. I've always assumed they approve of me, but it's nice to hear. Gives me a little boost. Can't imagine why a compliment like this would make Kell so upset.

Kell's mom pauses to lift her water glass to her lips. "So what we want to know is, why not pursue Kell? Some of the best couples we know were born from friendship. Her father and I met at a teaching conference and became friends first before we ever dated. You can't honestly tell me that it's never crossed either of your minds."

No wonder Kell is practically running from the table. Judging by the turn this conversation is taking, I guess she hasn't told them about our fake relationship. It's not my place to say. Instead, I force a chuckle. One hand rubs at the back of my neck while the other drums on top of the table. "Well, Kell is awesome. I wouldn't say we never—"

"They're joking. Seriously, this is their idea of a joke." Kell pops up straight in her seat. She shakes her head at her parents. But her face is a bright shade of red. Looks like a strawberry.

"Leave Ash alone and let's decide on our orders before the waitress comes back." She picks up the stack of menus in the center of the table and hands them out. I bury my head in one. Her parents look at me over the top of theirs. So much for a nice, easy meal.

"I'm sorry if I made you uncomfortable, Ash." Kell's mom pats my hand. She's a nice lady. Kell's right about her being too involved, but at least she tries. My mom has never asked about my relationships. I don't think she cares. In fairness, Mom has been that way since Dad died, that is, not interested in much.

"Not at all," I say. "Kell is a big part of my life. Believe it or not, we get that question a lot." I try to smile at Kell, but she won't meet my eyes. All of a sudden, she's too absorbed in the menu for anything else. The rest of the lunch I talk to her parents about my last few movies. Turns out they're as big of fans as they claim to be. They even remember little things about my characters I've already forgotten. Kell stays pretty quiet until we're done. I fight her parents to pay the bill and Kell sends me a small, whispered thank you.

We don't talk much until after we leave the restaurant. I get a text just as I'm pulling up at home.

Kell: *I'm so sorry about my parents. When they get worried about me, they start throwing me at random men. I guess today you were the lucky guy!*

Ash: *They're fine, Kell. Lunch was fun.*

Kell: *Thanks again for the reservations. My dad still hasn't stopped talking about the grilled shrimp.*

Ash: *Anytime.*

My chest is tight. I let my finger hover over my phone before shooting off another text.

Ash: *For the record, it's definitely crossed my mind.*

There. It's out there. She has to remember the conversation, seeing as she reacted to it just like I could have predicted. If she hadn't changed the subject so forcefully, I would have told her parents the truth. That it's crossed my mind a hundred times in a hundred ways. Especially over the last few weeks.

She doesn't text back right away. I picture her sitting on the little sofa in her apartment. She's probably staring at her phone in panic. Another minute passes before I get a response.

Kell: *Ha. I remember! Glad we didn't go there in college and glad this time around it's not real.*

College. I blow out a breath. She thinks I'm talking about that party in college when I tried to kiss her. As if that even counts as an attempt. Is that the only time she's thought twice about me? My hand rakes over my face. I'm such an idiot. To think that Kell would ever consider me as anything more than a friend. A colleague. All those things but never relationship material, not in real life. The old sting flares up, the fear that I'll never be taken seriously. I text her back and squeeze my eyes shut tight.

Ash: *Yeah, me too.*

The home gym seems like a good place to work out my frustrations. I find Jonah already there lifting weights. "Hey, where were you earlier? Ryan wanted wings and there was no one here to outvote him."

"I went to lunch with Kell and her parents."

Jonah sets down his barbell. "Yeah? How was that? You talk to Kell about anything?"

"No."

"Why not? I'm telling you, the more I think about it, the more sense it makes. You two would be good for each other."

"It's not gonna work, man. Just drop it."

He holds up his hands in surrender. "Fine."

I pull my phone from my pocket and shove it at Jonah. Maybe he'll leave me alone if he knows how Kell really sees me. A friend. Always just a friend. "Read these texts. This sound like someone who wants anything more than friendship with me?"

Jonah's face shifts as he scrolls through our conversation. He shrugs. "Maybe not yet. Maybe she just needs you to show her what it would be like. If she hasn't thought of it as a possibility, there's still hope."

I take my phone back. I don't know when this became so important to me. When I decided this thing with Kell was real. At least on my side. "How do I do that?"

Jonah's eyes go wide. "Uh, I have no idea. Do romantic shit. Stop treating her like a friend, for starters."

"I don't treat her badly." I take offense to that because I've always tried with Kell. Maybe I'm not perfect, but she has to know that I would never hurt her.

"I didn't say you do." Jonah is clearly fed up with me. "You don't treat her like a girlfriend, though, and that's the problem."

No idea why I let Jonah talk me into having this conversation when his advice doesn't add up. It's not like I can start kissing Kell or showing up at her house like I would a girlfriend. Things are already confusing with the show, and I'd be lying if I said I hadn't been using it as an excuse to touch her more often. But I can't transfer that to outside of filming. Kell would be freaked out, for one thing. "But she's not my girlfriend," I say.

"Exactly," Jonah says, clearly proud of his logic. It makes sense in a twisted way once I think about it. If I treat Kell like I would a woman I'm dating, then she'll see me in that way. As someone who'd make a good partner.

Okay, romantic. No idea what Kell views as romantic since that's not a conversation we've ever had. She doesn't strike me as a flowers type of girl. Her perfect day would be stacked full of work. I remember once in college she cried tears of joy when a professor pointed out her essay as the best example of work he'd seen in years. I thought she was dying until I realized what was really happening. What am I supposed to do with that? Compliment her into my arms?

"Guess I'll have to think about that." I snatch Jonah's hand weights and start warming up. The tightness in my muscles is a good distraction. Counting reps keeps my mind busy too. Mind and body both occupied, I should be able to zone out. But Kell is still there in the back of my mind. I know one thing for sure—lunch with her parents is not the way to her heart after all.

CHAPTER TWENTY-ONE

❀ ❀ ❀ ❀ ❀

Kell

*C*laudette hands me a strip of shimmery gold fabric. The light catches it and it looks blue, and I turn it another way and it looks pink. I'm mesmerized. "What in the world are you going to make with this?"

We're spread out on the floor of her apartment as she sorts through potential fabrics. She decided she has too many and needs to get rid of a few stacks to make room for her favorites. So far, the donation pile is looking suspiciously slim. "That I'm saving for a special occasion."

I laugh as I fold the fabric neatly into the keep pile. "Like what? A striptease?"

She huffs and tosses a bit of felt at me. It hits my forehead and flutters to the floor. "No. This beautiful fabric would be wasted on a striptease. Duh."

"I'll take your word for it," I tell her, picking through the remaining stack. My eye catches on a patterned swatch and I scoop it up. It's pale pink with red cherries polka-dotted throughout, so subtle you have to look closely to distinguish them. I love it.

"That's very you," Claudette agrees with my unspoken awe. "I'll save it for you, promise."

"Thanks." I hand it over reverently. My friend is amazing at what she does. We have a rule between us that if either of us finds the perfect fabric, we save it. Then, when something happens that calls for a special dress, Claudette starts working on it, giving the fabric life. I've bought other Claudette originals over the years, but I've only earned one special dress: the one I wore the night Ryan, Ash, and Jonah were named hottest acting brothers in *Entertainment Magazine*. It was a small victory, but it represented so much more to me. It meant that we'd come far enough to be recognized, to be celebrated. And I was a part of that. Claudette made me a navy-blue dress with shiny brass buttons, and I wore it to a party Ryan hosted that weekend. It's hanging in my closet still, never to be worn again, but I keep it like a trophy.

Whatever I do to earn this cherry dress will be equally great, and I can't wait for that moment. Claudette's last milestone dress was an all-velvet green minidress that she made for herself after winning yet another design award because she's impressive like that. I borrowed a professional backdrop from my photographer neighbor two apartments over and took pictures of Claudette in various poses before we went out to dinner. It was like a mashup of middle school and the Oscars, and the photos will probably never see the light of day, but it was so much fun either way.

Claudette runs a finger over the fabric. "This would make a good second-date dress," she says innocently.

"Not first date?" I get it enough from my parents, but Claudette is there too, always hinting that I should really be dating more. To be fair, I've gone on exactly zero dates in the past six months, which is an embarrassing fact I don't plan on sharing with anyone.

Claudette casts me a sidelong glance. "It's been a while since you've had a second date."

Her bluntness has long since stopped hurting me, but ouch. It stings to hear the truth put out there so plainly. We both know the reason for my lack of dates. I've spent the better part of the past several years waiting around for Ryan. Which, if I'm being honest, has led to zero actual dates and a whole lot of sitting on my ass feeling lonely. "You're terrible," I mutter.

Claudette shrugs. "Just saying. You should work on that. No better way to move on than to, you know," she waggles her eyebrows. "Physically move on."

"What about you? Maybe you should take your own advice." Claudette hasn't dated since she broke up with her boyfriend a few months ago. We talk about everything, but she doesn't have much to say on the subject of her five-year-long relationship. It would worry me more if she weren't a perpetually well-adjusted person in general.

She whacks me in the arm. "We're not talking about my love life, we're trying to fix yours. I told you, I'm taking time for me. I spent a quarter of my life with Max, and now I have stuff to figure out."

I purse my lips. "Maybe I'm taking time for me, too."

"No, you've taken time. You haven't had a solid relationship since high school. It's time, babe."

"That's a lie! I've dated at least six guys since high school."

"For a few months at a time each." She softens. "I'm not trying to shame you. I just think you're ready. This obsession with Ryan was holding you back, but now that he's officially unavailable, you have a real chance to find some happiness."

"I'll have you know that I'm already happy."

"Good. Then the right guy will just add to that." She shoots me a triumphant smile, aware that she's proven her point.

I push myself up to stand. I'm still covered in little strings of fabric that I try to dust off with my hands.

"Okay, you've convinced me. Let's go out tonight. We'll do something fun."

Claudette pumps a fist into the air. "I have been waiting for this moment." She scurries off, rustling around the room looking through her stacks of fabric. She evidently finds what she is looking for and holds it up in a fisted hand of celebration. "This is going to be so perfect, Kell, you can't say no. Please just try it before you turn it down."

Things never go well when she starts by assuming I'll say no before I've even seen her design. Even though I trust Claudette implicitly and I consider myself her number one fan, our styles tend to differ.

"I won't say no." I hold up a finger. "But I'm not going to say yes until I see it." That feels fair enough.

Claudette must agree because she pushes the shimmery golden minidress into my arms and squeals. "You're going to love it."

There's no weirdness between us as we both strip down to our underwear to try on dresses. We're like sisters who have spent so much time sharing the same spaces that it doesn't faze me when Claudette unhooks her bra and pulls it through one sleeve of her shirt while we're watching a movie on a Sunday night. She doesn't blink twice when I am battling my chronic illness and need a restroom every thirty minutes. She's the best friend I've ever had, full stop. I step into the gold dress and Claudette gathers up an armful of options for herself, saying, "I'll know once I try them all on."

Claudette is a genius, proving that I never should have doubted her, even for a second. The gold dress fits me so well that I'm suspicious she sewed it just for me, even though she insists it was for a client who ended up trading it in for a different design. It's shorter than I normally wear, ending just a few inches below my butt. The fabric feels like soft, buttery leather but looks like a high-end gown. And it shimmers in the light, changing from a warm yellow to a deep, majestic gold depending on which way I turn. I feel like a princess wearing it.

She opts for a sage green dress that looks like the replica of something worn in the early nineties. It has matching puffy sleeves and a cutout back, and the whole thing ends mid-thigh. It's not something I could pull off, but of course on Claudette it looks like it was taken straight off the runway.

"I guess we should go somewhere," I say, feeling much more excited than I should for a woman with no plans at all. The last time I spontaneously did something fun with my best friend was too long ago to remember. We used to do cool things, things like picking up guys at a red light or dancing in the street at three a.m. Granted, I've always been a little too focused on school or work or projects to completely let loose. But when I first moved to the city and met Claudette through total chance, I wasn't the stress ball I am now. I used to know how to put work aside and give myself time to actually live. "Let's go out!" I say again.

"Yes." Claudette grabs my arm. From the gleam in her eye, I can tell she's been waiting for this moment. "I know exactly where we're going!"

CHAPTER TWENTY-TWO

✺ ✺ ✺ ✺ ✺

Ash

"*Y*ou promised me a full night of fun. A night off of work, remember?" Ryan pushes a glass into my hands.

Jonah and I exchange a look. Ryan bullied us into coming out with him tonight. Samantha has some work thing and Jessie is out of town visiting family. I have no one. So here we are. Brother bonding night.

Not that I dislike hanging out with them, but sometimes it gets old. Ryan loves the attention, eats it up. Jonah tolerates it. I appreciate fans. I wouldn't get good jobs without their support. I'd just rather keep my life as separate from work as possible, that's all. Going to one of the most popular spots in LA with Ryan by my side never results in lying low. This place is packed. Groups of LA's finest has-beens and wannabes fill the bar. They hold out their phones and take turns getting shots of their drinks, arms thrown around each other. And then they stand around some more while they post on their socials.

I haven't told anyone, but Judith got back to me today about the audition and she said it wasn't looking promising. It will only be a matter of time before I get word that they chose to "go in a different direction." I had a feeling from the way the casting lady had reacted. And there that fear is again. That I'm never going to be taken seriously. Never going to score the big roles I want. Tonight is about blocking it all out and forgetting. At least for a night.

I slap a smile on my face. "We're having fun," I tell Ryan, downing my drink. Jonah is already off in the corner texting Jessie pictures of his drinks. Ryan hasn't looked at his phone all night. Guess he's fine going a while without talking to his fiancée.

"You two are actors, right?" A short woman with bright red lipstick bats her eyelashes at Ryan. She looks way too excited to meet either of us. For a split second I wonder if she even knows who we are or is just taking a wild guess. Then she says, "I saw *A First Kiss Holiday* with my sister this summer and we both cried." She bites her lip and squints at my brother. "And you're in that spy movie, right? I think my younger brother saw that."

My mouth twitches. It's not often that someone is a fan of my movies and not Ryan's. Or if they are, they don't make the mistake of admitting it. I'm so tempted to look to Ryan to gauge his reaction. "Yeah," I nod, "that was a fun movie. Did you know that the original ending was supposed to have my character dying instead?"

Her eyes go wide. "No way. I wouldn't be able to handle that. It's perfect as is."

Holiday is not my favorite movie I've ever done. Not something I'm ashamed of either. It's a solid love story, even if it's all fake. Nothing ends up like that in real life. There are no feel-good family Christmases where people make mistakes and everything is magically forgiven. And the beautiful girl falls for the dumb guy at the end just because. There's no reason to spoil anyone else's fun and point that out though.

The woman, Shea, gives me her number and leaves to find her friends. I watch her walk back to them and whisper. Her head jabs in my direction. Ryan eyes me.

"What?" I save the number in my phone and slide it back in my pocket. Shea was cool. I rarely call women after they give me their number. Most of the time it's because I don't think they really mean it. They just get caught up in the moment of seeing someone from the movies and offer up a number. But this woman seemed genuinely interested in, well, me.

"Nothing. Just happy to see you having a good time for once." Ryan lifts a shoulder.

I roll my eyes. "I'm going to look for Jonah. You promised me burgers after this."

The crowd is thick as I try to inch through it. People stand in packs, drinks in hand. Some of them bob to the music. Some of them are lost in it. There's a nice balance. I'm more the subtle sway kind of guy. I turn to survey the room, still not seeing Jonah.

I do see Ryan. He's back where I left him. A group of laughing women all around him. Typical. He's not technically doing anything wrong, but I wonder what Samantha would think. I try to put myself in his situation and can't figure it out. If someone like Samantha—or Kell—wanted to be in a committed relationship with me, I would have no problem spending nights with her. Days. Whatever she wanted.

I reach the door to the outside, thinking I'll check for Jonah. Shea is there and her eyes light up when she sees me. "Hey. I didn't think I'd see you again this soon."

"Yeah. I'm looking for my other brother. Ryan is, uh, busy."

She laughs. Her fingers touch my arm. "Do you think your brother will be okay without you for a minute? Come sit down with me."

Jonah is most likely busy talking to Jessie. He doesn't care if I find him. We all know how to make it home on our own anyway.

Shea leads the way to a small corner booth near the door. I slide in, but instead of taking the bench across from me, she scoots in close on the same side. "So are you working on any other movies right now?"

Her smile is cute, lips full and red.

"Just finished shooting one. I'm not supposed to talk about it though." I wink. Not really true, but it feels like mystery is the way to go here. If she's a fan of movies like mine, she'll likely see the trailer when it releases in the next few months.

"It must be really fun, doing something you love and getting to share it with fans."

I stop. It's not often that I think about my work in that way. "Yeah, it can be fun." Feels like a jerk move to complain about making money doing movies when fans like Shea get so much joy from it. Kell has said similar things before.

"What do you do?" Enough talk about me. I'm getting curious about the woman beside me.

"I'm a nurse. It's not exactly fun, but it is rewarding. My dad was a nurse, and I've known that I wanted to do the same since I was a little girl." We're sitting closer now. Her hair brushes my arm.

"That's amazing. I have a lot of respect for nurses." Shea isn't the typical groupie that Ryan usually finds at these types of places. She's kind and smells nice. Cute with a career that doesn't have anything to do with the way she looks.

"Thanks, Ash." Shea's hand goes to my shoulder. She urges me closer and gives a nervous little laugh. I could easily go in for a kiss. It's clear that she wants me to kiss her.

Not so clear is what I want. Shea's eyes linger on my mouth. And then I don't have another second to think about it before she's kissing me.

It's nice. Soft. There's no spark or anything, but it's a first kiss. She pulls back and grins at me. Not shy at all.

"I have to go, but I want to see you again. Call me?"

I nod after her and she disappears into the crowd. Figure I should look for my brothers now. Jonah might be ready to leave. Ryan might need an intervention.

I almost run straight into Judith. She looks out of place wearing a dark-green pantsuit next to the party crowd. Why is she here? She waves her fingers at me. "Don't worry, we already got all the footage we need tonight. You boys have fun. And say goodbye to Kell for me, will you?"

The hell?

Judith jumps into conversation with another guy who's suited up, making it clear she's done talking to me. My eyes search wildly for any sign of Kell. She's not here. Why would she be? And why do I get the feeling that Judith being here isn't a surprise to some of us?

Then I see her. She's staring straight at me from the door of the bar. Kell's eyes are wide and her mouth open. I don't need to ask if she saw me with Shea—it's written on her face. I step toward her, her name on my lips, but Kell turns and rushes outside and I stand frozen with a pit in my stomach.

I swing back to Ryan. He's still talking animatedly and nothing about his body language lets on that he knows about any cameras. But my eyes narrow as I scan the crowd again. One. Two. Three familiar faces. All holding small cameras pointed at my brother and me.

No wonder Jonah disappeared.

I push through the room and shove an elbow into Ryan's side. "You should have told me they were going to be filming tonight."

"Relax, bro. Did you read the contract? They're always filming. That's the whole point."

When I turn my back on him, I hear him launch into detail about our reality show to his captive audience. I leave him behind and go out into the street to look for Kell.

CHAPTER TWENTY-THREE

✿ ✿ ✿ ✿ ✿

Kell

hat the hell, Ash?

$\mathcal{W}$ I speed walk down Sunset Boulevard, past a slew of other glitzy bars with lines out the door. The women waiting there are hoping for a fun night when something magical might happen, and an hour ago I was naïve enough to be one of them. Of all the clubs in the city and all the nights to choose to change up my comfortable routine, why did my plans have to align with the Matthews'? It should be none of my business what they do on their off time, but that's not how this works, unfortunately for me. All of their business is my business. Whatever the public sees, I need to see and know, but better and more as that's the only way I can do my job.

And tonight I saw Ash ramming his tongue down a woman's throat. I have no idea if he saw me, but I'm guessing he didn't because he was too busy with the aforementioned woman. I almost tripped over my own feet trying to get out of there as quickly as possible. Since Ash's breakup with Celeste, I haven't had to think about him with another woman. It's been a while since Ash has shown an interest in anyone, and I got used to it being just him. Seeing Ash's mouth on a beautiful stranger's made me hot and itchy all over, like some terrible allergic reaction. I guess I didn't realize how much I'd be affected by seeing him with someone else. Whatever romance exists between us is pure fantasy, made up for TV ratings and keeping producers happy. It's not like I don't know that. It's not like I think that I have some claim to Ash because of our history or even our present.

It's just that seeing him with another woman makes me want to claw my eyes out.

Pretending to be his girlfriend hasn't been all bad. I've always wondered, ever since that almost kiss back in college, what it'd be like to see that side of him, the softer romantic. I glimpse it occasionally in moments when he has his guard down. Even back then, up until the second that his lips nearly grazed mine, I hadn't been sure of what I'd do, if I'd pull away or let him kiss me and see where it went from there. For all this time, I always thought I made the right choice. But now, there's a small part of me that wonders if I let something great pass me by. Ash has already proven that he'd be a near-perfect boyfriend, and maybe, given the chance all those years ago, we'd be in a real relationship right now instead of an increasingly confusing made-for-reality-TV one.

My apartment is technically within walking distance, but I lean against the outside brick of an Italian restaurant emanating drool-worthy smells of cheese and garlic and order a ride. I sigh. I was actually having fun, which hasn't happened in a pathetically long time. Claudette and I were dancing, and I was wearing the dress that made me feel like someone else, someone much more relaxed and spontaneous. Before she had to leave for a late-night client emergency, Claudette was trying and failing to convince me to go up to the redhead in the corner who looked scarily like a young Prince

Harry. Maybe he *was* watching me, but I wasn't ready. I'm not ready for some new guy to come trample all over my life, not when I still have to operate in very close proximity to the last one.

Once the driver has dropped me off at my apartment building, I trudge inside and kick off my shoes. My computer is warm and heavy on my lap when I curl up with my blanket on the sofa.

Work-life balance and all that means that I should wait until actual work hours to check my inbox. I don't prescribe to that because I'm clearly a masochist. I spend an hour organizing final details for Jonah's new brand collab before I let myself take a break. I scan my emails and click a recent one from Judith labeled, "Matthew Film Review." The only other film I've seen from the show so far was from the first day, and it was actually impressive. The guys were just how they are in real life—one part awkward, one part endearing. And a big part ego, especially in Ryan's case. I could see it being an entertaining show for a certain kind of audience, and that's all show business really is—finding the perfect audience.

The raw footage Judith sent over starts with the photo shoot day from last week. I spot myself in the background within the first few seconds and drag my mouse until it's skipped past that part. I will avoid reliving myself on camera for as long as possible, thank you very much.

I keep scrolling and, wow, the footage includes clips from tonight. As frustrated as Judith makes me, I have to admit, she's dedicated to her job. There they are at the same VIP big-shot club I was, just the kind of place that Ryan loves to brag about getting into. It's never been Jonah's scene and hasn't been Ash's thing for the past year or so, but the camera doesn't lie. I drag my mouse along again to skip through. If anything too outrageous happened, other than what I saw, I doubt Judith would have buried it in an email with a dozen other clips. About halfway through, Jonah slips through the crowd and goes outside with his phone. I don't even have to guess who he's talking to since Jessie isn't there. Those two are one hundred percent committed to each other. It's nice to see.

Speaking of commitment, Ryan isn't shy about talking to every woman who crosses his path. A gorgeous woman with ruby red lipstick comes up to Ryan and Ash, but her focus seems to stay on Ash. I snort. I'll bet Ryan did not see that coming.

I skip through again until I'm nearly at the end. I feel a bit like a spy scrolling through such recent footage, almost like I'm seeing private moments I shouldn't be. Then again, such is the nature of a reality show, for better or for worse.

My breath is held tightly as I watch Ryan hold court with half a dozen beautiful women. They hang on his every word and laugh at the end of every joke, right on cue. I expect the usual pang of jealousy to hit me, but it doesn't come. Instead I zoom in and frown at the way his hair looks too thick with hair product. The dimple on the left side of his chin looks manufactured. His smile is too smarmy.

And, holy crap, it's actually working. Claudette and Ash both told me I'd be able to move on some day, and I'm starting to think they were right. Ryan Matthew has lost his charm for me, and that's a huge step.

The smile on my face is wiped away by the end of the footage still rolling on my computer. Ash is back with the woman, the woman I saw him with. The one he kissed. I close the file before it plays out on my computer screen. I already saw it once, and that was enough.

My phone rings with an incoming call from, who else, Ash. I let it ring as I toggle over to another page on my laptop and train my eyes on my work. It's late, and Ash can wait until tomorrow considering how busy he looked earlier at the bar.

Kell: *I'm not answering calls right now.*

CHAPTER TWENTY-FOUR

✿ ✿ ✿ ✿ ✿

Ash

*J*t's not morning yet. It can't be. Stiffly, I sit up in bed and tap the screen of my phone. It lights up with a text.

From Shea.

Shea: *Last night was fun. Dinner sometime? Let me know what your schedule is like.*

It doesn't surprise me that she's the type of woman to take matters into her own hands. Normally I wouldn't see the harm in getting dinner with her. Shea is interested in me. She was fun to hang out with in the brief time we talked last night. But I spent the better part of the hours after I left the club trying to get ahold of Kell. After she ignored my first few phone calls, she sent a terse text that essentially told me to stand down.

I scroll back to the last text I sent her.

Ash: *Sorry to call so late. I was worried about you after you left the club. Are we good?*

I thought it was decent, but she left me on read.

So, no matter what, I can't focus on anything else until I talk to Kell. The only thing that I'm perfectly clear on from last night is that she's mad at me.

After getting ready, I find her in the front living room talking to Jonah and Jessie. At first glance everything is normal. Kell is talking in a low voice and Jessie is by her side nodding enthusiastically. Jonah stands a little apart. But as soon as they spot me, they all go quiet.

Jonah raises his eyebrows in some lame attempt to communicate with me. I don't know what the hell he thinks he's saying. "We've got things to do," Jessie says pointedly and drags him out of the room until I'm left alone with Kell.

For the first time, this doesn't feel like a good thing. She doesn't say a word but sits on the end of the sofa. I swallow and sit next to her while still leaving enough space so she can't smack me if this conversation goes wrong.

"Are you going to tell me what happened last night?"

Her head snaps toward me so fast. She doesn't say a word, but her eyes speak volumes.

I hold up my hands. "I get that you're pissed about something." Still not sure what it is. "But seriously, Kell, I was worried about you. You just ran out of there and wouldn't answer my calls." I remember the reality show all of a sudden and curse under my breath. My head swivels, looking for Ryan's hidden cameras or a well-camouflaged crew member. I see none, thankfully.

Kell's answer comes in a harsh whisper. She's thinking of the cameras too. "Well, I didn't want to talk to you if we're being honest. I was embarrassed. You made me look like an idiot, Ash."

"How? How could I embarrass you?"

Kell's eyes flash. "The last I checked, we're supposed to be in a relationship." She turns away. Her shoulders hunch like she's folding inward.

"Right . . ." I'm not sure what she wants to hear from me. We're pretending to be in a relationship. *Pretending* being the operative word. She's made sure to make that clear over and over.

"Last month I was in the tabloids with headlines claiming I was trying to steal Ryan away from his fiancée. And now, probably literally as we speak, there are going to be stories about you kissing some girl you met at the club on top of leaks about the two of us from the show promo. Do you not see how pathetic that makes me look?"

"You're not pathetic."

I rake a hand through my hair. If I say that none of this ever occurred to me, it will only make her madder. But honestly? None of this ever occurred to me.

"Well, thanks. That solves everything." She gives me a weak smile. Sarcastic as ever but at least she's not giving me the cold shoulder anymore.

"What can I do to fix this?"

Kell lets loose a long, slow breath. I watch the movement of her chest and feel tightness in mine. I really screwed up.

"There's nothing to do. It already happened, and I'm sure the story is out there, so now we ride the publicity and use it to our advantage."

This sounds more like the badass I'm used to. "Okay, so, it's not bad press? For the show?"

"No. No, if anything, it's good for the show. It gets your name in the tabloids more and gets the show more visibility. I'm sure marketing will be happy with us."

"I really am sorry," I say again, but Kell stops me.

"Apology accepted. And I owe you an apology too. I overreacted because I was caught off guard, but at the end of the day, you're right. We're not in a real relationship and there's nothing in either of our contracts that says we can't date outside of the show."

"It still shouldn't have happened."

She narrows her eyes. "Judith and Aaron will be thrilled with the extra drama, so there's that. I'm sure they don't mind at all."

"I'll make sure they know it was a one-time thing." Knowing that Kell cares who I'm seen with in public is enough for me. I'm not going to put her through it again.

We reach a tentative truce, and Kell sits back on the sofa. Every part of me wants to pull her into my arms. I'm not supposed to be the one hurting her. That's Ryan's thing and he's done it enough for the both of us. But there's making things right and then there's beating a dead horse, so I keep myself from apologizing another time for good measure. Kell says something about contracts, and I get a text from Jonah to meet him for a workout.

While I walk to the other side of the house, I text Shea and tell her I had fun last night too. I don't make any plans with her and hope it's letting her off easy. Shea seems like the kind of person who won't have trouble moving on. Not like me. Dating has never been easy, but ever since Celeste my luck has run out. And now, it would be a lot more convenient if the one woman I care to date actually wanted to date me back.

CHAPTER TWENTY-FIVE

⁂ ⁂ ⁂ ⁂ ⁂

Kell

J officially suck.

I avoided Ash and didn't take his calls all because of some very not-my-business kiss. About mid-tirade was when I realized that I have absolutely no reason to be as mad as I was.

Ash is never going to run off and get engaged without giving me a heads up. He's not going to do anything off-the-cuff or image wrecking, so why did I think it was any of my business who he kissed last night?

Ash kissing a mystery woman adds to the drama of the show. It's a good thing, and not one person working in Hollywood could argue that it isn't. The cardinal rule of this industry is that all press is good press, and I know this. For the first time since working with the Matthews, I've messed up and let my personal feelings trump business.

It's a problem when my unhappiness with work rubs off on everyone around me, I know that. But the only solution I can come up with wouldn't make anyone any happier, so we're stuck. All that remains to do is to be better at my job and not take it out on my clients, especially not Ash.

When there's nothing left to say, Ash goes to find Jonah for their morning workout, and I head upstairs. I have contracts tucked in my bag for Ryan to look over, but as soon as I knock on his door, I know I've made a mistake. The sounds coming from inside are unmistakable. Instead of hanging around, I run the other way, not stopping to look back. There's involved manger and then there's TMI, and this is too much for me, no doubt.

I end up in the kitchen, standing at the oversized island and staring at a bowl of untouched fruit. Three days a week the guys have Ava, a retired chef, come in and cook for them. She always does extra things like leave them special fruit and fill the freezer. They used to rave about how amazing it was, how cool and convenient. Now, I feel like they barely even notice that their lives are wildly different from the norm. There were certainly no girls hidden away in bedrooms back then. Instead, it was the four of us all the time, oohing and aahing over every magical step of newfound fame.

The Matthews used to be the most solid thing in my life because I knew exactly where I stood with each of them. Jonah was the easy client who never made things hard, Ryan was the one I would have given anything to be with, and Ash was my best friend.

Now Jonah is getting fined left and right. Ryan is nothing more than a client. And Ash—I wish I knew where I stood with Ash. There's this tension between us now that wasn't there before.

Maybe what I've always heard is true—platonic friendships can only end one of two ways, they fizzle out or erupt in sparks. Maybe we're fizzling.

I suck in a deep breath and look down at my hands. I don't want to lose our friendship, but I'm not sure what I can do to reverse the strain of passing time. I already made a big deal about Ash with another woman, so anything I do now will look like me marking my territory.

That's not what I'm doing, right?

Am I jealous that Ash is dating again and I'm not? Ryan is engaged and Jonah is practically married, but Ash and I have always been the single ones in the group. And even when we've had significant others, it's been long distance or a fellow workaholic, some arrangement that left us mostly to our own devices.

Normally I'd call Claudette or show up at her apartment and word vomit my fears until she talked sense into me. But she left today for a whole week of working an event in Paris. Lucky duck. Even if I wanted to crunch the numbers and figure out the time difference between us, I don't want to bother her. She deserves to have fun without hearing my constant drama. I sigh and stare back down at the rainbow assortment in the fruit bowl. My hand closes around a perfect-looking peach just as Ash walks into the kitchen. I freeze, feeling guilty for a reason I can't quite pinpoint.

He cocks his head toward the bowl. "No one cares if you take a peach, Kell. Take all of them if you want."

"Thanks." I bring the fruit to my nose and inhale. It smells amazing, like nectar and flowers rolled into one. I hop onto one of the stools at the island and bite into it. My mouth explodes with juice. Ash busies himself with his phone at the other end of the kitchen, so I fill the silence with bites, focusing fully on eating. I haven't had time to eat yet today. Maybe that's all my stomachache is.

Jonah's voice carries down the hall. "Ash? You want to play basketball with me and the guys today?"

A pair from the camera crew follow him, but Jonah acts like he doesn't notice. He brightens as he comes into the kitchen. "Hey, Kell. I didn't know you were still here."

My peach has been reduced to a pit and I have nothing more to hide behind. I walk to the sink and wash off my face and hands.

"I came by to drop some contracts off," I hedge, and Ash doesn't correct me. Technically, I did come to drop off contracts for Ryan, but I chickened out and will have to send them electronically and call it good.

Jonah starts to say something else, but now that the camera crew is here, I'm focused on not wasting this chance. This is something I should have done first thing anyway. I suck in a breath and walk straight to Ash, who is still leaning against the far kitchen wall scrolling on his phone. I am hyperaware of the turn of the cameras tracking my every move. "We need to talk," I say in my most important voice. "I know about last night."

Ash blinks slowly and repeats my words. He probably thinks I'm officially losing my mind. "Last night?"

"You were with another woman. Are you seriously going to pretend like you didn't get all cozy with someone while you thought I wasn't there?"

Ash takes half a second to catch on and then his mouth shifts from slack-jawed shock to quick understanding. He holds out a hand as if reaching for me, and I step back, feigning an indignant huff.

"Don't touch me! Not after you kissed someone else."

"You know it's not like that. We never said that we were exclusive, Kell. You were the one who said we should keep our options open."

I cock an eyebrow. "That doesn't sound like something I'd say."

Ash's smirk is just subtle enough that I don't know if it will translate for the cameras. It passes between us as somewhat of a secret, making the shared joke of what we're doing even sweeter because it's something the show can't capture. They don't know that this isn't real. The rest of the people with us in the kitchen just stare. Even in my peripheral vision I register Jonah's bug-eyed gaze of total confusion. No one besides the two of us can decipher the truth from the lies in this conversation, and honestly? It's exhilarating to hold that power for once, to be the one in charge of this narrative. It's fun.

"Call me when you are ready to be honest with yourself, Ash. I'm not sticking around to be anyone's side chick." I huff and ready myself to march away, thus ending the single most thrilling role of my meager acting career.

But just as I rotate Ash catches my hand and pulls me back. I spin into his chest, landing flush against him, pressed up so tightly that I feel the thrumming of his heartbeat right against mine. This is new.

My eyes flit up to meet his, and I'm supposed to be confident and aloof right now. I'm supposed to be playing the role of the jilted lover to really sell the whole story, but my body clearly hasn't gotten the memo.

Before I can push away, before I can do anything, Ash lifts a hand to my chin and tilts it upward. His mouth meets mine in a fleeting kiss, so quick and whisper-soft that I have no time to even feel it. His lips brush mine and then they're gone, taking all my confidence in what I think I know with them.

"You're the only person I'm dating. The mistake I made last night won't happen again. I swear." He steps away gently, dropping my face and hand.

Because I'm an acting novice and also because I've been rendered completely speechless, all I can do is nod.

CHAPTER TWENTY-SIX

❀ ❀ ❀ ❀ ❀

Ash

"*L*et's get you over here with your brothers." Judith drags me by the arm. Her grip is as persistent as she is. My brothers and I and the rest of the filming crew are gathered out on the sidewalk in front of our house. I'm holding a leash with a dog attached to the end of it. Everyone's acting like it's not weird that there's a random dog here. We don't have any pets. Not enough time for one, plus Jonah is allergic. His eyes swelled up to golf balls when we were kids after I brought home a stray cat. The dog is cute but obviously nervous. A tan lab-mix puppy with big brown eyes and trouble walking on a leash.

I told Aaron we don't take family walks. No reason to. He called one of his aides and thirty minutes later they brought over this little guy from the closest shelter. Guess he thinks the puppy solves that problem. When Kell parks and walks across the driveway to us, she gestures to the puppy, who is trying to chew my shoe while I'm wearing it. "Did I miss something? Whose dog is this?"

She crouches to check his tag and scratch behind his ears. Kell snorts. "His name is Ryan?"

I bend down to confirm, and sure enough, the dog is named Ryan. Aaron's aide must have done that on purpose. Kell and I lock eyes and burst out laughing. "Yeah, kind of perfect," I say. I sidestep as dog-Ryan tries to lick my socks. "He's from the animal shelter. For this footage of us going on a walk."

"I've never seen the three of you on a walk in my life. This isn't *Pride and Pretty People*." Kell smirks. Referencing movies I've done in the past never fails to bring her a sick sense of joy. The contemporary Jane Austen spin-off I did at the beginning of my career is one of her favorite punch lines. To be fair, it was a terrible movie.

"Let's get moving!" Aaron cups his hands to his mouth and divides up his filming crew so they're circling our group. We each get mic'd up and start walking. The sidewalks are narrow and hardly fit two people at once. Instead of walking in a group like I'm thinking Aaron imagined, it's more of a two-by-two march.

The hardest part is talking without it sounding like forced conversation.

Not surprisingly, Kell has a talent for pretending to know what's going on. "We should get Gatorade." She fans the back of her neck with one hand and looks up at the cloudless sky. It's early October and it's still burning up outside. Halloween is going to be a sweaty mess if things don't start cooling down.

"Yeah. Gatorade sounds great." I keep a straight face at the bold placement of Jonah's newest sponsor. It's hard to miss because the logo is on the back of his shirt and on the hat he's wearing today. No idea how Kell pulled that one off since it's a pretty big deal, but I'm happy for my brother. It's all part of his brand rehabilitation, and Jonah is set on making it work.

"This is such a cute puppy," Jessie coos. She bends to nuzzle the fuzzy top of dog-Ryan's head.

Jonah slips an arm around her waist. "I don't know if we're ready for a pet."

"I want this dog." She pets him again and dog-Ryan pulls against the leash while wagging his tail at super speed.

"I'm allergic," Jonah protests.

I hand Jessie the leash and she and Jonah start arguing about when they think the right time to adopt a puppy is and whether or not allergy shots actually work.

The rest of the walk is uneventful. The cameras pan over Ryan and Samantha for most of the time, which is fine by me. I figure Kell and I have put in our time lately.

After about twenty minutes, we straggle back to the house and Jonah and Jessie head inside. The film crew puts away their cameras as soon as we scatter, and Ryan walks Samantha to her car. Kell passes dog-Ryan's leash from hand to hand. "Do you think we should have held hands during the walk? For the show?"

"I think we gave a good enough performance the other day. We probably don't have to worry too much about convincing anyone." I raise an eyebrow.

She shakes her head, laughing. "Okay. You have a point."

This is the first time either of us has mentioned the scene in the kitchen. I finished our staged argument in the kitchen with a kiss that I don't think either of us was expecting. Of course Aaron and Judith ate it up. My gaze burns into hers as I tilt my head. I wish that I could see into her head and figure out what she's thinking. Sometimes I think we know each other inside and out. Other times, Kell is a mystery. Softly, I tell her, "I really appreciate you doing this, Kell. It means a lot to me. This is above and beyond manager duties." She agreed to this setup because it benefits me and the show, and that's the only reason. I honestly don't think a better manager exists.

She lifts a shoulder. "It's not so terrible."

We grin at each other until she breaks. "Anyway, I'll be here all week for filming. They want to squeeze in some more shots of me doing manager things. And, you know, relationship things."

"And you're okay with that?" Last I saw, she wasn't loving being on camera. Though we did have a good time with it during our fake fight. I've never seen Jonah so confused.

"I'll survive. Judith seems to think expanding the cast will make the show better. That's coming straight from Aaron. I trust her judgment on this, and at least I have a pretty great costar."

"You're pretty great yourself." I take advantage of her offer to hold hands and lead us inside the house. No cameras are watching, and no one is around to care. But I figure we might as well practice, right?

The rest of the day is filled with lines half-memorized on the spot. Aaron reviewed some of the home footage we sent in and rewrote some of the conversations. Feels ridiculous having a fake fight over eating Jonah's yogurt stash. When he caught me the other day, he passive-aggressively grabbed a pen and wrote a big *J* on the tops of the remaining yogurts.

In Aaron's version, Jonah and I face off in the kitchen. I strut into the room like a college freshman who's just seen his first sorority house. Jonah takes one look at me and bolts up. "You've been eating my yogurt," he says in a voice that's almost a growl.

"It's just yogurt, bro. It's not a big deal." I duck into the fridge and grab the last remaining strawberry yogurt cup. It's been placed strategically in the center of the shelves.

"Put it down. I'm not joking."

"Or what?" I stare him down while peeling back the lid and bringing the cup to my mouth. Slowly, while maintaining eye contact, I stick my tongue into the yogurt.

Jonah yells something unintelligible and dives for the yogurt. I hold it over my head just out of his reach, but Jonah uses his muscles to his advantage and manages to pin my arms. "Drop the yogurt," he grunts. Per Aaron's suggestion, I do. I drop it right on Jonah's foot, spraying strawberry-colored goo everywhere. And then Jonah does what he does best and curses like a sailor. And there you go. The Matthew brothers at their worst in a bite-sized kitchen disaster. It's not at all real, but it's exactly what the show ordered.

After we both clean up, I wander into the kitchen to find Judith with Kell and a small gathering of crewmembers. While Judith whispers with one of the crew, I try to catch Kell's eye. I'll kick Judith's ass if she gives Kell trouble, and I need her to know that.

But Judith tells the crew to cut the cameras and motions me over. "I just talked to Aaron," she announces. "Early testing for your relationship is great. Sample viewers are invested."

"That's good news." Kell tosses me a proud glance. There's no better proof that we make the best team.

"It is." Judith raises both eyebrows. "People love relationships. But do you know what they love more than a happy couple? They love two people in turmoil, which is why we're breaking the two of you up at the end of the show."

"Wait, what?"

She tsks. "I know. But let me and Aaron worry about this, okay? We're the brains here, honey. We're going to leave it on this little cliffhanger so people are desperate for more. It's going to work out so much better than the original plan."

She pats me on the arm and walks from the kitchen. I turn to gape at Kell. "This doesn't make sense. Why even ask us to be together in the first place?"

Kell shrugs. "Actually, it sounds like a smart idea. Judith has no tact, and she could have worded it better, but she's probably right. People will care *more* when there's something to fight for."

Still doesn't make sense to me, but if Kell's on board, so am I. "You should probably break up with me, then. Don't want anyone thinking I'm the villain."

She smacks my arm. "Hey! I don't want to be the villain either. But I agree that it should be me since Judith and Aaron clearly want you to play the role of single heartthrob next."

I narrow my eyes. "Heartthrob? Do people still say that?" And before Kell can answer I add, "Are we getting old?" When we first met, I was young and invincible. Unbeatable. Wasn't even that long ago, but it feels like forever.

"We're in our twenties. You were named Hottest Bachelor *last year*." She shakes her head. "We're definitely not old yet. We just have a long history."

Mention of our history snaps me to attention. Kell's face is soft and reflective. I like the way she talks about our friendship. Like it means as much to her as it does to me.

"What are you two whispering about in here?" Ryan leans against the hallway wall next to the kitchen.

Kell's eyes cut to the cameraman who has followed Ryan in. This is what I was afraid of. The whole thing stinks of another reality setup, and I should have known that no quick conversation with Judith is what it seems. He walks to the island and folds against it, his elbows down so that he's at our level. "I have a funny question, Kell."

"Okay." Her lips form a thin line.

"You and Ash have been friends since the very beginning. Was there ever anything happening between you? I mean, while we're on the subject, what exactly is your relationship?" He waves his hand between us with another smirk.

I want to slap it off him.

Should slap it off him.

But the cameras. We're almost done filming, and if Ryan would just shut up we could power through. If only I could air Ryan's dirty laundry without hurting Kell in the process. He's the one who took advantage of Kell's feelings. That's impossible to bring up without dragging Kell down though.

Kell tilts her head. "Where's Samantha? Why didn't she stay and hang out longer? Busy schedule?"

Opening and closing his mouth like a fish, Ryan makes a non-committal noise. "Sam's been busy, yeah. She's going to try to stop by on Monday."

Nine times out of ten, Kell knows something I don't. I can't help wondering if that's the case now. I hadn't noticed that Samantha has been missing. Now that she brings it up, I can't remember the last time Ryan voluntarily brought her up in conversation. Every scene she's filmed has ended with her quickly driving home.

Ryan spins around and mutters something about going out. He leaves the kitchen in painful disgrace. The camera guys follow him. Maybe they're hoping for a confession from Ryan. That, or a fight with Samantha, if that's where he's going.

"I think we ruined his plan."

Kell glares in the direction of the leaving cameras. "I'm not so sure it was entirely his plan." She's not going to start bad-mouthing Judith on air, I know that, but we're both thinking it. Judith is a pain, but crossing her is career suicide.

"Everyone always wants to assume we have some sort of romantic history." She shakes her head. "I mean, we didn't back then, and we don't now. They act like a man and a woman can't be good friends."

"Technically, for show purposes, you are my girlfriend," I remind her.

Kell shrugs like none of that matters. "Yeah, but the point is, we've only ever been friends."

Never fails to point that out. I'm not oblivious. I know what it means when a woman makes sure to call herself your friend. She's drawing a line. It says what she's feeling loud and clear.

"Maybe we could have been more." Too much truth falls out of me before I can stop it.

Nervous is the only way to describe the way she laughs. "Yeah, I guess so. If we'd gone through with that kiss in college." She narrows her eyes. "But you would have gotten bored with me. You broke a lot of hearts back then. And then what? We would have never spoken again, and we'd never have teamed up." She gestures around us. "And this wouldn't have happened." Kell's cheeks go pink. "I mean, maybe it would have. You are a pretty great actor. But I wouldn't have gotten to be a part of it."

"No way. Not without you. I'd still be scooping ice cream," I say, referring to the part-time job I had before acting could pay the bills. I balanced a job handing out ice cream and a couple of indie films for the first two years. Kell made a habit of stopping by for free cones weekly.

Kell only wrinkles her nose. "I doubt it. Someone else would have made sure you were seen by the right people."

"I wouldn't be here without you, and we both know that."

We don't look away for a minute. I've always loved Kell's eyes. The way they feel like a reflection of who she is on the inside. Warm, quick, guarded.

I should say something. But it's a little too mushy for me, so instead, when she tries to stifle a yawn, I move away.

"You should sleep over tonight. Take one of the guest rooms," I tell her.

She stretches. "The drive isn't that bad. You know I'm weird about sleeping in my own bed."

"Have you been feeling okay?" I take in her appearance to look for clues. No circles under her eyes. No too-pale face.

"I'm just tired. I'm planning on taking my medication this weekend, so you don't have to worry about me." Her arms cross over her chest, pulling away. Kell gets mad about anyone checking up on her. She's always been too independent for her own good. But telling her that is out of bounds, even for me.

"I don't worry. I know you're strong as hell. But you put everyone else first. You have to take care of yourself. We'd literally fall apart without you."

I don't know how she does it. Then again, I don't get how she manages all the things she does.

"No one's going to fall apart," she assures me as she heads to the door.

CHAPTER TWENTY-SEVEN

❈ ❈ ❈ ❈ ❈

Kell

*B*y the time I get home, I'm so tired that my limbs are wobbly. It feels a little like I'm dragging myself inside my apartment as I scoot to my bed and flop over onto my pillow. I've been working nonstop lately. But also, Ash is right. My medication has been staring me in the face every morning and I've ignored it in favor of rushing out the door. It's possible that I may be pushing myself too hard.

Ash is always there, noticing every little change. He's more worried about my health than I am. As much as I wish I could argue that this is a total one-off, the truth is that this happens more than I care to admit. And the closer it gets to the time the next dose is due, the more my body slows down. I hate feeling limited. Even though I know it's well-meaning, I also hate that Ash called me out on it. After all the times I've had to physically pull him out of bed in the mornings, it doesn't sit well that he's scanning me for signs of sickness.

I know how to handle my own illness just fine by myself.

Speaking of calling people out. My teeth grind together. Ryan had to have been put up by Judith for that ridiculous question. But put up or not, he knows better than that. I thought he cared about me more than to try to humiliate his brother or me. I could see it in Ash's eyes, the urge to point out that Ryan was actually the only one to explore anything more than friendship with me. I almost wanted to say it myself. Before I can steam about it too much, my eyes grow heavy and it's impossible to stop from falling asleep.

Dragging myself up, I cross to the kitchen and open the fridge to stare at my waiting medication. I should really inject myself and get it over with so I don't have to worry. But I'm so tired. I close the fridge and curl onto my bed.

Tomorrow. I'll definitely have time for my medication tomorrow after I get some sleep.

❀ ❀ ❀ ❀ ❀

When morning comes, I'm not prepared for the stinging light from the sun pouring through my bedroom window. I fell asleep without washing my face or removing my makeup, and my mouth is sticky and dry like it's stuffed with cotton.

It's not a good way to convince anyone, including myself, that I'm doing a good job at taking care of my body. To make amends, I scrounge in my freezer for some frozen fruit and blend it up with a scoop of the protein powder Ash insisted I try last Christmas when he gifted me every flavor ever invented. I add a splash of almond milk and watch as it all blurs together into a pleasant peach shade. Honestly, I don't know if I'm doing the whole healthy thing right, but fruit is good for you, right?

I drink my smoothie at the table while I scroll through emails on my phone. My stomach is bloated, full and hard and uncomfortable, like it doesn't really appreciate my efforts at breakfast at all. I gulp sips of water and scoop up a handful of Tylenol as I rush out the door. No, I'm not feeling any better than I was last night, but I've got to channel the Matthews and *act* like I'm fine. That's all I have time for.

CHAPTER TWENTY-EIGHT

✿ ✿ ✿ ✿ ✿

Ash

"It's too early," I slur as I roll over. I grab a pillow to smash over my head. Bright lights fill my bedroom.

"You asked me for a wakeup call." Kell's voice holds a touch of amusement.

I'm starting to think she does this for fun. That she likes torturing me more than is necessary. I groan. "Asked for a phone call at eight. It's not eight."

Her words are singsong. "Oh, yes, it is. It's eight-oh-five. I've been knocking on your door for four minutes, and you didn't answer, so I decided on a more hands-on approach."

The end of the bed bounces. I blink one eye open to see Kell sitting there staring at me. She's definitely getting some sort of sick pleasure from this. What is it like to be a morning person who has their life together?

"What's wrong with you?" I struggle to sit up. "Why are you so happy so early in the morning?"

She shrugs one shoulder. "Deal with the devil. I'm not supposed to talk about it."

"Give me fifteen minutes." I squint one eye open and look at Kell. Her hair is pulled back into a fluffy ponytail low on her neck. She's wearing a loose dress and her face is pale. It's early, but still. We should *both* be sleeping in more than this. No matter how bubbly she sounds, she doesn't look quite right.

"You have five," she retorts. "Judith wants us shooting as much as possible outside this morning. It's supposed to rain later."

No way is it going to rain. It's been clear all week. I checked the forecast yesterday and everything was clear. "Judith doesn't know what she's talking about," I grumble.

Kell pretends to look scandalized. She covers her mouth with a hand. "Watch your tongue, Mr. Matthew. Here's a lesson for you. If Judith Young says it's going to snow glitter balls in July, you go with it and offer to shovel her driveway for her."

My eyes roll. I get it, but respect only goes so far. Judith tried to set up Kell for an awkward moment yesterday. I'm not going to bend over backward for a bully.

"'Kay." Kell pats the bed. "I'll leave you to your shower. Meet me in the kitchen after?"

Once I'm showered and dressed, I make my way to the kitchen as promised, but it's empty. I open the fridge and scan the items. Jonah's yogurts are there front and center. Might be a trap, but I don't care. I grab a peach yogurt and a spoon and sit at the table. Looks like I wasn't late after all. Everyone else must be struggling to wake up too. Sticking to this early schedule is probably the hardest part of the show.

"Ryan, stop."

Kell's voice is muffled but I'm sure it's her. I don't see anyone else around, so I spring up and listen by the half wall leading to the living room. She's sitting on the sofa with Ryan. There's space between them. I blow out a sigh from my nose. She scoots farther away from him. The distance between them is encouraging. I don't know what they're even doing together. "This is inappropriate. You shouldn't be telling me this."

Probably means I shouldn't be hearing it either.

I blow out a breath and retreat far enough away that I'm no longer listening to their conversation. My phone is barely enough distraction, but I train my eyes downward. A minute later, I see Kell out of the corner of my eye. She storms down the hall with her head held high.

Ryan follows her. He rounds the corner into the kitchen. Almost slams into my chest. His eyes are wide. Wild. "Did you hear all that?" he demands.

I puff up a bit. My anger is less after watching Kell handle herself. "Some of it. You gonna leave Kell alone? You have to talk to your fiancée."

"Samantha and I aren't doing well." Ryan's mouth is drawn. "Things haven't been great. You have to talk to Kell for me. I get that I messed up, but I don't want to lose her."

My chest hurts. "As a manager or what?"

"Anything. I don't know why it took me so long to realize, man, but Kell is special. Please, just tell her how sorry I am. Tell her that I can be better." Ryan doesn't beg. Doesn't toss around words like special. Any other circumstance and I might feel bad for him. I might even be happy that he finally cares about someone other than Ryan. But he did this to himself and there's no shot in hell I'm letting him mess with Kell again.

I push past my brother. "I'm not saying any of that. Kell deserves better and you know it." Even Ryan can't be this stupid.

"Where are you going?"

"To talk to Kell. About nothing to do with you. Clean up your own mess for once." I walk from the kitchen with my fists still clenched. Part of me hates that I overheard all of that. The other part of me wants to celebrate the fact that Kell told my brother off finally.

I try to find Kell, but she avoids me for the rest of the day. Judith's crew packs in filming and reshoots for hours straight. The most I see of Kell is across a room, her arms crossed and her jaw locked tight. Ryan tries once and Kell turns her back and leaves the room without a word. At the end of the day, I wait outside for Kell to get in her car, but she's already gone. She must have sneaked out early.

CHAPTER TWENTY-NINE

✿ ✿ ✿ ✿ ✿

Kell

yan's voice is deep with emotion. "I can't stop thinking about you. I'm sorry, but I can't just push that down and ignore it. I've tried."

My head spins because I'm still not sure how a conversation beginning with "How are you?" could turn into a confession so quickly.

"You're engaged," I tell him flatly. I stand and smooth my hands over the skirt of my dress.

"I'm your manager. I will be here if you need to talk career moves, but otherwise, I'm not open to talking about relationships or your personal life." I turn and pause. "Oh, and I think you should call your fiancée. You two need to talk."

"Kell, wait." Ryan is up and following me. Because of course he can't accept the word no.

I sharpen my voice in answer. "You're an idiot, Ryan. And I should have done this weeks ago, but if you pull something like this again, you're no longer my client. This isn't going to work for me anymore."

Ryan stands alone, frowning as I walk away. I don't look back. I just keep moving.

I spend the entire day simmering over Ryan's confession. To think that a few weeks ago I would have killed to hear him say those things. And now it makes me sick to my stomach to know that he actually thought I'd be happy to be the woman in between him and his fiancée.

The day is a blur, and before I know it, I'm at home in my bed, holding a heating pad to my stomach in vain.

Filming today was going through the motions, trying to make myself look okay when I was hurting. Inside and out. The stress over Ryan's confession has only made my stomach issues worse, or at least left me with no choice but to face them. My doctor's office is closed, but the on-call nurse sent over prescriptions to my pharmacy. Now I just need to summon the energy to drive there.

Ryan kissed me two months ago. He said things I'd waited years to hear, like how great we'd look together if we dated, how happy I made him. At the time, it felt like righteous wish-fulfillment, like I'd waited long enough and been patient enough that I was getting my reward. Now the thought of a relationship with Ryan as a reward makes me ill.

We would never have worked—*will* never work. And the fact that he had the nerve to first ignore me and then get engaged to someone else only to turn back around and try to rekindle something that was never even there in the first place?

Ugh. The audacity.

The longer I sit here on my warm, comfortable bed, the more I realize I'm sick to my stomach in more ways than one. I rack my brain but can't remember for the life of me when I last took my medication. I know I've been saying I'd do it for a while now, but my life is busy. Most of the time when I get home I squeeze in as much work as I can before my eyes fall closed.

Someone knocks on the door, and I duck down further into my blanket, hoping to ignore it. Whoever it is knocks again, calling, "Delivery!"

I drag myself from bed and open the door to Ash, and then take an automatic step backward, wondering why he's here and what he might need from me. "Hi." I try but fail to put on my work mask. "Is everything okay?"

Ash's eyes go dark as he studies me. His mouth is a sharp slice against his face, turning downward. "It's not. That's why I'm here. You're not okay."

Before I can protest, Ash grabs my hand and squeezes it gently. "I'm coming inside, okay? Let's get you sitting down."

Part of me wonders if I really look so bad that he can tell I'm struggling to stand straight. Another part of me wants to fight him on this. I came home so I could be alone. I don't want anyone, even Ash, seeing me like this.

But I step aside and let him in anyway, mostly because I'm too tired to argue. When he enters, something plastic in his hand crinkles. He holds it up for me to see. "Groceries?"

I make a small sound of appreciation. I don't know how he knew that my fridge was verging on empty, but he's right. My excuse is that I'm barely home enough to cook anyway.

Ash puts one hand on the small of my back and softly pushes me toward the sofa. He goes straight for my yellow blanket, draping it over me and tucking in the sides until I'm completely wrapped up like a burrito. Then he crouches next to me and opens the grocery bag. "Gatorade, soup, crackers, and these gross fruit-flavored mints you like. Um, I thought you'd want comfort food."

"I heard you with Ryan." He sets the stack next to me on the couch cushion, in easy reaching distance.

My bottom lip tugs downward, quivering. My hands cover my face but not before it's completely obvious that I'm tearing up.

"You're being too nice to me," I cry. It comes out all squeaky and whiny.

Ash's face tightens, and something akin to anger flashes there again. "Ryan wanted me to talk to you. Convince you that he's sorry or something."

He shakes his head. "His actual words were 'tell Kell how special she is and how sorry I am.'"

"What did you say?"

"Hell no."

I breathe out a sigh of relief. "This isn't about Ryan. I don't even care about what he thinks anymore, to be honest with you." I gesture to my traitorous body. "I'm just really, really tired."

Ash looks me over like he's searching for battle wounds. "You said you were going to do your injection two weeks ago, Kell. And then you said you were going to do it this week. You gotta take care of yourself." Ash's furrowed brows are the ultimate mark of disapproval.

"I know. I've been busy. The medicine has been sitting in my fridge, but I get home and I check emails and then I fall asleep, and I've felt fine, you know?"

Clearly, I don't feel that way anymore. The sweat accumulating on my brow is more than enough without the soft groans of pain that keep slipping through every few minutes. I clutch my stomach as another wave hits me, the strangling feeling in my gut growing with every second.

Ash's gaze rakes over me, discerning in more ways than one. "Have you called your doctor?"

I nod. "He sent a prescription for a steroid and told me to take my injection ASAP. And then call him in two days if I haven't started feeling better."

"Let's do the injection, and I'll run to the pharmacy while you sleep it off." Ash is already walking toward my fridge, determination set in his jaw.

"Ash." I shake my head. "You are terrified of needles. You don't need to do this. I'm a big girl. I do the injection all by myself every eight weeks."

"I'm not leaving you until I know you've actually done it. Where is it? Fridge?" He motions to the appliance in front of him.

"Top shelf. I need the alcohol swabs too."

I slide the blanket off and sit up slowly and carefully. Ash comes back, holding the boxed syringe in one hand, frowning at the instructions on the back. "This goes into your stomach?"

"Hand it over." I reach for it, but he shakes his head, holding it just out of my grasp.

"I can help."

"If you pass out on me, that's not exactly helpful." His face is ashen, and I've seen him around pointy things one too many times to trust that he won't get sick.

Ash's shoulders square. "I promise that I won't. I want to help. If you want me here?"

Oh, now he's asking. The truth is, I've never injected my medicine while anyone else watches, but the idea doesn't scare me. It might be nice to have someone to talk me through the brief sting after the needle goes in.

"Maybe just hold my hand while I do it? You can talk to me and distract me, too, if you want."

Ash's hand is warm and steady in mine.

"Well," he says quietly, "Ryan also said that things weren't going well between him and Samantha. Which makes sense because I haven't seen her around the house lately."

With my right hand, I grip the injector tightly and push the needle into my stomach, an inch or so below my bellybutton. There's a weird sort of tingly pressure at the spot where it goes in and then just a cool stinging sensation. I hand the used needle to Ash, and he disposes of it in my sharps container.

He presses a pink Band-Aid over the spot and slowly rolls my shirt down over it.

"Thank you," I say. "And I didn't know that about Samantha, but she seems nice, so it's probably for the best for her."

Ash's voice is right next to my ear, sounding against my neck with warm vibrato. "Can I go to the pharmacy for you?"

I'm too sleepy to argue and too comfortable cuddled on the sofa to convince myself to drive to the pharmacy.

"Okay," I murmur, laying my head back down.

CHAPTER THIRTY

✿ ✿ ✿ ✿ ✿

Ash

*K*ell is out like a light. When I get back from the pharmacy she is softly snoring into her yellow blanket. Kell's always sworn she doesn't snore. Seems like the wrong time to prove her wrong with video evidence.

Instead, I set her pills on the table and stand in the kitchen. I set a supermarket bouquet of yellow gerbera daisies on the far counter because I know yellow makes her happy. Her place is kind of a mess. Kell's the one organizing and taking care of us. Usually her stuff is clean. She must have been too exhausted to do anything else after work this week.

And now I know why.

The least I can do is help a little. I run the hot water and soak the few dishes in her sink. Wipe down her table and counters. Bag up trash and take it out to her building's dumpster. When I get back, her eyes are open and she's blinking at the door.

"Why does it smell like bleach in here?"

I sit next to her, looking her over for signs of sickness. A second later her head lands on my shoulder. Flowers. Her hair smells like some kind of flowers. No idea which ones, but I want to buy dozens of them and keep them around the house.

"Thank you." Her voice is a soft hum against my shirt. "For coming over. I didn't want to admit it, but I was kind of falling apart. Today was hard."

"You've been there for me more times than I can count. I'm just glad I got a turn to help you." Kell is not the easiest person to help. She's had something to prove for as long as I've known her. It's one of the things I love about her. But no one can do it all alone.

"I guess I can be kind of a perfectionist." She sighs. Her eyes fall closed again. Her breathing is even but not heavy.

I laugh a little, nudging her. "You guess?"

She elbows me, but I catch her arm. No idea what I'm going to do with it, but I don't let go. Kell's gaze slides over me. She hooks her arm through mine and snuggles in closer.

"You're going to do great at whatever movies you pursue, you know that, right?"

Her head is nestled right under my chin, so I angle down to look at her. We weren't talking about my movies, so I have no idea where this came from. "I'm not so sure. The movies I've done in the past—"

"Are great in their own right," she says, cutting me off. "I'm not the only one who's a perfectionist, Ash. I know you want more serious work, but give yourself credit. You've worked hard these past few years and you have a lot to show for it. You should be proud. I know I am."

Damn.

I blink, not sure what to say. "Um. Thanks."

She tilts her head up and laughs softly. "What? It's true."

Our heads are so close that the air between us warms. My eyes drop to her mouth.

I'm not about to go there. Kell isn't feeling well. She's leaning on me as a friend. I'm not going to pull a Ryan and take advantage of her while she's not feeling her best. I reach out and pat her head. It's getting dark out.

"You should get some sleep. I'll stay here on the couch in case you need me." I reach for her blanket and stretch it over me.

Kell's eyes flash with confusion. "Oh. Well. You don't have to stay."

"I want to."

I watch her walk slowly to her bedroom and close the door. I find the linen closet and an extra blanket and pillow buried under a stack of fuzzy towels. One arm stretches behind my head as I try to get comfortable.

I can't decide if I imagined that moment between us. I know I felt something because I care about her. Of course I do. She's everything I could ever want in a woman. Everything I don't deserve. The truth is that she's too good for Ryan, and I hate to admit it, but that means she's too good for me. I never thought it was a problem until earlier. I never thought Kell could look at me as more than her buddy from college. Every hint I've tried to drop has gotten promptly shut down.

❀ ❀ ❀ ❀ ❀

Sunlight hits my eyes too soon. Kell's tiny sofa makes a crap bed. My body aches in places it shouldn't. I stretch and wince my way to standing.

"I've been watching you sleep on that sofa for an hour, and I feel so guilty," Kell calls from the kitchen. Vanilla hits my nose. I inhale and smell more spices and warmth. She's been baking. "Maybe I should buy a bigger couch?"

She stands in front of me with a plate of muffins. "I made you a thank-you breakfast. I don't have a chef, so you're stuck with my recipes."

Kell gestures to the table, where scrambled eggs sit in a bowl. Another bowl of sliced strawberries is in front of my chair. "You should have woken me up." I'm embarrassed. I stayed over to help her, and now she's trying to take care of me again.

"You know your muffins are my favorite," I say, sliding into the seat and taking a muffin in one hand and a scoop of eggs with my other.

She grins and sits across from me. Some pink has returned to her cheeks. The dark circles have ebbed. Seems like a full night's sleep has done her some good.

"You're feeling better?"

"I'm feeling a little better," she confirms. "On my way, thanks to your help." She takes a scoop of eggs onto her own plate. Maybe to show me that she's fine.

"That's good."

I bite into a muffin and groan. "So good."

After we eat, I clear the table. "Thanks for breakfast. Don't tell Ava, but this was the best breakfast I've had in years."

"In that case, you can come over for breakfast anytime. I'm completely open to flattery."

I offer to clean the kitchen because I want Kell to rest more. The only way she'll do that is if she feels like she has to. I fill the sink with warm water and suds and start scrubbing. Mom used to say that she hated cleaning the house, but she liked the time it gave her to think. Sounds about right.

One dish goes in the soapy water. I scrub it clean and then I rinse and dry. Repeat with the next dish in the line. In between, I replay the moment on the sofa with Kell. I could have kissed her. Maybe I should have.

If Ryan still hasn't chased her off completely with the things he's done, I don't want to be the one to officially send her over the edge. I should tell her how I feel. But then again it plays right into what we've always said: friendship first. Friendship before everything else.

Putting that into perspective means that pursuing a risky romance is out of the question.

"You're staring a hole into my sink." Kell laughs. She walks up behind me with a questioning look. She takes the sponge from my hands and drops it into the sink. Turns the water off. Positions herself between me and the next stack of dishes.

"Are you okay, Ash? You look like you're really deep in thought."

I shake myself out of it and flash a lopsided smile. "I was. I know I get called a himbo a lot online, but I swear I'm smart sometimes."

Kell glares at me. "Himbo? What are you talking about?"

I shrug. "You know. Guys like me. Attractive but dumb. It's okay—I've been called it a half a dozen times this week according to my Google alerts." It's not supposed to be an insult. Still messes with me though.

"Don't do that." Kell puts a hand on my arm. "Don't repeat trash reviews like that. You're smart and you know it. Since when do we let actors' roles define who they are as a real person? You don't see Tom Cruise jumping off of buildings downtown. That's not who you are in real life."

I look at where she touches me. "Sorry. Yeah, you're right. It's hard to get that kind of stuff out of your head sometimes." I meant it as a joke, but she's right. If I let what movies I do define me, then I'm no better than Ryan.

"I can only imagine. But I hate to think that you let any of it get to you. Challenge yourself for *you*, not to try to change for some loser who doesn't even know you." Kell is indignant. On my behalf. She's an angel.

"You give good advice." I try and fail to swallow down the gratitude in my voice. There's something about the way she's always ready to go to bat for me. It does things to me that it shouldn't do.

"I try." Kell's hand slides up my arm. She grips my bicep. Her tongue reaches out to lick her bottom lip.

What I would give to watch her do that for the rest of my life. My body tenses.

Her hand slowly makes its way to my neck. Then my face. She cups my jaw and traces the lines.

I go still.

Kell is touching me in ways she never has before. Ways I have only dreamt. I don't know what any of this means.

She urges me closer, pulling me toward her. There are questions in her eyes. For once she isn't voicing any of them. I part my lips to ask something. Anything. Like what the hell is happening.

Kell's mouth covers mine. Instinct takes over and I kiss her back. My hands tangle in that sweet-smelling hair. She moans against my lips. It's this soft, throaty sound. I want more of that sound. The hand on my face tightens.

And then it leaves my face. Kell pulls away with her arms up in defense. She shakes her head. "I'm so sorry. I don't know what that was. I just got caught up in the moment and I—"

I press Kell against the kitchen wall. Her bottom lip goes between my teeth, and she stops apologizing. I kiss her with equal force to the kiss she initiated. Every question, every thought, every almost-moment between us all these years gets poured into the kiss.

My hands find hers and I lace our fingers together. Still pinning her to the wall, I raise her arms over her head. With my mouth, I explore the soft skin between her shoulders and neck. Her breath is hot and ragged. When I come back to her lips, she gasps into me. Holy hell.

I don't know how I survived this long without kissing her.

So many wasted years.

"More. Please," Kell breathes into my mouth.

I don't wait for her to ask twice. Kell handles my chin. Her thumb strokes the stubble I've let grow there. She swallows, throat bobbing with the motion. I kiss her softly once. Twice. Three times.

Control shatters. My lips bruise into hers. Kell's hips buck against my body. My tongue sweeps into her mouth, deepening the kiss until I'm desperate for more. More of Kell. More of her kisses. More exploration.

Just more.

I want to wrap myself around Kell and do nothing else.

But we have time.

I really think we do.

I press one more kiss to her lips and release her hands. "Kell . . ." I can't think of the words.

Kell raises both brows. She lets out a breathless laugh. "I'm starting to feel really jealous of your costars. I'd kill to get paid to kiss someone with your skills all day."

"I don't kiss them like that." I don't kiss anyone like that.

She looks almost shy when she smiles back at me. "That's good to know."

I want to stay here with her all day. Want to do more of what we just did. Right as I open my mouth to tell her so, my phone rings.

I bite back a swear. "It's Ryan." He's already texted me and now he's calling. Must be something good. Of course he'd interrupt now.

Kell nods. "I'm going to take a shower and get ready for the day. I'll be quick."

I sit on the sofa and answer, my voice clipped. I could be kissing Kell right now. "What's up?" The bathroom door closes, and I try not to think about Kell in the shower.

Ryan scoffs into the phone. "That's what I want to know. Where are you? We're supposed to meet Judith's buddy. You promised you'd check it out."

The last thing I want to do is go with Ryan and Jonah to this meeting. Not even sure what it's for. But Ryan thinks he's the boss and Jonah already said he'd go so I can't not show up. "I'm at Kell's."

"Did you talk to her?"

Of course that's what he cares about. "Already told you, not doing your dirty work for you."

"You don't have to be a dick about it."

I switch my phone to the opposite hand and stand. "I do when it's the only way you'll leave me alone about it."

Ryan's voice is tight as he bites back. "The only reason you're hanging all over her is because you think you have a chance with me out of the picture."

"I've always spent time with Kell. Nothing has changed." Just because Ryan's too wrapped up in himself to notice doesn't mean I haven't been paying attention to her. I've always seen her.

"She wanted me first," he says. I can practically see his smirk. "We were almost in a relationship before I met Sam."

My hand squeezes the phone so hard it cuts into my palm. I try not to raise my voice but fail. "Listen to me. It doesn't matter what happened, any relationship with Kell is strictly professional, and that's it. It's not up for negotiation. Please tell me you know this."

"Sure. Whatever."

There's a scuffling sound and Ryan yells at someone. "Ash?" Jonah's talking now. "Can you come to this thing? Ryan won't leave me alone until we go, and Jessie says she's going to move out if he doesn't stop circling the house."

"Fine," I grind out. I'll do it for Jonah. "Text me the address. I'll leave right now."

CHAPTER THIRTY-ONE

❀ ❀ ❀ ❀ ❀

Kell

ny relationship with Kell is strictly professional, and that's it. It's not up for negotiation.

"You have to stop panicking." Claudette hands me an open bag of chocolate chips with concern on her face. I snatch up the bag and pour a handful of chocolate morsels into my hand. I shove the handful into my mouth. Chewing, I say, "I can't stop. I did a bad thing, and everything is ruined." Ash's words replay in my head on a torturous loop. Even worse is that he was talking to Ryan, of all people. Hearing him say that was more painful than any punch to the gut could be.

"You don't know that. You're just assuming that everything is ruined. Ash is probably completely chill about the whole thing. He could have been talking about any situation with any one of them. I don't know why you jump right to rejection like this."

Sweet, naïve Claudette. She doesn't know Ash like I do. After I pounced on him, I thought he kissed me back. In the moment, it felt like he did. But fear has taken over, and I can't trust my memory, not even from a few hours ago.

And maybe, as much as we both like to insist that we've never considered more than friendship, we both have. It's normal to be curious about these things. If I was wrong, if the kiss wasn't what I thought, then Ash is probably panicking like I am, worried that our professional relationship is as doomed as our years of relatively easy partnership.

So while it's normal to wonder, it's not so normal to act on those questionable feelings and sabotage a friendship, which is what I'm so afraid I did. What I'm pretty sure I did. The one thing I never, ever wanted to do because things with Ash were fine the way they were. How am I supposed to show my face after kissing two out of three Matthews?

I know exactly how this happened, too. We never should have let ourselves get pulled into this fake dating scheme for the show. We were perfectly fine and happy as friends and then we started holding hands and Ash kissed me and now . . .

Now we're here. Fake dating Ash has been nice. If I'm being honest with myself, it's been better than nice, and it's hard to make myself remember that it's not real. And maybe that's why it's hard to think of Ash as *only* a friend right now, because I've seen firsthand what it could be like if we let ourselves be something more, and it's so good and easy.

I add the rest of the chocolate chips to my mixer, the final ingredient in the cookies we're baking. Claudette is at my apartment for an emergency strategy meeting. I called her the second Ash left, knowing that I'd need my best friend to talk it through with.

I know that what I need to do is talk to Ash and make sure he knows that nothing has to change between us. Claudette keeps bugging me to text him, but text doesn't seem appropriate in this case. I'm also keenly aware of the hazards of talking about it in person since his house is mic'd up essentially everywhere. The only thing more degrading would be for our conversation about this to be publicly broadcast. I honestly don't think I'd survive that.

"Did he look freaked out?" Claudette watches me with half amusement, half concern.

No, he didn't look freaked out at all. Not much fazes Ash Matthew, but when I kissed him, I think part of me expected him to recoil in horror. Especially after our text conversation the other week about how we were glad we never kissed in college. He didn't recoil. Didn't do anything except kiss me back so hard that my toes curled.

"He was fine." And I know the next question before it even leaves Claudette's mouth. "But I heard him on the phone. Ryan called and then I got in the shower, but I didn't start the shower because I was kind of eavesdropping."

"And? What did he say?"

"He told Ryan that there was no way we'd be in a relationship other than a working one. He was very clear." It was so mortifying that instead of facing him again I just yelled goodbye through the bathroom door and waited until I was sure he was gone.

"Why did you kiss him exactly? You didn't really make that part clear in between all of your freaking out." She puts a hand on her hip. "You initiated a kiss, were surprised when he kissed you back, and then completely lost it after the fact, and now you regret it ever happened. Help me understand. What am I missing here?"

If only it were that easy. "It's Ash. He's my friend, not to mention my client, and the brother of the guy I just recently stopped pining over." I pop another errant chocolate chip in my mouth. "But he's amazing. And there was like this magnetism that kept drawing me closer to him all night and this morning. I regret it ever happening because I thought I was going off signals. But obviously I was reading the signals all wrong because it's been years since I've had a normal relationship with a man."

As cheesy as it sounds to say out loud, it's somehow true. I'd spent the night alone in my bedroom thinking about how Ash had shown up and known exactly what I needed. How he always did. And then I'd woken up, set on making him a very friends-only thank-you breakfast, but the moment we locked eyes again, my skin sparked. I didn't wake up and choose to kiss him. It felt totally beyond my control, to be honest. And even though Claudette is the most understanding friend in the world, and I tell her almost everything, I can't admit all of that.

Having that foundation of friendship with Ash already in place makes the prospect of being with him romantically even easier. I'm more comfortable with him than almost any other person in the world, and certainly any other person I've dated. That's the thing about Ash—he's been here in front of me all along, checking up on me and having my back and a million other small, indispensable gestures. And somehow, I never realized that he was everything I ever wanted and more until we kissed. The truth I can barely even admit to myself is that I like Ash as more than just a friend. I really, really like him.

Claudette is moving around the kitchen, letting me inwardly spiral while she listens. She sighs. "But why the regret? If he kissed you back, he can't say that it was all you. Maybe he just thinks of you as a friend or maybe he's lying to Ryan. Because, you know, it's Ryan and he's horrible. But a kiss like the one you described is definitely mutual."

Because of all the previous reasons why it would be a bad idea, him and me. Because of the same friendship that makes it so tempting to fall for him in the first place. "Because looking back now with a clearer head, I'm not one-hundred percent sure that it meant anything more to him than taking care of me because I was sick."

Claudette makes a strangled noise and almost spews coffee. "I want a nurse like that the next time I'm sick."

"I'm serious. I was miserable and he helped me out and then I made him breakfast and made a move on him. How do I know that he just didn't reject me out of obligation? He basically said as much on the phone."

She picks up my phone and slides it across the table toward me. "There's this new invention. The kids call it texting. You ask someone a question and if they don't hate you, they answer."

We get the cookies in the oven and sit on my sofa. "If I swear to talk to Ash, will you please tell me about your dating life?"

Claudette thinks I don't notice all the maneuvering she does to steer the conversation away from her. She's fiercely private, even with me, and sometimes I worry that she holds too much in. I take a page from her book and drive the conversation away from myself for a moment. I can't stand to keep talking about this when it's so freshly awful in my mind.

"There's nothing to tell." Claudette twirls a piece of hair around her finger. "Like I told you, I'm working on myself. You'll be the first to know when I'm ready to start dating."

I bump her with my shoulder. "I better be."

Claudette is always there for me, even when I create terrible messes like this one. I don't know if I'll ever get over the embarrassment of kissing Ash only to find out that he was not at all on the same page. It occurs to me, not for the first time, that at least our fake relationship was destined to end, giving whatever we were outside of the show a clean break as well. Soon enough, I won't even have a pretend boyfriend. But at least I have Claudette. And cookies.

CHAPTER THIRTY-TWO

✿ ✿ ✿ ✿ ✿

Ash

*J*t feels like I'm floating. Jonah is in the sitting room of the office we're meeting at when I get there. No sign of Ryan. Jonah looks at me funny.

"What's up with you? Did you see the girl from the other week again? From the club?"

I shake my head. "No."

Jonah grins. "I've never seen you look so happy. I need details."

I sit on the chair across from him. Smile won't leave my face. "I was at Kell's apartment."

Jonah's eyes go big. "All night?"

"Yeah, but not like that. But I think we're on the same page now."

"You finally told her how you feel, huh?" Jonah leans forward. Rubs his hands together.

"Didn't have to. I think I made it pretty obvious." Holding Kell while she touched me. Kissed me.

Yeah, it was like a dream.

Jonah shakes his head. He frowns at me. "But she definitely knows where you stand? You made it clear that you want to be with her and so did she?"

I ruffle my hair, feeling suddenly frustrated. My little brother is being nosy like usual. I don't need any second-guessing going into this. Not when things are finally going amazing. "Trust me. I know Kell. And she knows me."

He claps me on the back. "I won't say anything, but I'm happy for you. Kell too."

"Thanks. Where's Ryan? We waiting on him?"

Jonah casts a glance at the closed interior door. "He's in there talking. Said he'd get us in a minute."

"Any idea what this is even about?" All Ryan said was that he had an "opportunity" he wanted us to get in on. Can't be all that great. The only reason I agreed was because of Jonah. That was before Ryan tried to pull the crap he did with Kell. He's lucky I'm even speaking to him after that.

"No idea." Jonah stretches. "So how does this work? With Kell being our manager, are we going to have to watch you all over each other while we're trying to talk to her?"

I pick up a pillow from the chair next to me and launch it at him. Jonah laughs and swats it away.

"Who's all over each other?" Ryan opens the door and stares between us.

"Get this," Jonah pipes up before I can signal not to say anything. He just freaking said he wouldn't say anything. Kell can't want Ryan knowing her business. "Ash and Kell."

Ryan scoffs. "What about Ash and Kell?"

"None of your business." The stare between us is long and hard. He's going to find out eventually. Kell might not be thrilled with me telling him, but I don't care about stepping around Ryan. He's never bothered to do that for anyone else.

"You're dating Kell?"

I grit my teeth. "Why would that be so hard to believe?"

I walk over to him. Get in his space.

His jaw works like he can't decide what to say. "I guess it isn't. She has a thing for Matthews."

My hands go up and I shove him in the chest. "Shut up. You don't know what you're talking about."

Ryan says something I can't hear because all the blood is rushing to my ears. He pushes me back and jams his shoulder against mine. Somehow Jonah gets right in the middle of us and uses his body as a barrier. Damn his obsession with building his arms.

"Everyone needs to calm down. We're not doing this. We're not fighting."

My breath comes heavy. I point a finger at Ryan. "Stay away from Kell."

"Kell is my manager, same as you. I can talk to her whenever I want. As a matter of fact, I might go call her right now." Ryan's phone lights up in his hand as he waves it around like an idiot.

A throat clears loudly. Behind Ryan a familiar cheery voice calls. "Boys? In here please." Judith pokes her head out. She acts like us fighting is nothing surprising. Maybe it's not.

Jonah looks at me with wide eyes, and I nod to tell him I'm all right. We follow Ryan into the cramped office and sit in the three chairs facing Judith's desk. Pushed up next to her desk is another chair. A tall, thin man with a black mustache grins at us.

"Howdy."

Apparently, he's a cowboy. Ryan gestures. "This is Norman Cherry. I met him through Judith, and he wanted me to introduce him to my brothers."

Ryan nods at us. "These are my brothers, Jonah and Ash."

"Nice to meet y'all." Norman frowns. "Everything okay? I heard a scuffle out there."

"Ash gets worked up like that." Ryan doesn't even try to hide his smug smile in my direction. "But we're cool."

Steam hisses under my skin. I'm anything but cool right now. The hell am I even doing here?

Norman doesn't seem to mind the tense vibe in the room. "I've been a manager for going on twenty-three years. My success rates speak for themselves, but I can give you my clients' information if you want to ask them the hard questions. They'd be more than happy to speak up for me. Managing sibling groups is my specialty. You've heard of the Olsen twins and their sister Elizabeth Olsen, the Scarlet Witch? The Hemsworths? The Baldwins?"

I guess Jonah is thinking what I'm thinking because he turns to Norman. "Sorry to be rude, but we already have someone who takes care of booking and things for us. Kell is our manager."

"She's also their college friend. It's very unconventional," Judith pipes in. Ryan nods. He's pro Kell one minute and siding against her the next. What gives?

Norman shifts in his seat. "What I provide is more of a direct route. Your manager might have been the right choice for you up until this point, but you're in the big leagues now. One person can't keep track of all the publicity, scheduling, and scouting for three men. Hell, I don't think one person could even do that for one man. It's too much to ask."

He has a comforting southern accent. His voice is calm and steady. He sounds so confident, but he's wrong. Kell does all of that and more. She does it better than anyone. I don't know what Judith and Ryan are playing at here, but I'm not about to screw over Kell. Couldn't pay me to even want to.

"You should listen to him. Have you ever thought about what Kell wants? She's tired, man."

I can't believe Ryan has the balls to talk to me like this. Can't believe he's stupid enough to think he knows anything about what

Kell wants. Jonah's forehead creases with worry as he catches my eye. Don't fight, I know that's what he's thinking. Not here.

I swallow through a tight throat. "Kell loves being our manager. We would be nothing without her."

Standing, I try to smile through closed teeth at Judith. Maybe salvage that relationship. But I'm not going to buy into this agenda. "Thank you, but I think I'll stick with my current manager. She hasn't done me wrong yet."

I walk out and sit in my car. Hands on the steering wheel, I exhale slowly. What the hell. Had I known what I was going to be walking into, I never would have come. Never would have considered it. Kell doesn't deserve this kind of disrespect. I could still be back at Kell's apartment.

Ryan planned it this way. Knew I wouldn't come if I knew what it was about. So much of me wants to drive away, but I wait. Twenty minutes after I leave the office building, I spot Jonah striding toward me, his hands in his pockets, eyes on the ground. When he stops, I roll down my window. "Did you sign anything?" I manage to ask without sounding as angry as I feel.

He levels me with a hard stare. "Of course not. I stayed and heard them out, that's all. I owe a lot to Kell, and you know that."

"Then why even stay?"

Jonah sighs through his nose. He rubs at his temples. "I don't know. Because part of me thinks that Ryan is right about Kell. We've always said that she's too good for us, right?"

I don't want to hear it. All of this feels like the sickest, deepest betrayal. Kell would be heartbroken if she knew where we were. "We have a contract with her. This is messed up," I snap. I should go straight back to Kell's apartment and tell her everything. I should, but I'm not going to. Not until I figure this out.

He nods as we both watch Ryan walk from the office. Ryan makes his way to my car. But I leave Jonah and pull out before Ryan can get close enough to say anything.

CHAPTER THIRTY-THREE

✿ ✿ ✿ ✿ ✿

Kell

My brain is screaming at me to be reasonable and text Ash, but my heart knows that this is a conversation better had in person. As awkward and painful as it may be, we're not going to get anywhere by ignoring each other. Virtual or otherwise. So, even if Ash tells me that he kissed me back out of pity or because it just seemed like a fun thing to do at the time, he's going to have to tell me in real life. Even though, thanks to overhearing his phone conversation with his brothers, I already know his feelings.

I figure it's the mature thing to do, something two adults who want to remain friends no matter what should do. That doesn't mean it doesn't scare me half to death.

I take twice as long standing in front of my bathroom mirror as I usually do. My hair won't sit the right way, my makeup looks like it was drawn on by my preteen self, come back to haunt me, and I officially have nothing to wear. Everything is a mess, including my jumbled nerves.

The drive to the Matthews' house is one traffic jam after another. Not that that's unusual, but it's so not the morning for it. I'm stuck in between two school buses full of kids who look like they're going on a field trip when it hits me. Ash hasn't bothered to text except to say that he wouldn't be able to come back over after all, so I haven't talked to him since he left my apartment almost twenty-four hours ago. It's not so farfetched to think that he's giving me the silent treatment on purpose.

I'm sure he doesn't know what to say about our kiss. Knowing Ash, he doesn't want to hurt me or jeopardize our friendship. He's seen me post-Ryan and he most likely sees me as too fragile to handle the rejection.

I sigh through my nose and let myself inside. The house is quiet and still. There's not even the hum of machinery thanks to all of Ryan's fancy gadgets that promise complete silence. It's eerie and leaves me even more unsettled.

"Looking for me?" Ryan's grin says he's never been happier to see another human being in his entire life. It's only after this many years that I'm starting to see his acting skills come in handy in the day-to-day, too. It definitely makes me wonder how many times in the past I've been fooled by a well-delivered line. Ash is an actor by trade too, but he keeps the façade out of his personal life. I've never once felt like I was getting something other than the real person with him.

"Actually, I needed to talk to Ash about something. Is he here?"

Ryan casts me a weird look. "Oh. You wanted to talk to Ash? It's not about the thing from the other day, is it?"

I blink. What the hell? "What thing?" I hedge. It's strange to think about Ash coming home to tell Ryan all about our kissing. But he did tell him something over the phone, so maybe they share more than I know.

Ryan reaches for me. "I don't want to talk for my brother, but I'm sorry if it hurts you. That's something I know none of us want."

I step away and force a smile. I'm not having this conversation with Ryan, and I will not cross any of the lines he's so bent on wiping away. It's a relief that I'm not even partially tempted. "Thanks. So, Ash? Have you seen him?"

"Do you want me to tell him you were looking for him? He went with Jonah to play basketball. If you need someone to vent to, I'm always ready to listen. I know we're in a weird spot, and I'm sorry about that. I miss talking to you." Ryan's eyes are puppy-dog big, hurt with eagerness mixed in. He looks ridiculous.

I blink. I don't owe Ryan one more minute of my time. This is an uncomfortable enough conversation without involving him. Inviting him in would turn this one-sided attraction into a Jerry Springer–style saga that I'm just not ready for.

"No. I'll try to get him another way." I turn, and it hits me that walking away from Ryan has never been so easy.

I text Ash because it's faster, and he doesn't need to see my face when we have this conversation. So much for being mature.

Kell: *Stopped by but Ryan said you're playing basketball. Just wanted to make sure we're okay after the weirdness from yesterday? We got it out of our systems, so I think we're good now.*

I can't bring myself to turn around and drive back home. I take myself to In-N-Out and order a strawberry milkshake. My car radio lands on a sad song by Billie Eilish, and before I know it I'm clutching my milkshake and singing my heart out into the straw while parked in the parking lot. My phone buzzes with a text, and I reluctantly turn the radio down to a soft blur of music.

Ash: *I'm calling you.*

The next second my phone lights up, but I swipe to ignore.

Kell: *About to go into an important video call, but don't worry. All good.*

He calls again, and as much as I don't want to because I don't know what to say, I answer. "Did you get my text? I really can't talk right now."

"I got it. Are you at home? Can I stop by and bring you dinner later?"

This isn't how it was supposed to go. If Ash is so desperate to make sure we're on the same page as friends, then why is he making it so hard on me? I slurp the rest of my milkshake. The cold sweet taste lingers on my tongue. "I have plans with Claudette."

"Kell."

I take a shaky breath with the phone tilted away.

"Kell. Please. I know that I'm not good at these kinds of things. I know that this is new for us. But please. Can we just talk?"

"Okay." I swallow. I nod even though I'm alone in my car and he can't see me. "Come over tonight. I'll be home."

The call ends, and I squeeze my eyes shut. It's been a long time since I've wanted something new. I've gotten so comfortable with my career and my friendships and my sense of self. Changing any of it up makes my stomach roil.

But oh, I think I really wanted this.

I wanted to kiss Ash again. I wanted him to be the person I go to, and I wanted to be that person for him. How am I supposed to hide from Ash when he's so sweet and so patient with me? Maybe Claudette is right—that things could work between Ash and me. We've been friends for long enough that I doubt there would be any surprises in a relationship. It could be a quiet, welcoming, settling into more-than-friends territory. Really, it might not change much at all, except to make things better.

But none of that matters when Ash doesn't see me in that way. Nothing can change that. The best I can hope for is that when he tries to let me down easy, our friendship remains intact. I can't lose that.

That's what I tell myself all day long, like a battle cry, as I work and stop to steal long glances at my phone clock. It might not change much at all. It might not change. The chant sticks in my head until it almost convinces me.

By the time Ash texts to say he's picking up ramen and coming by, I'm too antsy to wait. I slip on shoes and stand in the parking lot, next to the guest space where Ash usually parks. His smile lights up as he pulls into the spot a moment later.

"Hey. What are you doing out here?" He steps down from his truck, his hands full of plastic bags that hold delicious-smelling things. My nervous stomach groans.

I take one of the bags to keep my hands busy. "Waiting for you actually."

"Oh." Ash stops, turning a concerned frown on me. "Are you trying to get rid of me?"

"No, of course not. I just . . ." I level the plastic bag in my hand and spin it slightly. "I want to . . ." I laugh. "I'm hungry."

Ash raises his brows. "Wow, okay, don't worry. We've got food. Let's go."

We reach my apartment, and I close the door behind us. Ash puts the food on the table and starts unpacking while I get two spoons and something to drink. We sit. My thoughts suddenly freeze. No inner chanting, just silence and nerves that clench my jaw shut.

The last time Ash was here in my apartment, I kissed him. And then he kissed me. I wonder if he's thinking about that too, about how his body pressed into mine so tightly I could feel every bit of it. Or how soft his lips felt, even when his kisses became hungry and hard. Thankfully, I can blame the heat of the broth for the flush rising up my body.

Ash puts down his spoon and looks at me with wide, open eyes. "Kell."

The way he says my name makes it sound like a prayer. It almost breaks me. I want to believe that this is possible, that it's something I can trust in. And if either one of us puts words to what may or may not be happening here, it could all fall apart. Blow away with the wind as easily as a scrap of paper.

When I don't answer him, Ash returns to his noodles. "Hope Claudette was okay with me ruining your plans," he says, his mouth half a smirk. He knows very well that my plans with Claudette were fake. Sometimes I wonder if he knows me *too* well.

"She was. She is." It's true enough, given the fact that Claudette would be thrilled to know that I'm talking to Ash just like she advised me to. She'd be happy to hear that I'm sitting down with him in real life like a real adult.

Ash tilts his head like he's considering me, but he doesn't say anything for a long moment. Finally he says, "Didn't really think we needed to talk about what happened yesterday, but maybe we do. I want us to be thinking the same thing."

I nod. "Yeah, I think it's a good idea to talk about it."

"Right." Ash reaches a hand out. I rest mine on top, letting his fingers graze mine. It's a silent agreement between the two of us. His thumb rubbing the side of my hand. My pinky shaking because my heart is moments away from crushing into pathetic dust.

"That text you sent. What was that you said, about getting it out of our systems? Is that really what you think?" A hint of frustration colors his words. Maybe he's been holding back his annoyance with me this whole time. It's not the easiest thing to talk about, so I'm not going to apologize.

This isn't where I expected him to start. "I don't know," I admit. "You're dating other people, and I respect that, and I don't—"

"Is that what you think? That I'm dating? I'm not dating, Kell. I'm not even talking to other women." His voice rises, almost like he's offended I'd assume that.

"But a few weeks ago . . ." I stop. There was Shea, the girl from the bar. I know they'd been texting.

"I know you want to just be friends," I finish.

Ash's mouth falls open. "Me? *You* were the one who saw me as just a friend. For so long. You can't keep doing this, Kell. You can't keep putting the blame on something else. Either you want to be with me or you don't, but please don't leave me hanging. It's torture."

"What—what do you mean? Do you see me as more than a friend?" My hand grips the top of the table. I can't comprehend the turn this talk is taking. Just let me down easy, I want to say. Stop dragging this on and say what you came to say.

"Yes. For years," he says softly, and I shake my head. This doesn't make sense.

Ash is still talking, saying words that don't add up. Can't add up. "I have wanted this for years. Have wanted to be more than just your buddy for so long. I can't remember a time since I met you that I haven't hoped for that." He swallows, his throat moving tightly. "Even if I tried to convince myself otherwise."

A stuttering gasp slips out of me. "Why did you never say anything?" But I already know why. Because I wasted time loving other men, ones who weren't my friends first, or even second. Giving men attention who weren't Ash, who didn't care about me the way Ash always has.

"Listen to me. I want this." He ducks his head and meets my eyes straight on. "Do you?"

I nod slowly, and that's all it takes. Ash rises from his chair and scoops me into a hug, his arms wrapping around my back, pulling us close together. He spins me around then sets me down looking intensely at me again. "Are you sure?"

My head tilts to meet his and I find his mouth and kiss him in answer. His tongue teases along my bottom lip. We kiss again, and I feel it in my toes, my stomach, my heart.

It's new but it's familiar already, this feeling of being physically close with him.

"I want to try too. I think we could be good together. I mean, we've been pretty great together all these years. It would just be a little different." I am breathless with relief and want.

"We *are* good together," Ash insists. He puts his hands on my shoulders and looks at me with a perfect, full smile. "It doesn't have to be that different. Except the kissing. That's got to change. It needs to happen much, much more often."

My smile matches his because this is wild and it doesn't feel quite real yet. I had only started to imagine a possibility of Ash and me together like this, and now here it is. Our heads gravitate closer until we're breathing the same air, the same universe. The Hollywood Christmas Parade could storm through my apartment, and I wouldn't notice, wouldn't care. Ash is the only living being I can think about. His lips brush over mine, just a whisper of a touch, so soft and barely there that my stomach flips in anticipation. And then we're kissing again, but it's fast and urgent, back into less familiar territory of wanting more and more of each other.

My teeth catch his bottom lip, tugging not-so-gently. He lets loose a sound that's a cross between a groan and a sigh. His tongue teases my lips, slipping into my mouth until the kiss feels somehow more intimate than I've ever been in my life. My body flushes with heat and it pools low, building an ache.

Ash is hard against me, pressing into my stomach against the thin fabric of my T-shirt. I swallow, my throat suddenly dry. He looks down at me with a question and there's no other answer than *yes. So much yes.* I nod, probably too eagerly because he pulls a gorgeous lopsided smirk, his eyes crinkling at the edges. I should be embarrassed to feel this much this quickly, should be worried about what he might think, but I'm not. I'm so happy I could crack.

Not right now, though, because I would really hate to crack before I get to see Ash Matthew naked. Ash tugs me with him, still kissing my mouth as he backs us toward the bedroom, to my bed. It's made, obviously, the sheets tightly tucked in and the pillows neatly lined up near the headboard. None of that matters as we land on the bed, me on top of Ash, my body pinning his.

He feels so perfect underneath me, like the world's best place to lie down, ever. I'd gladly trade my mattress in for the chance to lie on him every night of my life. And I paid a lot of money for this mattress.

Ash's eyes bore into me. His lips find mine once more and the kiss is so soft, so tender and sweet, that a wave of timid anxiety washes over me. Suddenly, I'm all too aware that I'm kissing my best friend. I'm in bed with Ash and thinking about him in an entirely new, not-friendly-at-all way.

"Kell?" He touches my face.

I inhale. "I'm okay. I'm good."

He shifts, holding me as he does so that I end up curled into his side. I'm the little spoon, and holy crap I love it so much. Ash's voice is in my ear, steady and reassuring. "I'm just happy to hold you. This is enough."

A thrill runs down my spine, but I'm not sure I feel the same about it being enough. I've had only a few hours with Ash, and I'm greedy already for all of him. I turn slowly to face him, our bodies flush, my curves bumping against his hard lines. Our foreheads press together, and I feel the rise and fall of his chest at the same time my own heartbeat drums in my ears.

I kiss him. I let my hands drop to his chest.

Ash kisses me back with sudden urgency, crashing against my mouth until my stomach swoops and my head feels underwater. Everything is foggy and warm as my shirt pulls over my head and Ash's does the same. Our skin burns together.

He looks at me and shakes his head, unbelieving. "Kell." His voice is barely above a whisper. "You're *beautiful*."

This is real. It's happening and it's real and not for anyone else to see or dissect. Everything changes in the next seconds, minutes. Our friendship will forever be altered, but I can't bring myself to worry or care. Beyond how *right* it feels to be with him in this way.

"That was," I struggle to catch my breath afterward. I shake my head because I don't know how to put words to what just happened between us.

Ash kisses me, one hand wrapped around my waist, one hand threaded in my messy hair. "I know.

"Judith and Aaron are going to be happy about this. Us, for real." Ash softly brushes the tips of his fingers over my stomach.

The words feel like a vise. "We can't tell them. I think that this should stay between us for now."

Ash stares at me. The hand that rests on my waist moves, leaving the bare skin there cold. He's bordering dangerously close to judgy eyes.

"Only because of the show, Ash. I just don't want this thing to be fodder for the reality show. That means more fake drama and more people in our business. I just think it would be better for everyone if we keep this to ourselves until shooting wraps. And then we can try to figure out how to navigate us in real life."

"Jonah and Ryan would know." He offers this like it's entirely obvious and not at all exactly the point.

The familiar panic rises in my chest. I wrap my arms around my naked body, suddenly very aware of the fact. "They can't. No offense, but Jonah is the biggest gossip I know. He'd tell Jessie and Jessie would mention it to one of the crew and before we knew it Ryan would be barging in to try to sabotage things." I sigh, overwhelmed by the mere idea of it.

Ash sets his jaw. "I want to really be with you. I'm not going to be your dirty secret."

The words prick because of Ryan, how he always treated me, and I wonder for a second if Ash knows that. I swallow. "Of course not. That's not . . ."

"When filming ends, we'll pretend to break up but keep seeing each other in secret, and then what? Are you embarrassed of me?"

"No. Ash, no. That's not what I mean at all. I just don't think I can handle a high-profile relationship. I don't want my life in tabloids." I look into his eyes. This is going to work. I think it really might. "I promise that this has nothing to do with you, and it has everything to do with me. I can't handle the outside attention right now." I suck in a breath.

He takes a minute to think it over, and I try not to panic that it's all going to implode before it even begins. But then Ash's hands go to my cheeks, gently cupping either side of my face. "Okay."

"Okay? I know it's a weird ask, but it would make me feel so much better knowing that it's our secret for now. No one else can ruin it."

"Whatever you want, Kell. Seriously. I don't mind keeping you all to myself. As long as that's all you're worried about."

"Thank you." I press my lips to his. With the level of drama currently in the Matthews' house, I want to keep this one thing out of the spotlight. It's too fresh, too fragile to be bandied around where other people can look and talk about it. They can have the show and the staged pictures of us. But when we're really together, I don't want it to be on display as someone else's entertainment. I can't stand the idea of this being cheapened.

CHAPTER THIRTY-FOUR

✿ ✿ ✿ ✿ ✿

Ash

Kell is on my mind from the moment I wake up. Yesterday was so good. We finally talked it out and said how we feel. Turns out Jonah was right about a lot of the relationship stuff. I never would have guessed that Kell was on the same wavelength as me and doubted how I felt. I could have laughed if I weren't so damn relieved to find out the truth.

I send her a text because we don't have to play games anymore. I want to see her. Can't get enough of seeing her.

I hear back from her almost immediately.

It feels like we're a real couple now. Her issue with not being together on camera makes sense. Not telling Jonah and Ryan makes sense too. I just wish things were different because I'm ready to shout from my bedroom window how happy I am. Being with Kell is better than I ever knew. I have thought about holding her like that for years, and honestly, I never thought it could happen.

But I can wait.

Once filming is over, we'll tell the world. We can figure out a way to take things public without compromising her privacy. Meanwhile, I'm going to spend as much time as I can alone with her. I pick up her favorite herbal tea from the place by her apartment and get an overpriced coffee for myself. I stop for a box of doughnuts with pink sprinkles.

At her door, I knock, then wonder if I should have called and given her my ETA. She said she wanted to see me, but she might have things going on. She's a hardworking woman.

Kell opens the door with a soft, happy smile. "I thought maybe you'd have other plans today."

I wave the doughnuts at her. "Never too busy for you. Besides, I don't usually do a lot on Sundays." I bounce on the balls of my feet, feeling like a shy teenager. Kell's never had that effect on me, but it's different now. Seeing her brings back the events from last night. The memory of touching her. Of her body responding to mine like we'd been doing that our whole lives.

She leads me inside. "I guess we typically don't see each other much on weekends. I know that Ryan likes to go out a lot. I kind of figured you went with him."

The fact that she knows Ryan's weekend routine and not mine sucks. Easy to change that. She just needs to spend more time with me. Funny how our friendship never extended past work hours in the past. Guess there was no need in the past. "I don't like to go out anymore. That ended for me once I realized everyone at those Hollywood clubs is there to play a social game I don't want to play."

She raises an eyebrow. "But you went out with him a few weeks ago. You met that woman. Shea."

I sigh. Stretch my hands behind my head and sit on her sofa. Gotta set some things straight. "I did. She was really nice." I look directly into Kell's eyes and hope she sees how sure I am. "But she wasn't you."

Kell's mouth forms a small O. "That's good to know." She crashes next to me and buries her head in the crook of my shoulder. Her face softens. Another second and she crawls, slowly, into my lap. Her arms wrap around my neck. "Thank you for being patient with me. For waiting for me."

I hate that she wants to thank me for doing the easiest thing in the world. Hate that my brother played a part in making her feel like she wasn't worth waiting for. "I'd do it again in a heartbeat," I promise.

I run a hand over her hair. It's swept up into a messy bun-type situation. I pat the top and it bounces back at me like a fluffy stress ball. "What about you? Are you working today? Going out?"

She shakes her head. "Before you got here my only plans were to try out a new recipe my mom sent me and resist the temptation to look at my emails." She looks sheepish. "I don't know if you know this about me, but I'm a little bit of a workaholic."

That cracks a smile from me. "I can help with the second thing on your list. Maybe the first, too, if you want the help." Distracting Kell from work is exactly the reason I'm here. I can think of much more interesting ways to spend our time.

Mouth lifting up in one corner, Kell gives me a dubious look.

I chuckle. "Hey, I'm a crap chef, but I can follow a recipe. Or lick the spoon. Whichever."

She stares into my eyes. "That does sound hot. It might be fun to cook together."

"Mm hmm." I'm not thinking about cooking. I'm not thinking about anything other than Kell sitting on top of me. The smell of her surrounds me. Her soft skin brushes against mine at every angle. It's suffocating in the best way.

Can't even stand up without the evidence of what it's doing to me becoming too obvious. I swallow. "What's the recipe?"

"It's shepherd's pie. Potatoes, ground lamb, green beans, and brown gravy. You'd like it."

Kell never stops surprising me. I guess I've survived off her muffins for so long I didn't stop to think she might make other things.

"Sounds amazing. Should we start it up?"

She tilts her head and pretends to weigh her options. "Okay, fine. I'll let you help me later. But first . . ."

Kell's lashes close over her eyes. She moves closer and her face fills my vision. Her lips graze my neck. Slow, painfully delicate kisses brush from my chin to my collarbone. Like an agonizing march to seduction.

Groaning, I tilt my forehead against hers. "You're killing me."

I've seen Kell as an ambitious student. Kickass manager. Loyal friend. Never like this, though. She's something else entirely. Someone else, and it's the best kind of privilege to see this side of her.

When she opens her eyes, they're deep brown and brand new. Different and just for me. She doesn't laugh. I half expect some kind of nervous giggle, but she's the picture of serious determination. Our faces still pressed together, she whispers to me, "I want to spend all day with you. Right here." Her hands brace on my chest.

The air leaves my lungs. I don't have a way to say what that means to me. There are no words good enough. I nod. My hands go to her hips. Don't know who folds first, but our lips crash and we're kissing like it's the last thing we'll ever do.

A pattern starts. New favorite game. Kiss. Soft moan. Kiss. Kiss. Moan. Kiss. Bite. And again. And again.

Today is not long enough. I want tomorrow and the next day and the next week and month. I don't want to scare her, so I just hold her close and enjoy this moment.

Her hands fold their way in the back of my shirt. Twisting the fabric until it's stretched and knotted. About as wound up as I feel. Every kiss inches the shirt farther up my skin.

Kell makes a frustrated sound with her teeth. "I can't get this off you."

A laugh barrels out of me. "Is that what you're trying to do? I thought you were going to strangle me with it."

She gives me a look and I laugh again. My chest feels light. She pointedly tugs on the shirt again, and I pull it off. Toss it over our heads to the rug. Her eyes widen as she stares. Been working out with Jonah but I'm not a bodybuilder by any means.

One finger skims along my stomach. "I've seen you without a shirt before, um, obviously. But other than yesterday I tried not to ogle you." She blushes. Swear it's the cutest thing I've ever seen.

I spread my arms. "Ogle all you want. It's all yours."

She grins and runs a hand over me playfully. Then her hands go to her dress. I watch, mesmerized as she shifts in my lap and slips it over her head. She settles back close to me wearing only her bra and underwear. Somewhere in the back of my head I register that they match. Green and lacy.

When I was seventeen and Ryan was starting college, he liked to throw out advice. He told me once that women only wear matching underwear when they're hoping to have sex. Stupid, I know. But it makes me happy to think Kell thinks about me like that. Makes it feel that much more real. Like yesterday wasn't a one-time thing for her either. That she really does think this could be a thing, an *us*. I brush a hand over the top of the lacy bra. "This is nice."

Kell's eyes flicker over my face. The heat I see there makes me touch her again. Her skin is smooth, warm. "It's my favorite set," she admits.

Face to face like this with her mostly undressed, my tongue sticks in my throat. I'm not smooth enough to find the words. I wish I could channel some of the characters I play. In romantic comedies the guy always says the right thing. Always makes the girl swoon. I can't think of any words good enough for Kell.

She brings her lips to mine and kisses me. Her tongue sweeps against mine. My breath comes short and fast. Kell's hands slide low to my hips. Lower. She unbuttons my jeans and—not fast enough—my boxers are gone. I'm still kissing her when I hear her unleash a loud breath. My chest puffs up. Can't help it.

Then my hands are on her and she's staring at me like I'm beautiful. Perfect. Fascinating. All the things *she* is. We're tangled on the sofa together. Our skin is slick. Kell fits into my arms like no one else. And I can't stop touching her. Never want to.

And then we're lost in each other.

Afterward, I don't know how long we spend just lying here. "Kell?"

Her eyes are still closed. She looks peaceful leaning against me, completely lax. "Hmm?"

"Should we make that recipe now?"

Kell's eyes slowly flutter open. "One more minute. I'm comfortable here."

Kind of hard to argue with that.

✿ ✿ ✿ ✿ ✿

I'm in the kitchen baking with Kell when my phone rings. She's pulling open cabinets and drawers in a frenzy. She lines up a bunch of different sizes of measuring cups. A bowl. A spatula-looking thing that bends at the end. Then she looks back down at the recipe on her phone and scoots to the pantry.

I stare at the name on my screen.

Mom.

It's rare for her to call. Jonah talks to her the most and she texts occasionally. Honestly, we don't really talk much at all. We tried some after Dad died, but neither of us had a lot to say. Kind of fizzled out after that.

Kell is still in the pantry when I go to the living room to take the call. "Hey, Mom." I sit straight-backed on the edge of the cushion.

"Ashley." Her voice is soft. Warm. "I haven't heard from you in a while, so I thought I'd call. How are you doing?"

Dad was the parent I went to when I had questions. When I wanted someone to teach me basketball. Help with homework. Someone to complain to.

Mom made me after-school snacks, and she drove me to my first audition. Some local mall open call that I never heard back from. She's always been there for those kinds of things. Not talking though.

That was Dad. After he passed, Mom said even less. We tried for a while but fell off. Now I get news from Jonah because of course Jonah talks to Mom every week. Hearing from her never fails to make me feel guilty.

"I'm good, Mom. Work is good. Just been busy."

"It sounds like it, with your new show and all that. And Jonah mentioned you're auditioning for some new types of movies. I think that would be great, honey."

A lump catches in my throat. I may not talk to her as often as I should, but Mom is still the same. Never fails to make me feel good about myself.

I open my mouth to respond when Kell bursts into the living room. She's balancing bags of chocolate chips.

"I can't remember. Do you like white chocolate? Because I can add it to some of the cookies and leave them off the other half if . . ." When she sees I'm on the phone, Kell trails off. Grimacing, she mouths, "Oops, sorry."

On the phone, Mom inhales sharply. "Is that Kell? Am I interrupting a work meeting? I can call back another time."

One more glance between Kell and my phone and I sigh. "No, it's fine. It's not work. I'm at her house."

"Oh." Mom's voice climbs an octave. "I see."

I can hear the question she's not asking. "We're making cookies," I say. Doubt that will be enough to satisfy her curiosity.

I follow Kell back into the kitchen, and she shoots me a questioning look while she sifts flour into a measuring cup. Feels like I'm trapped between the two of them. I don't know how much to say. Or what to say, really. As ready as I might be, I don't think Kell's wanting to DTR yet.

"That sounds really nice. I'm glad you two are still so close," Mom says finally. She's letting me off the hook, and we both know it. I hope that I can tell her more about this thing with Kell soon. I know it would make her happy.

"Yeah, it's great," I agree. "Anyway, auditions are slow around here. But I am pushing hard for a movie about the Great Depression." I sit back. Take a breath. Judith let me know that the movie was still looking for its lead. I might still have a shot. "It reminds me so much of Dad."

"Oh," Mom sighs. "That would be perfect, Ash. I'll keep my fingers crossed for you."

After promising that I will keep her updated, we say goodbye. Kell comes to sit on the sofa next to me. "I didn't even realize you were on the phone," she groans. "Sorry if that made things weird. That was your mom?"

I ease Kell's head onto my shoulder. Let her lean into me. "It was," I say. "We haven't talked in a while. And don't worry, you didn't make it any weirder than I did."

Nodding, Kell's lips sweep my neck above my shirt collar. "Your dad's death must have been really hard on her."

Somehow Kell understands this about my family. She sees as much as she listens. Doesn't judge but understands. I love her for it.

The realization shakes me, but I can't bring myself to say the words out loud. With Kell wanting things to be secret. With all the changes in our careers. I want to be sure about how she sees us. Yeah, I love Kell. She's been a special person in my life for a long time in one way or another. It's evolved into different things.

What I feel right now is more.

"It was hard on everyone, but especially Mom," I say. "I think she wishes we still lived close. Maybe she feels like we left her."

Kell shakes her head. Puts a hand on my shoulder. "I'm sure she doesn't think like that. The times I've met her all she talked about was how proud she is of the three of you."

I kiss Kell's forehead. "That's good to hear. Speaking of being proud of work accomplishments, have I told you lately that you're really good at what you do?"

She laughs and the vibrations shake my chest. "I thought I'd get better at it the longer I was your manager, but honestly, lately it seems like I'm getting worse." She purses her lips. "It's changed a lot, huh?"

The unhappiness sneaks in sometimes, and it's painfully obvious to everyone but Kell. It's what Jonah and Ryan were talking about. Why they talked to Norman Cherry. And why I haven't blocked his number yet.

"It has," I agree with her. I wait for her to say something else about it, but she doesn't. Instead Kell kisses the edge of my jaw and I'm undone all over again. This woman kills me in the best way.

CHAPTER THIRTY-FIVE

✿ ✿ ✿ ✿ ✿

Kell

J'm supposed to be cool, calm, and collected about anything and everything to do with the Matthews. It's literally my job. But I've officially lost my ability to *not* melt into a puddle on sight of Ash Matthew. I thought his rabid groups of fans were weird before, but they have nothing on me.

After spending the entire day—and night—together, I can somewhat proudly say that I am addicted to the way he smells. I always appreciated his efforts at good hygiene, but holy crap on a stick, I want to bottle him up and sniff him all day long. It doesn't make sense that we've been in each other's lives for so long but I'm just now really seeing him. I can't believe I wasted so much time thinking I cared about Ryan. I can't believe I wasted any time at all on other men. Ash is everything I ever wanted, and I didn't even see it.

It physically pains me to send him home, even knowing I'll see him over there soon. Claudette has been texting me nonstop for updates, and I'm half afraid she's going to barge through my front door any second and demand to talk. So maybe it's okay if he leaves for a little bit.

"Sure you don't want to drive with me?" Ash picks up one of my hands and kisses the top, letting his lips linger there temptingly. "We can make up some believable excuse."

He kisses my hand again. "Or just tell them the truth."

I shake my head. No, I'm sure that I don't want any of it included in the reality show. We've talked about this, but I don't blame him for asking again. Part of me wants to announce it to the world too. Logically, it's probably not a huge deal. But emotionally, I can't handle it quite yet. Today is the last day of shooting for their show and as weird as it might be to figure out a new dynamic, I don't want to hide this away after shooting ends.

I bite my bottom lip. "We'll tell everyone soon, I promise. Drive careful. It looks nice out, but my weather app says it's supposed to rain."

Ash waves my words away. "I'll be fine."

It's a joke at this point because rain has been in the forecast all week and we've still had nothing but sunshine and the occasional misguided cloud. If it does rain, it probably won't be anything other than a light sprinkle, one that the dusty lawns in LA desperately need.

I go inside to text Claudette and invite her to come over for some of the remaining muffins. She doesn't text me back, but two minutes later a knock comes on my door. I open it to Claudette grinning so widely her face might break. "I was in the neighborhood," she starts.

We collide into a hug. "You are ridiculous," I tell her.

She preens. "I am the best friend you will ever have. Now tell me everything that happened between you and Ash. Everything, everything."

After I fill in Claudette and she hugs me so tight I can't breathe, we make plans for breakfast next week and she goes. As I'm getting ready to get in my own car and make my way to the Matthews' house, I get a text.

Ryan: *Can we talk after the wrap party tonight? Got some work questions.*

Kell: *Of course. I'll find you after.*

The usual dread doesn't take hold of me. Talking to Ryan isn't talking to the man who ignored and tossed me aside anymore. He's just another playboy client. And it feels so good to come to terms with that. To realize that what almost killed me just last month holds no power over me now.

I think about that on the drive over, but mostly I think about Ash. How much he's surprised me lately. Clearly I was living life with blinders on to never realize that he had feelings for me. It's hard not to wonder what direction things would have taken if I'd realized my own feelings earlier. If instead of chasing after a destructive crush on Ryan, I would have let Ash kiss me way back when. Maybe we could have skipped years of drama and been living our happily ever after all this time.

When I walk inside the house, I can still conjure up the way it felt when Ash kissed me. The focus in his eyes when he leaned over me, a bead of sweat on his back. Not driving over here with him was a mistake because I'm apparently addicted. Too many years *not* touching him and kissing him has left me depleted, desperate to be with him.

Inside the Matthews' house is chaos with almost every front room taken over by crew and equipment. Still, I feel Ash's gaze on me immediately, like he's locked in on me at all times. At least the urge is mutual and we're both obsessed.

Before I can do anything, Jessie takes my arm and leads me down the hall, leaving the guys alone with the filming crew. "Is it true?" She stops us at a portrait I've always hated hanging on the wall. It's Ryan, Ash, and Jonah standing with their arms folded and looking seriously into the camera. None of them will give me a straight answer on whether or not they really believe it's art. It looks like something shot in the early 2000s in a mall. "Ash came home so happy, and of course he refused to say anything. I just assumed . . ."

My smile answers for me. The corners of my mouth lift before I can stop myself. I've never felt this way about a guy I've dated before. I haven't had that instant smile response, but every time I think about being with Ash, my face has a mind of its own. "No comment?" I say weakly, still smiling like a goof.

Jessie squeezes my hand. "I can keep a secret, I swear. I'm so happy for you two. You have no idea how stressed out he's been about this. He was so sure that you didn't want to be more than friends. After the text—"

"Wait, which text are you talking about?"

"I know I wasn't supposed to know about it, but Ash showed Jonah your conversation, and you know what it's like. Jonah told me about it." Jessie waves it away like it's nothing, but I can tell it was a big deal, at least at some point.

My smile turns to a frown while I try to remember what text conversation she's talking about. Ash and I talk all the time, but until very recently we hadn't talked about anything especially personal.

Something stirs in my memory. Ash said he wanted to be with me from the beginning, and he's made similar jokes before, but I never paid them much attention. I guess because I thought they were just that—harmless teasing that he didn't really mean. "Are you talking about that text about how we almost kissed in college?"

Jessie nods. "Yeah. In his guy brain I guess that was you saying 'stop trying it's never going to happen.'" She puts pressure on my hand again. "I'm glad he was wrong."

"Me too." I step away, looking back down the hall at where I left Ash. I can't believe he thought I was rejecting him. I really can't believe that what I saw as a theoretical question was actually a come-on. Maybe I wouldn't have been ready for him a few weeks ago, since my brain was still so stuck on Ryan. Maybe it would have made things harder.

"I'm going to go make sure everything is good to go," I tell Jessie. I stop by and make relatively painless small talk with Judith. I thank her for convincing me that the show was the right direction for their careers. The compliment is bitter in my mouth but it's necessary. Judith knows show business and I would be foolish to not recognize it. She's apparently feeling gracious enough to take the compliment without any argument because she pats my hand and says, "We really should work together more often."

Working the room a little more, I pass Jonah, who asks if I've seen Jessie and I point him in the direction of his girlfriend. Ryan catches my eye from across the room where he's chatting with one of Aaron's assistants.

I'll deal with him later.

But Ash. Ash watches me steadily, his eyes tracking my every movement. He is so handsome standing there waiting for me, a small smirk on his lips. They twitch slightly when I check for anyone watching and wink at him.

I nod my head in the direction of the far hall. "I have some things I need to talk to you about before filming," I announce in my most managerial tone.

My hair bounces with each step, and I can feel Ash's stare on my back. Even without seeing his face, I sense we are on the same page. Anticipation is thick with each passing second we sneak farther away from the main part of the house, toward the rooms.

"Am I in trouble?" he asks, pushing open his bedroom door and shutting it behind us.

"That depends on whether or not you make us late for the first scene."

"Can't make any promises." Ash's mouth finds mine.

He pushes us back onto his bed, and the weight of his body covers mine in a blanketing of arms and legs and torso, all muscled and sturdy. We tumble against the plush mattress. I breathe in his smell, so familiar and still somehow new. Cinnamon cologne and a clean-smelling shampoo that combine perfectly. Ash moves over me, his arms forming a cage around my body. His eyes are intense, hooded, and a focused kind of gray I've rarely seen on him. "Never thought kissing you would be like this." He ducks low, kissing me again.

"Like what exactly?" I smile against his lips even though I know the answer. I feel it too. When we touch each other, it's charged with something—more. Something hard to explain but so easy to convey when it's the two of us. I want to hide in here with him for so much longer than we have. For now, it's so much easier to wall away this part of me, keep it separate from the rest of my life.

CHAPTER THIRTY-SIX

✿ ✿ ✿ ✿ ✿

Ash

*K*ell is so beautiful looking at her should hurt. I can't believe I get to touch her like this. Hide away and be with her. The way things were between us is gone. Now it's different in so many ways.

She has to be feeling it too. Whatever this is between us, I'm not making it up. We've said things, done things that have changed us. Feels like there's no going back now. At least I hope not. Her eyes meet mine, and we stay like that until I inch closer. "Kell."

She makes a little *hmm* sound, her lips parting just barely. One of her hands lifts to my chest. She pushes her palm against me. I swallow. Wonder if she can tell how fast my heart is pounding. Being closer to her does things to me. Kell was right. She might have a point about keeping things secret. As much as I want to show her off, sneaking around is hot. Feels like I have her all to myself for once without having to compete for time. I wish we could stay hidden away for the rest of the day.

Forget about filming.

Her hand warms me through my T-shirt, and I can't drag my eyes away from her slightly open mouth. Those soft lips and the curve of her cheekbones. My fingers itch to reach up and trace her face, cup it in my hands. I can't make myself stop touching her.

Kell sucks in a breath, her shoulders shaking with the movement. She stares at the clock on my bedside table. My own breath catches. I didn't realize the time. Kind of melts away when we're with each other. Everyone is probably wondering where we are. "Ash," she says, and a little line forms between her eyes. "We have to get back. We should—"

"What's going on in here?" Ryan flings open my bedroom door. He looks between Kell and me. He's changed clothes for some reason. He's wearing one of those mesh button-up shirts that I used to think no one wore in real life.

Of course he would.

Before I have time to react, Kell jumps away from me and plasters on a fake smile. I know it's fake because I have her real smiles memorized. All of them. This one sits right between polite and panicked. She doesn't look at Ryan or me. Her eyes stay locked on the bedroom wall. "Just going over some contracts, but I think we're good, right, Ash?" She doesn't wait for me to respond. "I'm going to go find Aaron and make sure everything is good to go for today."

And then she's gone. Runs down the hall faster than paparazzi chasing a story. Runs without looking back.

I hope she's not rethinking everything. But, knowing Kell, she could change her mind about me in a second. Decide I'm not worth the trouble. I whirl on Ryan. "What are you wearing? You look like a Jonas Brother."

He looks himself up and down and shrugs. "I was going for Harry Styles." He tucks his hands in the pockets of his frayed pants. "You just don't know how to dress, but I don't see how that's my problem."

I don't understand how we're related sometimes. At least I never let fame change me like this. I should have Mom email me pictures of Ryan's outfits in middle school and sell them to the highest bidder. Might be too harsh though. "Whatever. Don't let yourself into my room again. Try knocking."

Ryan leans against my doorframe. "Why would I need to knock? Kell said you were just talking work. Anything else you were doing with our manager on your bed would be kind of inappropriate, wouldn't it?" He lifts an eyebrow. Guy's clearly pleased with himself.

He can think what he wants. I promised Kell I'd keep quiet, and I'm going to. I shoulder past him and head back to the living room. Ryan follows because he doesn't know how to leave me alone. He's right up on me when he says, "I've got some work of my own to talk with Kell about later today. Think we should use my bed or is she partial to yours?"

I turn. My hand reaches out and grabs the neck of Ryan's shirt. I slam him against the wall. Fire snaps in my veins. Fills me up so much I have to bite it back down. He can give me shit all he wants, and I'll take it because I'm stuck with him. Kell is a different story. "You leave her alone."

Something's wrong with Ryan because he doesn't look mad at all. Looks like he wants a fight. His mouth curls into something cruel. "Come on, baby brother, hit me."

Too late, it dawns on me what's happening. I look over my shoulder. A camera crew. Shit. Two guys both holding small portable cameras and an intern with a mic pointed at us. I'm not mic'd up yet, but I wouldn't be surprised if Ryan is.

I loosen my grip on him and lean close. "Are you really that desperate for fame?" So desperate that he'd sell me out for a fake fight. Bait me just for views like I'm no one to him. We used to care about each other more than that. I thought we still did, even with the stuff he's put everyone through this year.

Ryan's reaction is quick enough to blink and miss. Just a hint of the guy I thought he was. Maybe some regret. Then he's shrugging me off and moving away. I stand alone and stare after him. I really don't understand. Ryan's career is bigger than any of ours. He never fails to remind us that he's made the most money out of the three of us. Is the most successful. The most wanted. Just now I'm seeing that he's the least happy.

Jonah comes hurrying down the hall and looks me over. "I just heard about what happened. You okay?"

The house is loud with chatter. I can hear Ryan in the front room still steamed. Probably giving an on-camera interview about our almost fight. As for me, the anger drains as quickly as it came. I know that Kell can handle Ryan, and that's good enough for me. "I'm fine. Not sure Ryan is though. Any idea what he's thinking?"

Jonah spreads his hands. He looks uncomfortable for a moment. "I'm not sure if this is true or not, but Jessie heard that Samantha broke up with him."

Samantha hasn't been around the house lately, but I didn't think much of it. Honestly, I got the impression that his relationship with her wasn't all that important to him. A breakup could explain the erratic behavior. Ryan doesn't do well when he isn't coming out on top. What are the odds there's no wedding after all?

I run a hand over my face. "Should someone talk to him?"

Not me. With Kell's and my relationship and Ryan's mood swings, someone else would be better at figuring him out. Anyone else. Used to be that I could trust Ryan with anything. He's my big brother, always will be. He just needs to get it together.

Jonah must be thinking the same. "Let's give him space. I think it's a lot right now for him. He isn't thinking straight."

"Yeah. Okay."

I'll give Ryan space as long as he doesn't start more fights. I feel for him about Samantha, but it's not like he didn't have it coming.

Dude's got to get some things together before he pursues another woman. I actually liked Samantha, but she's probably better off.

Jonah goes and I check my phone. Another text from Norman, the last person I want to hear from right now. He's persistent, not obnoxious, and not ready to take no for an answer. What kills me is that he's starting to wear me down.

More and more it's starting to make sense in my head. If Kell isn't my manager, then our relationship isn't as public. If Kell isn't my manager, or Ryan's or Jonah's, she would be free to do something new. Not feel tied down to us because of loyalty or obligation or whatever else. The issue is, how the hell do I broach the subject without hurting Kell. If it isn't what she wants and I'm off base, she could hate me. Stuck either way. I don't know what to say to Norman either.

Just keep putting it off until things settle down. Maybe it will work itself out.

Or maybe everything will blow up in my face.

CHAPTER THIRTY-SEVEN

❀ ❀ ❀ ❀ ❀

Kell

*T*he rest of the day goes off without any further drama. My head is still spinning from what happened with Ryan and Ash. The guys don't always get along, but physically fighting is a whole other thing. And according to Jessie, Ryan might have instigated the fight on purpose for the show.

He's really supposed to talk to me about these decisions. Maybe that's what he wants to go over in our talk later. At the beginning of the day, I was wary of meeting with him, but now it seems like a necessity. I need to find out where his head is at.

We hold an after-party at the house with drinks, catering, and Jonah's playlist. The guys play basketball on the half-court as the sun sets an orange-pink in the sky. Jessie sits next to me in a plush outdoor chair, and we cheer for them fighting over the ball like it's the last slice of pizza on family game night. Some things never change I guess when it comes to working with your siblings. I think they're going to be okay. I'll talk to Ryan and figure out what's happening with him. The end of this show is the conclusion of one chapter and the beginning of many more. I'm proud of all of us.

I walk Judith out as she follows the last of Aaron's crew. "Thank you for everything. This turned out really good for the guys' careers. I owe you thanks for that. It's been an interesting ride." One I never want to ride again, but still. My clients are happy, I should be happy, and in a way I am.

"And you were a good sport about dating Ash for the show. I have to say that I was surprised you agreed to that. The only other thing we need out of you at this point is a breakup."

The breakup conversation between Ash and me is supposed to be intimate and raw. We agreed beforehand to film it ourselves and send Aaron the footage later on. "I've been meaning to talk to you about that. What if we didn't break up? Ryan and Samantha already kind of did the whole ending a relationship angle."

Judith touches my arm, her tone light. "Oh no. It still needs to happen. If you thought this was a lot to handle, you need to prepare yourself for season two. The more seasons, the more drama necessary."

I'm sorry, what? I stare at where her hand rests on my elbow, desperately wishing she'd move it. "Did you say season two? Is that a for-sure thing?"

She nods, holding her eyes wide. "It is. I got the call this morning and all three of the brothers signed the contract. Exciting, isn't it? I hope you're prepared for even more cameras, bigger parties, and some surprise guests! I have to run, but I'll be in touch."

Judith finally lets go and leaves me on the front porch gaping after her. She and the other half a dozen cars pull away, and I blink, stunned. I don't know how she pulls the stuff she does, but she's good.

A second season of the show never even crossed my mind, to be honest. I've had colleagues get lucky enough for a pilot or maybe a short season, and they and their clients were thrilled. But those shows were always canceled before talks of renewal could start. A second season is a whole other animal. One that I'm not very enamored with, if I'm being honest with myself. Ultimately, these kinds of decisions are down to the guys and their goals, but I really thought they would have said no.

"These clouds look dark. Maybe it will rain after all." Ash's voice in my ear runs a shiver of pleasure down my spine. He's solid at my back, and I want to turn and let him take me in his arms.

Season two. Of course he would want that.

Why wouldn't he?

But if I even let out a hint of my feelings, Ash will change his mind and turn down the show and choose me. I know he will. That's a position that I never want to put him in, professionally or otherwise. So my choice is made for me. It was never even a choice after all.

Instead of leaning back into Ash's arms, I speak to him while still turned away. "I know I promised that this was only until after shooting ends, but I don't think I can do it yet. I have to stay in work mode. The line is too blurred." I shake my head, stepping away from him. Filming will never really be over, not when there's a season two. And maybe season three and beyond. Anything that happens between us will eventually be caught on cameras, and not regular cameras but ones poised to take hold of the storytelling and turn it into something ugly. I'm not ready.

I hurry inside before I have to see his reaction. I know I can't avoid it forever, but at least for the next few hours I will. Maybe then I can come up with something coherent, some believable reason why we can't be together for real. One other than the truth—that the lifestyle he loves so much no longer fits me.

Ryan is waiting for me at the front door, his eyes weary and heavy. Despite how angry I am with him, I remain neutral because I am, after all, still a professional. "Where should we talk?"

Ryan gestures to the unused office space, and I follow down the hall. I pull up two chairs and sit to face him, gesturing for him to sit too. "Want to tell me what today was about? I feel like I'm out of the loop here, Ryan, and it's kind of my job to know."

"Everything's falling apart." He sinks into the chair, folding up on himself. He looks like an overgrown child.

He's not usually one to mince words. Ash is the guy who can struggle to put a full sentence together, but Ryan loves to hear himself talk.

I shake my head. "Can you please elaborate? Help me help you."

Ryan's head sinks into his hands, and he groans, mumbling something unintelligible. I'm starting to worry about being in a room alone with him until he lifts his head, and I see his face soaked with tears.

"Ryan?" He's starting to scare me, and I wonder if I should have held this talk somewhere closer to the other guys.

Just in case.

"I messed up," he rasps. "I really screwed up everything good in my life, including you."

The words should have more of an effect on me, but I don't feel anything but sorry for him. He's right—he really has messed things up for himself.

"What happened?" I ask.

"It's Samantha. She broke up with me."

So Jessie's source was right.

"Everyone gets broken up with eventually. It's nothing to be embarrassed about, even if it was a fiancée instead of a girlfriend." I shrug. "Look on the bright side, at least now you don't have to go through with a wedding." I think we all knew that Ryan is not a marriage kind of guy.

Ryan shakes his head. "She broke off the wedding because of me. I only proposed to her in the first place because of Judith."

My forehead creases as I try to process. "I'm sorry, what does Judith have to do with this? She didn't even approach me about the reality show until after the news broke."

Ryan ducks his head. "Yeah, that was her idea, but it seemed like it all worked pretty well. I didn't get that movie I wanted—you know, the Ryan Reynolds one? And Ash got all these new projects and Jonah was starting to get more recognition. It scared the shit out of me. So Judith told me about this manager, Norman. She said that he could make my career. I never meant it to spiral into this mess, but I thought it was worth a shot."

After several seconds of staring at him, I nod numbly. None of this makes sense. I don't understand. "Okay, so you broke the terms of our contract and sought out the advice of someone who is not your manager." The anger I'm trying to hold in takes over, because how *dare* he?

"And not only that, but you also met a fan of yours, and after barely knowing each other at all, you proposed to her as what? A publicity stunt? To get a reality show?"

Ryan nods. "Pretty much," he says miserably.

I can't say I feel bad for him at all anymore. He deserves every bit of that misery. Not Samantha though. As much as I didn't want to admit it, she was great. And clearly, she was way too good to be with Ryan, in a real or fake relationship.

"So that's why you're crying over Samantha breaking up with you, because you didn't get to do it first and alert the media beforehand?" He's really sick, and I hate to admit it, but I expected better of him. Ryan never used to be this bad. A little full of himself, sure, but not like this. I don't even recognize this man, the one I spent too large a chunk of my twenties daydreaming over. That version of Ryan Matthew likely never existed. My heart squeezes as I realize the full weight of how stupid I've been. Ash was the only real man all along and I ignored him for a *fantasy*.

Ryan's tears have dried up but he's still sniffling as he explains. "It started as a publicity stunt, and I told her as much from the beginning. But Sam is amazing. She's so much more than I thought she was. I fell for her, for real, right away, but I kept letting other things distract me."

I flare my nostrils. Ryan can't leave people alone—he has to poke at them until things get raw. He did it to me, stringing me along for years, and to Ash, teasing him until he fired back. "Like your obsession with one-upping your brothers?"

He flinches. His eyes are red. But how am I supposed to believe he's really sad? I refuse to buy one more sob story. "Among other things, yeah. Like I said, I see it now. I did everything wrong. I tried to make up for it by introducing the guys to Norman after Judith pushed me in that direction, but . . ."

Someone knocks on the door. Jonah, Jessie, and Ash stand outside the partially open office door. Their faces match the stricken look I'm sure I have. They've all talked to Norman. And they all signed on for a second season without even mentioning it to me. Something tells me that I wasn't supposed to know about that, this favor Ryan did for them. Everything spins, but I somehow keep cool. I have to, because what else do I have left?

I look at them and then back at Ryan. I'm so done. So entirely, absolutely done. I've known it for a while now and tried to desperately fight it, but enough is enough. I grit my teeth. "Needless to say, Ryan, our contract is broken, and you will need to look for new management effective immediately. I wish you luck in the future."

Turning back to Ash and Jonah, I swallow. Some huge part of me is screaming inside. I don't know how to do this. I don't know if I'll ever be able to forgive myself, but also—I feel like I owe it to myself.

This is the much harder blow to deliver. It's hard even if what Ryan says is true, that they met with another manager behind my back too. "And to you two, I'm sorry to do this this way, but I'm retiring as your manager. I will give you both as long as you need to find someone new so that you're not left wanting, but this is it."

Ash's hand lands on the back of my shoulder, tentative and soft. It says so many things that he's not saying out loud. I nod at him, sighing. I have no idea what this means for our relationship, or even our friendship.

I march down the hall and swing open the front door. Hand still on the doorknob, I freeze. Rain thunders down, mixed with huge, golf-ball-sized hail and winds that render the trees sideways. It looks like I'm not making any sort of grand exit, not tonight anyway.

CHAPTER THIRTY-EIGHT

❀ ❀ ❀ ❀ ❀

Kell

*T*hrough the dark and noisy patter of the rain, my phone chimes at one a.m. with a text. A consistent stream of thunder has growled overhead for the past several hours. I groan and reach for it on the bedside table where it's not charging because the power's gone out. I'm still awake because it's impossible to sleep on this guest bed. Something about it is too plush, too comfortable, too unfamiliar. When I complain after staying over, the guys tease me that I can't handle luxury. But it's more that I can't handle change, especially the kind of change happening recently.

I made a lot of big decisions tonight, ones that fell off my chest like the weight of the world, but also broke my heart. I know that both of my big decisions hurt Ash, and I hate that. I swipe up to read his text, even though I can easily guess what it says.

Ash: *We need to talk about this.*

I flop over and groan into the silk sheets. I should have sucked it up and driven home tonight, storm be damned.

My phone buzzes again, lighting the screen with another text from Ash.

Ash: *Please, Kell.*

I apply lip balm, splash water on my face, and run my hands through my hair. My vanity stops me from doing anything less.

I pad upstairs to Ash's room and knock. I know avoiding him for any length of time after my declarations makes me a coward. I know he deserves more explanation, but so do I.

I'm not even sure I have the answers for myself, not yet anyway. Sometimes things just feel right and you try to move forward, hoping that you're headed in the right direction. I wasn't the one at fault here, nor was I the one to keep secrets.

Instead of waiting for him, I pull open the door and stick my head inside. It's dark, only the glow of his phone, open to our texts, lighting the room. "Hey."

His hair is a disaster, poking up from every angle like he's been tossing in his bed but not really sleeping. Just like I have. How does he manage to look heart-stoppingly gorgeous, even now, even with the sleepless vampire look he's sporting? He sits up in his bed and pats the space next to him. I sink down and tuck my legs under me, but I turn away from him, resting my back against his arm. "It's late, Ash."

"You were awake," he says with a short laugh that has no humor in it.

"I'm tired," I whisper. It's true, even if I doubt I'll be able to sleep. The emotions of the day are catching up to me and my brain is begging to shut down.

With a groan, he lies back down, pulling me with him until his arms wrap around me and I'm flat on his bed. The solid weight of his body behind me is too warm. The smell of cinnamon fills my nostrils. Every bit of me fights against this, the suspicion that he's my home, my best friend. I bite the inside of my cheek. "I thought you wanted to talk."

"I do want to talk, but I'm tired too. Hence, lying down. Help me understand, Kell. Help me know what you want from me. I'm trying not to freak out, but it's hard. I messed up, I know that, but give me a chance to explain."

What are we doing? Our friendship had been the one thing I could count on for the past five years, and now it feels like we're deconstructing it. I don't want to break a good thing. Not for ratings or publicity or anything else. "You don't need to explain yourself. I understand how career moves work."

As I inch away and put a respectable few inches between us, his eyes darken. "Is this about my brother? Still? Is that why you still won't admit we're together and why you don't want to manage us?"

"No, I don't care about what either of the guys thinks. I don't care about Ryan in that way anymore. I haven't for a long time. Please tell me you know that." The idea of Ryan finding me in bed with Ash once might have caused a sick twisting in my stomach, but now it does nothing at all. I softly push Ash away. I stand and give him a weak smile. It feels like one of those wobbly Play-Doh smiles I'd stretch over my face as a little girl, just to make my parents laugh. "I'm really tired."

Ash swallows. "I talked to Ryan and we're working things out. He made some bad decisions. We all did. The three of us—we just want what's best for you, Kell. If it's moving on from being our manager, we respect that."

"Thank you," I say, but the weight on my chest doesn't settle. "But I need more than just a professional break."

He's quiet for a long moment. "Then why did you come to my room?"

Ash doesn't talk to me like this. Not in this short, gruff way. We don't do closed off with each other. But this time I can't give him an answer. Not the one he wants, anyway. He should understand this, given the information he kept from me.

"I really wanted this to work," I offer, while knowing in my heart that it's not enough to say the words.

Ash shakes his head. "If you wanted it to work you would be fighting for it. But you're walking away, and I don't understand why. Don't tell anyone we're together. Don't be my manager anymore. But stay with me."

My eyes sting. As sure as I was earlier about how I feel about him, I'm not so sure what I want from life right now. His career depends on a good, reliable person, one who can be there for him in an unbiased way. And it snaps my heart in two even admitting it to myself, but that's not me anymore.

And if I'm not that source for him and won't date him in public, then what good am I? I'm only holding him back. "I'm not walking away. Please don't think that. Listen—you're getting a second season of the show. I'm so, so happy for you, truly. I just can't do it, Ash. And I won't ask you to give it up for me. Our lives are moving in different directions."

I sound like someone reading a script of a breakup.

Ash reaches for me, one hand extended, palm flat. "I don't want a new manager and I don't want the show. I met with him once because of Ryan, but it was never my plan to sign with him. I should have told you." His voice breaks. "Please, I'll do anything to make this work."

I break.

It would be so easy to take his hand and fall back into bed, into his arms.

To effortlessly slip back into the same patterns I've kept myself confined to for my entire working adult life.

"I want you to sign with Norman Cherry." I nod. "He's really good. I like him." Norman is a close friend of Judith's and the only manager she trusts. She told me so the last time we worked together, which I took to be a dig at me so I locked the information away.

Ash's brows furrow. "No."

"Sign with Norman and do the show. You won't regret it." I rest my hand on the bedroom door. Several feet away at his window, a flash of lighting snakes across the sky. "I'm sorry it had to end like this."

I stop in the hallway and text Judith, my heart racing.

Kell: *I audio recorded the breakup on my phone. Here's the file. This is all you're going to get.*

CHAPTER THIRTY-NINE

✿ ✿ ✿ ✿ ✿

Kell

*T*he roads are quiet and the house lights are still dark when I wake up the next morning. My phone was plugged into the wall charger as a good faith gesture, but when I tap the screen, I see that it barely has any juice left.

I'm running on fumes as well after a night of too little sleep and too much tossing and turning. Ash accused me of running away from him, but it seems like no matter how hard I try I can't leave the Matthews behind. I could go to my apartment and survive the day and maybe the rest of the week with no power, but I have little to no food in my kitchen. The guys, however, are well-stocked per usual. Honestly, though, I'm not sure that I'm welcome here after my announcement last night.

As if right on cue, Claudette calls me. I don't know how she knows when I need her, but she always seems to be tuned in. Her timing is amazing. "Hi," I manage to say before sniffing into the phone. It's impossible to pretend with her.

"Oh honey. What happened? You're supposed to be happy."

"I know. I don't know why, but I messed it all up. Can I come stay with you?" I wipe at the tears dripping onto my face, trying to hold it together.

At least until I'm out of this house.

She doesn't question me. "Of course you can. I have a couch with your name on it."

I throw my things in my oversized purse and tiptoe from the room. No one else is awake yet. Or if they are, no one stops me to talk. I run to my car and drive, bleary-eyed, to Claudette's apartment. She's waiting at the door with her arms outstretched for a hug. The minute I see her, I lose the mask and let myself fall apart. It comes out messy, my eyes burning red from sucking back tears too long and my lips quivering like a sobbing child. "It's over," I tell her again and again until my tears have stained my face and my throat stings. Claudette strokes my hair and shushes me softly, and I sit there knowing my whole world is falling apart.

When I've stopped leaving wet marks on her furniture, Claudette brings out her stack of board games to distract me, and maybe also because it's her favorite mindless pastime. We sit on the rug in her living room and move colorful plastic pieces around a board, and it's so normal, so achingly mundane. For a moment in time I forget to be broken.

Claudette picks a card and gets to move her game piece halfway across the candy-themed squares. I pretend to bump my knee against the board accidentally, leaving her piece sliding around. Claudette gasps. She throws a stack of game cards at me, and I retaliate by throwing my cards back.

"You've always been a sore loser," she says. She pretends to be mad but that's what I love about Claudette. She doesn't care nearly as much as I do. She's one of those rare human beings who is happy just existing. Who doesn't overthink or overextend herself, and who definitely doesn't care to work herself to the bone. Not even for a game of Candy Land.

"I didn't lose," I point out stubbornly. "The game wasn't over yet. If anything, it's a tie."

"A tie?" Claudette shrieks and dumps the rest of the cards over me, letting them rain onto my head.

I laugh. My head tilts back and I wobble with the weight of the laugh. I clutch my belly because the laugh hurts my sides. My eyes tear up and the laugh turns to crying so hard that I'm half afraid I'll drown in my own tears. I hiccup, unable to stop and catch my breath, but it comes out as more of a gasp.

Claudette scrunches up her face. She takes my hand and pulls me up. Then she brings me a blanket and a cup of tea, and I curl into an armchair. We sit without saying another word until the crying jag has passed again. I'm not sure if I have any moisture left in me at this point. I wipe at my eyes until they're mostly dry. "Thank you," I tell my friend.

"What are you going to do now?" she asks, sitting across from me with untouched dress designs in her lap.

I swirl the liquid in my mug, pretending to think. "About Ash or about my job?"

Claudette lets out a breathy whistle. "Good question. Both, I guess. You have some big decisions to make."

"I know."

"Are you at least excited about finding something new to do with your life? This has been a long time coming." She crosses her legs underneath her and leans forward.

My head clears a bit because Claudette is right. She's seen firsthand how draining my career was, both mentally and physically. I may have pushed my frustrations aside for as long as I could, but it's time. It's past time now. And the truth is that I do feel a spark of excitement about finding a new passion, one that gives me time to breathe. One that doesn't touch reality shows. "It's the right choice, even if it's hard. I know that."

Claudette tilts her head. "And Ash? Are you okay with leaving that? Because as your best friend in the entire world, I'm not so sure you're being true to yourself. Leave your job, yes, but leave behind a guy who's made you happier than anyone else?"

"It's not that simple." I hug the mug to my face. It's warm and calming, but it doesn't provide answers, unfortunately. "Sometimes love isn't enough in a relationship. There's things we want that are different, you know?"

She looks at me like I've announced I'm going to become a runway model. "Love? Are you in love with him?"

I blanche. The word came out of me before I could think about it, but it felt right. It feels right. I've always loved Ash as a friend, but when we crossed the line into relationship territory, my heart quadrupled in size. I can't imagine ever feeling that way about a man again. I swallow. "I think I might be."

"Wow." Claudette knows what a big deal this is, and she's probably one of the only people on earth who can appreciate what the Matthews collectively have meant to me. What Ash alone has meant. And how terrible it is that I'm not in a position to act on my feelings anymore *because* I love him. I can't make him miserable by holding him back.

"I know," I say, staring into what's left of my tea. Because I do know that *wow* is the only word that appropriately sums up this situation. I'm in love with Ash, and he has feelings for me, or at least had them up until last night. But our feelings don't matter because our goals don't align, so our futures can't align. I won't subject Ash to a lifetime of dimming himself because I hate the spotlight. And I won't force myself to like living adjacent to the fishbowl that is fame.

So there's nothing left to do but stay away and hope that things eventually hurt . . . less.

CHAPTER FORTY

❀ ❀ ❀ ❀ ❀

Kell

hen I arrive in Washington with two suitcases, my parents exchange worried glances as they pull me in the front door. "That's a lot of clothes for a holiday weekend," Mom says, a question in her voice.

"Can I stay for a week? A few weeks, tops." Technically I'm here for Dad's birthday, just a few days usually since it falls on Halloween and we make a big deal of it in my family. But it hit me as I was packing my things that I wasn't going to be able to stomach the next phase of my life without a distraction. Sitting alone in my apartment with no work and no definite direction is scary enough to send me running back to my parents' house. Luckily, I knew they wouldn't mind.

Mom's face softens, and instead of the barrage of more questions I expect, she nods.

"You're always welcome here." Dad's there at the door and they both wrap me in a hug until I have to push away. After I unpack in my old bedroom, I curl up on the couch while Dad brings me a bowl of warm popcorn, the butter still gleaming yellow on top. "I added extra for you," he says while patting my arm. It's still very new for me, letting other people take care of me. Even when I was a teenager living at home, I wanted so badly to be independent that I kept a wall up, a distinction that said *I can do it myself, thank you very much.* While part of me appreciates the coddling, the other half itches to stand up and be the busy one. I don't think I'll ever be able to break the habit of going and doing too much.

Dad sits next to me, watching and waiting until I meet his eyes. "Is this about work?"

I nod.

When I don't volunteer any more information, he slaps his knee. "Well, you have time to figure out what you want to do. That's the beauty of being young."

To Mom's credit, she listens from the kitchen but says nothing remotely close to "I told you so." They've spent the last several years not-so-discretely hinting that they didn't like the way I worked too hard. Also that I wasn't building a solid career by only working with the Matthews. It's too difficult to try to explain that it isn't the Matthews who are falling behind, it's me. After all this time, I'm the one who needs to step back and who isn't quite cut out for the lifestyle.

We settle into a far-too-comfortable routine in the days that follow. Mom and I make dozens of sides and desserts for Dad's big birthday dinner, even though no other relatives are able to visit this year. We obsess over pie recipes like our lives depend on it, and Dad tries to sneak in the house with a pre-smoked turkey like it's Thanksgiving morning, hoping to trick us into thinking he did it himself. Part of me feels like I've gone through a time machine and my life has reset ten years earlier. The other part of me is ashamed that I'd even want that.

I made a mess of things in LA, but that's my real life. That's where I belong. And as nice as this break is, I need to spend time figuring things out. After the bulk of the cooking frenzy dies down, I sit on my twin bed and answer every email in my inbox. Letting people know that I will no longer be managing the Matthews makes a lump form in my throat, because what now? I add to the end of each message that I will forward my new contact information when I've settled at a new job.

Through the regret and the confusion, one idea sticks around. At first, I ignore it because it scares the hell out of me, but the longer I sit in my childhood bedroom, the more intriguing the idea becomes. Seventeen-year-old Kell would never have dreamt that she'd even know a movie star, much less be instrumental in getting them roles. So why not dream bigger and show that starry-eyed version of myself that I can do hard things?

With my laptop still open, I start a new spreadsheet and then send out several emails. It's time to start building a team and seeing how much I'm willing to risk for a fresh start.

I work over the next day until my hands start to cramp from the constant typing, and then I keep going. Mom cracks open my door and says my name. "Dad got the pumpkins."

As tempting as it is to roll my eyes and tell her how busy I am, I stand. It's been years since I've participated in Dad's pre-birthday pumpkin carving tradition. When I go to the front porch, the morning chill bites at my skin through my thin pajamas. A misty rain has started to pepper the ground, but we stand out there anyway. Dad produces three round, bright-orange pumpkins with a flourish. My chest hurts when I realize he got me my own. It's a good thing I didn't say I was too busy.

"What are you carving this year?" Mom tries to peek at Dad's masterpiece, but he angles it away, a sparkle in his eye. Another part of the tradition. The carvings are an absolute secret until tomorrow,

Dad's birthday. As a kid, what I really wanted was for my parents to hurry up with the shenanigans and let me go trick-or-treating with everyone else on our street. Now a thread of shame curls around me at the memory. All Dad wanted to do was share his birthday with me, and he always made sure to be done well before dark.

"I'm trying out something new," I announce, trying to match the teasing in Dad's voice as I inch my pumpkin from their view.

His answering smile is worth a lot.

I pull up an image on my phone and sketch lightly with a pencil until I've got a crude likeness of my parents, their arms around each other. Yes, it's cheesy. But they've welcomed me home with open arms and no questions asked. I figure I can throw them a bone. That, and I do love the two weirdos, like, a lot.

We end the day with a family dinner out to Burger Hopp, the place just down the road from our neighborhood. My parents have gone there on the weekends for as long as I can remember. When I sink into an only slightly sticky booth across from them and take my first bite in years, everything tastes exactly how I remember it. If I were to close my eyes, it feels like I could transport myself back to sixteen-year-old Kell. I'd just gotten my braces off and wore my retainer religiously, even during the day even though the orthodontist assured me it wasn't necessary. I had my future mapped out: college, clubs, and then a career in LA where I'd be a boss lady, working until I proved myself.

What I'd give for a peek into what that overly ambitious teenager thinks of this version of me. She'd be thrilled with the numb, exhausted Kell of last month. The woman who couldn't even stop to take important medication on time. But what about this? This woman who's out to dinner with Mom and Dad just like old times and actually savoring every slow-moving, mundane second?

CHAPTER FORTY-ONE

✿ ✿ ✿ ✿ ✿

Kell

*T*he first week in November my parents go to a work dinner after failing to convince me to come along. I may be a sad, pathetic mess, but I'm not so low that I'm going to start following them around just for free cookies. Besides, I have real work to deal with now that my ideas are beginning to bear fruit. Also, I have all the cookies I want at home thanks to the new ritual Mom and I have of baking together on the weekends.

With the house to myself, I wander around in my pajamas making notes in the little notebook I found in my closet. Things are coming together easier than I imagined, and even though I'm terrified of another failure, a new career that pushes me to the brink of myself, I'm ready to take the risk. I snag a plate of Dad's favorite chocolate chunk cookies before settling on the couch and losing myself in planning.

The doorbell rings and I glance at the clock, surprised to see that so much time has passed already. Mom promised she'd bring me back something to eat after the party, and my stomach grumbles as I remember. I stuff the rest of the last cookie into my mouth and hurry to the door.

"Coming!" I slide through the front hallway in my socks, laughing at myself. It's been years since I felt so carefree. Maybe I should have quit my job earlier. When I start back to work, I'm not going to let things get so dire. I'm not going to work myself to sickness, eyes closing at red lights just so I can grab thirty extra seconds of sleep. I'm going to make room for happiness. I have to.

I unlock the door and my mouth goes dry. Ash stands there in the early winter drizzle, hands tucked into the pockets of his navy-blue topcoat. "Kell," he says, his voice warm despite the temperature outside.

"What—what are you doing here?"

He ducks his head and steps inside, rubbing his hands together as the warm air hits him. I gape, my mouth permanently open with shock.

Seeing Ash standing in my parents' living room is akin to watching a giant polar bear wander through the LA Fashion District. It doesn't make sense. It doesn't match up.

Ash swallows, working his jaw as he presumably tries to think of what to say.

"Did my parents call you?" I blurt. Suddenly it comes together—the convenient timing of their work party and Mom's insistence on me trying her new makeup. I've officially been home too long if I'm so easily worked over.

"No." Ash shakes his head fervently. "No, they didn't. I called them. You told Jonah that you were going out of town for a while, so I guessed that you'd be here."

I sigh. "If you had a work question you could have just said that it was important. I would have responded." I don't know if that's necessarily true, but I'd like to think it is. After all, I don't have any reason to hate Ash or avoid him. We're at an impasse, wanting to be together but unable to make it work. To keep talking like we did before is just asking for more hurt.

The frown between his eyes deepens. "I wanted to see you. Wanted to make sure you're okay."

Something tells me he didn't cross state lines to check on me, but I answer anyway.

"It's been a lot. I've never taken a break this long. I went straight from high school to the summer semester of college and straight from college into managing." I force out a laugh that I don't feel at all. "Who knew that there were this many free hours in a day? I'm figuring things out." I'm not quite ready to tell anyone aside from my parents what I'll be doing next, but Ash will hear eventually, I'm sure.

"I've been hanging out with my parents *a lot,* so just ignore me if I sound like I'm fifty-five instead of twenty-five." If I keep talking to fill the silence, there won't be room for anything else. For whatever Ash really came here for.

Ash doesn't laugh, doesn't even crack a smile. He just watches me with this eerie sort of patience. I have no idea what he's waiting for, given he's the one who showed up unannounced. Suddenly he steps closer. He lifts a hand like he might touch me, then leaves it hanging there in the air between us.

"I never sought out Norman. I want you to know that. Ryan set up a meeting and asked Jonah and me to come. Once I realized what was going on, I left. Told them all in no uncertain terms that I wasn't doing it." He sighs. "But I started to entertain the thought. Once I saw that you weren't happy in the job like you used to be." He sways slightly on his feet.

When I stare at him in silence, Ash closes his eyes and releases a slow, weighty breath. "I don't want to do this without you, Kell." His hand settles on my cheek. Despite the chill of his skin from being out in the cold, there's a rush of warmth.

I deflate. All the fast-talking energy whooshes out of me, and just like that, it's replaced by a shaky fear. I'm not prepared for this conversation.

My body refuses to agree with my head and I nuzzle into his hand. "Is that why you're here?" I swallow. "I don't know how to fix us."

I'm not sure if we're talking about our working or romantic relationship, but my answer stands for both. I still can't see a way forward, for us both to get what we deserve, no matter how badly I want to.

Ash opens his mouth like he's going to keep talking—

The door pulls open. Mom and Dad wear twin faces of fake surprise that quickly shift to pleased. No one can convince me that they didn't know he was coming. "Ash!" Mom wraps him in a hug and Dad swats his arm in a friendly way.

They're terrible actors, and I want to tell them so, but I can't bear to make this any more uncomfortable than it already is. I step back to put distance between us. This is too much, too much everything. Vaguely, I hear Mom insisting Ash stay the night to avoid traveling in this weather. My breath catches and my eyes snap back to attention. Ash looks right at me as he shakes his head. "I wish I could, but I need to get going. I flew up for a meeting in Seattle, so I figured I'd stop by here and say hi first."

He goes, giving me one last long, searching look. If he wants something from me, he doesn't say. He hurries away to whatever meeting he has in the city, and I pace the kitchen. Then I grab a green apple from the fridge and sit at the table. I snap my teeth into the apple.

Mom comes in and sits next to me. She rubs my arm. "Are you okay?" She doesn't know the specifics, but she knows that Ash has something to do with my coming home in the first place.

"I've felt better." I set my apple aside.

"Ash flew into Seattle, huh?" she asks softly.

I shrug. "I guess so. I didn't even know he knew anyone in Washington other than me." There's so much I should have said to him, and now I have no idea when my next chance to talk in person will be.

Mom tilts her head. "And he drove an hour out of his way to *stop by*?"

I give her a look. "Well," she says, "regardless, Dad and I have talked it over, and we're willing to convert the guest bedroom into an office. Maybe you can work remotely for a while, until you feel sure about things. You can stay at home as long as you need." She squeezes my hand. "It's an option."

It is an option. One that crazily doesn't sound half bad. I could see myself settling here, living quietly and slowly and embracing Friday nights at Burger Hopp. I could maybe reconnect with friends from high school and form a new routine, a new life. Instead of just Christmases and birthdays I could be here for all the holidays, all the old traditions.

But even though I've promised myself that I'll embrace *some* more time off, at the end of the day I love the hustle. I miss working hard on a contract and gaining that long-worked-for satisfaction of seeing it through.

And, fine, there is a not-so-small part of me that wants to return to my old life. I know I can't fix things with the Matthews completely, but maybe there are some relationships there that can be salvaged. I hope there are. Ash came to my parents' house to see me, whether it was out of his way or not. That means something, and it's hard not to hope.

Maybe not right away, but someday, Ash and I could figure out how to make our lives fit together. Even if I have to settle for only being his friend and nothing else.

And that's how I know—it's time for me to get back to my real life in LA.

✿ ✿ ✿ ✿ ✿

Saying goodbye to my parents is more emotional than I could have imagined. Somehow, they are dry-eyed and completely composed, and I am the one sucking back tears as I hug them on the front porch of my childhood home. Mom strokes my hair. She pulls back and smiles. "Kell, you're going to do great. You always make us so proud. And we're here when you need us."

I nod a wobbly response.

Dad pats my back. He says low in my ear, "You belong out there. That's where you shine."

That doesn't help things at all. By the time I'm in my car and turning onto the freeway, I can barely see the road ahead of me. I swipe away the tears like a human windshield wiper and steel my shoulders.

They'll visit again next month, so it's not the missing them that has me so emotional. It's the knowledge that for all the crap they give me, they truly have my back one hundred percent. For all their complaining over the years about my career, they've always been there to talk to, to lean on. It's somehow very similar to my own role, managing and supporting the Matthews. And going forward, managing a different group of new professionals.

CHAPTER FORTY-TWO

✿ ✿ ✿ ✿ ✿

Kell

*T*he spiral staircase to my new office is nowhere near as intimidating as it should be. Nothing is—not even the new faces, each of them watching me intently. They all look at me like I'm supposed to know the answers. I guess that makes sense, given I'm the boss. Starting a talent agency where I can function behind the scenes never occurred to me until the moment I realized that an ideal job would let me further actors' careers without ever seeing my face on the front page of a newspaper again. I loved the work I did in the early years for the Matthews. The struggle, the high hopes and the lows that pushed us through, it all made me feel like I was doing something very worthwhile. And I've hired a small team of new managers-to-be that want all of those same things. Together we're going to find fresh talent, people who just need a chance and deserve someone who won't give up on their dreams.

Getting here was not easy but it was never, not for one second, debilitating. The difference going forward is that I can put my organizational skills to use and let that part of myself thrive. I can pass on my knowledge of how the industry works without finding myself stuck in the day-to-day drama. It's a new challenge, one that I'm ready to face.

Coordinating over email and video calls hasn't been easy, but Claudette went above and beyond scouting the location for me and even hosting a few face-to-face interviews when I couldn't decide over the internet alone. That's another thing I'm learning to do: ask for help. Hopefully my mental and physical health are better for it.

My desk faces a big window with a view of a stretch of palm trees and then farther out, the highway. It makes me smile. So does the array of well-wishing flowers that were waiting for me when I sat down. I've been in training meetings all day, but now that it's late afternoon, I take the time to look at what's been sent. My parents sent roses and Claudette sent an eclectic bouquet of all different colors and types of flowers. I look over the fruit basket on my desk surrounded by cheerful yellow gerbera daisies before finding a tag reading *Friends first. Good luck at your new job. Love, Ash.*

Ash.

Tears prick at my eyes and the words on the gift tag swim in front of me. We've talked some since his visit to my parents' house last month. He had a question about one of his past contracts last week, asking if I could send the information to Norman. Afterward, I told him about my new job. He texted to say that he'd gotten a role in the Great Depression-era film he'd been auditioning for. We've kept in touch but never let the conversation linger, never gone past the most basic of pleasantries.

I miss him.

Admitting it even in my own head is hard. Because if I admit how deeply I miss Ash, what does that mean? We tried the relationship thing, and it didn't go so well. We weren't on the same page about work or publicity, and I messed it all up by quitting on him when it got hard. With how I left things, I'm not sure he's up for friendship, even with this gesture. I'd be stupid to assume that all of that is fixable, or that one good luck fruit basket means he's even still open to trying.

But maybe I'd be equally stupid not to try and see.

I push back from my desk.

It's my first day of work, but I've just decided that I have somewhere to be. Work doesn't have to be all there is to my life. I have to think about my heart—and my health too. And first, I need to stop by Claudette's apartment for something to wear. I leave with instructions for my new, eager managers, telling them to finish the contracts they're drafting and to go home early too.

Claudette meets me at the door of her apartment with a mischievous grin. "Well, well, well, what are you doing here at four p.m.? Don't you have an entire office to run now?"

Heart hammering in my chest I shake my head. "I know it's last minute, but do you have anything that fits me?"

Claudette waves me inside. "I'm offended that you even have to ask." She pulls her hand from behind her back and shoves a finished dress in front of me. I clap a hand to my mouth, in awe of her. It's pink with little cherries and makes me just as happy as the first time I saw this fabric.

"Who is this for?" I ask, cautious in my hope. "You said you would save the fabric for me." Finding this fabric and fantasizing about wearing it someday feels like years ago.

She rolls her eyes. "I did save it for you. I used your measurements from the last dress and made this one a few weeks ago." She lifts a shoulder. "I thought you might be in need of something special to wear sometime soon."

"You did this for me?" I take the fabric-turned-dress in my hands and marvel at it. Claudette deserves the world for sticking with me through it all.

Claudette pushes me inside. "Try it on and then you can get all mushy."

While I get dressed, Claudette fixes me with an unnerving stare until I turn, eyes wide. "What? Do I look stupid? Is my butt hanging out?"

She glares at me, throwing a wad of fabric. "No! I was patient with you when you didn't want to talk about Ash for almost two months. And I let you show up here and wear your dress without asking questions, but are you planning on filling me in? What changed, Kell?"

I look at Claudette and groan. She's right. "I'm sorry that I didn't talk to you first," I say, coming over to give her a hug. "Nothing changed, exactly, except I guess I did? I realized today that Ash and I didn't work the first time around because of me. First I didn't want to ruin our friendship and then I didn't want to wind up in another tabloid. And then I got my feelings hurt over work stuff. But it was just excuses. And now—now I guess I'm realizing that I want to be with Ash more than I care about all that other stuff."

Claudette puckers her lower lip. "That's so sappy but I love it. What are you going to do about it?"

I stand straighter and look at myself in the stand-up mirror in the corner of the room. The dress is perfect, just like I imagined it would be. It makes me feel feminine and brave at the same time. And it's the perfect thing to wear for what I'm about to do.

"I'm going to make sure Ash knows how I feel, and then it's up to him."

CHAPTER FORTY-THREE

❀ ❀ ❀ ❀ ❀

Kell

"*I*'m surprised to hear from you, I have to say."

The voice over the phone makes me want to roll my eyes on muscle memory alone, but I suppress the urge.

"I'm surprised to be calling you," I admit. I thought my days of calling Judith Holmes and asking for favors were over.

She sounds nothing but chipper. What I'm starting to realize is that there was never any true rivalry between us, just two different ways of working. Judith is me thirty years from now if I never took a break.

But maybe she never needed it like I did, maybe she functions differently and has never stopped thriving on the chaos. "Truthfully," she says, "I'm honored to help you. I hope you know that there are no ill feelings on my side from what happened. I never meant for any of it to be anything other than a good business decision."

I take a breath. "I do know that. Thank you. It's fine, Judith." It's easier to see now that I have the distance. Maybe none of them, except Ash, went about it the right way, but it was a career move and one that we all should have discussed.

After hanging up with Judith, I get in my car and try to breathe. Inhale. Exhale. Inhale again just for good measure. I've done a lot of brave things in the past few weeks, but matters of the heart are scarier than anything else. Keeping things bottled up is the easy way out, I know that now. What terrifies me the most is whether or not it's taken me too long to learn this lesson.

When I pull up to the Matthews' house, a crew of camera people surround the outdoor patio. It's a pretty winter night, still sunny enough to give the evening a soft kind of glow. I note with pride the bigger crew, more expensive-looking equipment, and larger cast gathered. They did it. They went from tentatively dipping their toes into the waters of reality television to fully embracing a second season.

And all the guys are better off for it. From various sources, I've been able to gather that Ryan has the big role he'd been gunning for, Ash has his serious films, and Jonah was moved to another, less family-friendly network where he can let loose a bit more. Maybe I am better off too, in a roundabout way. I am definitely feeling more optimistic for the future now that I've jump-started my career.

Season one of the guys' show is currently running. Only a few episodes in and people are loving it. The buzz online is proof enough that the next seasons will be wildly successful. Of course it makes sense, with how attractive the Matthews are, the fact that they all live together, and the never-lacking drama. The episodes practically write themselves.

I've managed to avoid watching any episodes, but I haven't been able to escape notice from fans. It's been okay though. No one has been too overwhelming, and it's been fun to confirm that yes, I really do know the Matthews in real life. Questions about the status of Ash's and my relationship are more difficult to answer. But facing my fears in that way has gotten me to this point, where I've realized I want Ash Matthew enough to handle a little healthy publicity.

The marker snaps and the camera crew starts following behind Ryan and Jonah. I can just make them out from my hiding spot behind a tall potted fern. They're talking about Ryan's birthday, making plans for a big party thrown at the house. I can't help it. I smile to myself at the sight of both of them. They were a big part of my life. Even Ryan, who has always conflicted me. I'm happy that he's doing well. I'm also really, really happy that I have no part in that. When I walked away, I realized we never even had a friendship, so without my feelings for him, there was nothing left. And maybe even more surprising was the fact that I'm not bothered by that at all.

And then my heart leaps into my throat and stays there. Ash. He rounds the corner, phone in hand. Jonah stops him and says something that I can't quite catch. My hands shake. Ash is beautiful. His hair is unruly and dark, and I itch to run my hands through it. The need to touch him altogether is overwhelming, and I can barely breathe through the wanting.

Ash walks toward me, a slight frown on his lips. He still can't see me because of the plant, but I can see him perfectly, and everything about him makes me *ache*. His eyes, which are the exact color of the sky right now, catch on the plant and he sputters as he finally sees me in my hiding spot.

"Hey—what?"

I step out, hands by my side in a truce pose. The reveal is not the big, dramatic, heartfelt scene I had in my head. It's nothing but pure awkward tension. I stand in front of Ash and try to locate my tongue so I can say *something*. Just, anything.

Ryan and Jonah are there in the background watching us. Everyone is watching us. Somewhere in the back of my head I acknowledge that this is good TV, and I hate that because this is my real life. These are my real, naked feelings.

"What are you doing here?" He crosses his arms over his chest. The way he looks at me doesn't say heartfelt.

I shake my head. The heat from the lights draws a bead of sweat down the small of my back.

"I'm here to see you."

"Why?"

I brush away lingering fern leaves and step closer to Ash. "Because I need to apologize for walking away from you. And for ending both our relationships—fake and real."

Ash already said his piece when he came to my parents' house, but I didn't tell him how sorry I was to see us end. He wasn't the only one at fault. We both made mistakes and choices that ended what was a great relationship. Being honest with myself, it was the greatest relationship I've ever had.

"And because I didn't handle anything that happened in the past month very well at all. I not only walked away from you professionally, but in other ways too." My chest heaves with a giant intake of breath. "I wanted to say that I'm so, so sorry."

Sending over the audio of our breakup is something that I've regretted every day since. It was rash and hurtful, but most of all it was petty. That was me desperate for a reason to end things so that I could avoid confronting my own feelings. That was the me I hope I've left behind.

The main camera pans in on me, and I can see the reflection of my own bated breath staring back. I look into Ash's eyes and they're warm, just like in my memories.

I want him to hold me, to not care who's watching and kiss me until I'm dizzy. Instead, he keeps me at arm's distance. "When you left without even saying goodbye, it kind of broke me, Kell. I thought we were doing something real. And then you acted like it didn't mean the same things to you." He swallows hard, his throat bobbing. "It felt like you were making excuses not to be with me."

Like a slap, his words cause a physical reaction. My chin wobbles. I never considered that it would feel like I gave up on him. To me, it was a mutually failed relationship. He wanted more exposure and I wanted less, so what else was there for us?

"I never meant for you to feel that way," I say through choked words. "I thought I was doing the easier thing for both of us. It wasn't though." I shake my head. "It was so hard being without you, Ash. And I never want to do that again, if you'll forgive me and let us please, just start over?"

I look at him and want to go back in time and fix everything. I breathe in through my nose to brace myself. "I love you. And it's okay if you don't feel that way about me anymore, but I had to tell you."

A long, painful string of seconds passes. Then Ash's lips crack into a smile and the next thing I know he is scooping me up and carrying me away from the cameras. He sets me down in the circle drive, where a row of cars, including mine, are parked off camera. "Say that again," he says, leaning into me.

"I love you." It's easier to say every time the words leave my lips. It's like breathing properly for the first time in my life, like coming up from underwater and appreciating dry land all over again.

I barely speak before Ash bends to kiss me, his arms pulling me up to meet him. Kissing him is like muscle memory, and my heart and my body know exactly what to do. I melt into him, my hands on his back, his hands on my waist. With a breath, I break off the kiss and frown at him. There's something I've wondered about for weeks. "Wait. What about your meeting in Seattle? What was it for?"

Ash's eyes crinkle at the edges. He tips his head forward and laughs, his shoulders shaking.

"What's so funny?" I frown back at him, not following the joke. I've wondered a lot about Seattle and what could have taken him there. The only reason I never asked before was because it didn't feel like I had a right to pry anymore.

"Kell. There was no meeting in Seattle. I didn't want you to think I was so desperate to see you that I'd fly to Washington just to talk to you for an hour." He shrugs. "But I was. I thought if I could just see you then maybe . . ."

Ash's lips quirk. "I should have known it wouldn't change things." But it did, and the fact that he went to such lengths just to see me confirms everything I've been feeling since then. "I wasn't ready then to admit how much you mean to me, but I am now."

I suck in a bracing breath. "I am in love with you, Ash. I have been for months—years, probably—and I only let myself start believing it after you came to my parents' house."

I shake my head. "I had things I needed to figure out for myself. It was never about you, it was about me. Does that make sense?"

He takes both of my hands and wraps them in his. Ash looks at me and I can't look away. I don't want to. "It makes sense. I love you. I love you so much. I'm so sorry about ever meeting with Norman. I'm sorry for the cameras and everything else that comes with my career. I wish there was some way to keep you out of it."

I shake my head. "I'm here because I've decided it doesn't matter more than you do." I gesture to the crew now surrounding us, unable to leave a juicy moment alone in hopes of getting usable audio at the very least. None of it scares me anymore because I was without Ash, and I realized that losing someone I love is much scarier.

"Let's figure out what this means for us," I tell him. I'm willing to meet him wherever he's comfortable. As long as Ash is in my life again, as long as he *loves me,* I feel like anything is possible.

Ash kisses me so hard that a flush washes over my body. We're still on camera, I have to remind myself. "I'm free on weekends," he offers with a cheeky smile.

"What a coincidence," I say, "I am too. Do you have plans Friday night?"

CHAPTER FORTY-FOUR

❊ ❊ ❊ ❊ ❊

Ash

"*L*et's go over this again."

Kell loops her arm through mine and smiles up at me. Best smile ever, every time. Hard to believe I'm the lucky guy who gets to see her face daily.

"You're going to be fine." I kiss the top of her head.

A bustle of reporters hurry past the corner we're tucked into. Red carpet premieres are no joke. Especially for this movie. The Depression-era drama that I've busted my ass over the past eight months is finally ready for public viewing. I'm not even nervous. Never been so sure of work that I've done. It's a really good movie, no matter what reviewers decide to say.

"I don't want to embarrass you," she argues. She adjusts the straps on the bright red dress Claudette made her. She's gorgeous and could never embarrass me. Premieres are a big deal in my world, but I'd never ask her to be here if she didn't want to. I wouldn't be here without her in the first place and that's enough for me.

"Do you want to meet me at the after-party? I don't mind doing this part alone."

Kell's lips part. "No, don't you dare do this without me. I want to be here. I'm ready." She throws her shoulders back and squeezes my hand.

Lights flash around us and we stand closer together as photos snap. We move down the carpet. A reporter hurries over. "Ash, congrats on your movie's box office numbers so far. How are you feeling?"

"I'm excited. Really proud of this movie. Mostly thrilled to be here with my girlfriend." I gesture to Kell, who beams. She's been my girlfriend since the moment she showed up at my house and told me she loved me. Six months have flown by.

The reporter tilts toward Kell. She leans forward to the offered mic but looks up at me. "I'm so happy to be here supporting Ash. He has been working toward this movie for a while, and he deserves all the success. He's amazing."

She keeps insisting that she's not good at this sort of thing, but as far as I'm concerned, she's perfect. Watching her makes me want to take off these stupid fancy clothes and go home. Holding Kell is better than any of this. My hand finds her waist. I lean down, my lips brushing her ear. "Let's get out of here."

She laughs softly. "No way. We're not leaving until we get the full red carpet premiere experience."

I grit my teeth. "It's not that fun. Let's go home and I'll show you fun."

Kell swats me with the back of her hand. She's still laughing at me. "Maybe later. Let's watch my new favorite movie," she says, pulling me with her to the front of the theater.

I'm supposed to be watching the screen, but I've already seen the finished product. Instead, I watch for Kell's reaction. She laughs at my favorite moments. Cries freely when my character's sister dies. Looks tortured when my character hasn't eaten a meal in a week.

Afterward, the theater breaks into applause, and Kell leans her head on my shoulder. "This fits you," she says softly. "I see what you meant by wanting this. You were amazing, Ash."

My eyes prick at her praise. Kell's opinion is the one that matters most. I didn't want her to feel pressured, but I've been waiting to hear what she thinks for almost a year. I kiss the top of her head. "Thank you," is all I can manage.

"We're going to the after-party." She stands with her hands on her hips. I can tell she's trying to look fierce, but it's just cute.

We can party somewhere else. I've already given gifts to the cast and crew and said my goodbyes. "We're not," I say. "We're going home."

Kell loves her apartment and doesn't want to live with my brothers. Can't blame her. We've started calling her apartment home, though I haven't officially moved in. She laughs when I say it now. "No, we're definitely going to the after-party first. You've earned the right to be celebrated, and I'm not letting you skip out."

She laces her fingers with mine and leads us through the theater. Makes small talk with as many people as we pass. When we're finally at the car, Kell sidles up to me. Stands on her toes to kiss my mouth. "I'm so proud of you," she says.

"I'm looking forward to my next movie. Heard the cast is A-plus." I raise an eyebrow, teasing. Kell's agency has cast two of the characters alongside me in my next period piece. She's doing amazing. Not that there was ever any doubt.

Kell nuzzles closer to me. I rub the back of her dress. "Maybe it's okay if we skip the party," she says. "If you really don't care."

"I don't." We get in the car, and I drive us toward her apartment, but she puts a hand on my knee. "Let's stop by your house first." I groan and give her a look that tells her how impatient I am to be alone, but she grins. "Trust me."

We walk into a darkened house. No one home on a Saturday night. My brothers have been spending more time together. Honestly,

I think it's good for both of them, especially since Jonah and Jessie have been "off" for a few months now. He seems lonely. And Ryan is Ryan. Maybe he's lonely or maybe just doing his own thing. It's hard to tell.

But the dark doesn't bother me. No need to bother with light switches. I pull Kell close. Press her against the kitchen wall. My hands reach for her ass—

The lights blink on and my brother groans. "Bro."

Jonah shakes his head, setting down the chocolate cake he's balancing in one hand. "That's inappropriate."

Ryan cracks a grin, too, but says nothing about Kell. He's taken to giving her distance. "Congrats on your movie, little brother."

Kell buries her head in the crook of my shoulder, her body moving with silent laughter. She lifts her head. "Surprise?" she says weakly.

I take her hand in mine and squeeze, turning to my brothers and the cake. "This is for me?"

Jonah slides the cake across the island. It wobbles dangerously close to the edge. "Made it ourselves."

Kell laughs again.

"Okay. We bought it," Jonah admits with a smile that says he doesn't mind being caught in the lie.

"Thank you. All of you." Kell slices the cake and hands it out, and it's a rare moment when all the people I care about are in one room. Getting along and everything. Managing the Matthews used to be Kell's job. Now we kind of manage ourselves. We're figuring it out.

But with Kell and me there's nothing to figure out. I'm just glad I finally convinced her that she and I were worth fighting for. After all the drama to get to where we are, the rest has been easy enough.

She bumps me with her hip and slides a bit of chocolate icing into her mouth with her finger. "Were you surprised? At least a little bit?"

My throat feels tight. "I was. I love you, you know."

"Oh, I know." Kell beams.

I watch her lick more icing from her fingers and bite my tongue. Forget cake and anything else. I can't wait to be alone with her.

CHAPTER FORTY-FIVE

❀ ❀ ❀ ❀ ❀

Kell

"Come here." Ash puts a hand on the small of my back and leads me out of the kitchen and down the hall.

"Where are we going?" I whisper, looking back at his brothers, who are all of a sudden completely wrapped up in a conversation of their own and refusing to make eye contact with me.

Ash opens the door and pulls me into his bedroom. He looks at me with serious, hooded eyes. "We're coming here. To be alone. Finally."

I sit on the end of his bed and smile up at him, my head tilted to the side. "What's the rush? I was enjoying the cake."

Teasing Ash never gets old, and neither does the shake of his head combined with a rush of pink creeping along his face. Not working together means that the only expectations in our relationship are the ones we set ourselves.

It's nice to know that whatever we do, whatever we say, it's real and it's just for us.

He stands in front of me, caging my body with his legs so I have to crane my neck to see him. "The rush," he says, reaching to put a hand softly to my face, "is that we spent all day doing other things, and now I want to focus on only you."

It's hard logic to argue against. My tongue sits heavy in my mouth, and I gaze back at him with matched intensity. I can't believe I get to kiss this man. Even better, I can't believe that he loves me as much as I love him. "That sounds nice," I say.

Ash bends down to kiss me, and I melt against him, letting my head fall back onto the bed. He sinks on top of me, rolling us farther onto the mattress before deepening the kiss. His hands find my hips.

With my hands cradling his face, we kiss until everything else blurs and pulls away. We could be in another country, at the opposite end of the world, and I wouldn't know, not when I'm so wrapped up in him like this.

Finally, we sigh and break the kiss, still in each other's arms. I blink at the blank wall opposite his bed. And then at the too-tidy corners of the big, empty room. A bed and a dresser are all he has. His room looks like nothing more than a prop. My stomach sinks.

"Ash?"

"Hmm?" His eyes are half closed, his fingers tangled in my hair and absentmindedly stroking the tip of my ear.

"Your bedroom is empty. You don't have anything in here."

He opens his eyes and looks around like he's not sure what I'm talking about. Then he shrugs. "I don't need anything. I have stuff at your apartment and whatever else I need is in my top drawer." He gestures to the dresser across the room.

I roll over until I'm sitting up with my legs tucked underneath me. My eyes widen as I voice a thought that's been sitting in the back of my head. "What if we find a new place together?"

Ash shakes his head. He sits up next to me. "You love your apartment."

"I love *you*. I want to live with *you*. And you've been spending so much time at my place that you clearly don't even treat this like your home anymore."

He's quiet for a moment, his body still as he thinks it over. "Are you sure? I don't mind staying at your place, Kell. It's enough room for now."

I take Ash's hand in mine. "I'm sure. It's a good idea, right? We should have a place that's both of ours. Preferably somewhere that fits us both."

"Okay." Ash nods, lighting up. This is a big step, but one I'm sure we're ready for. "Let's look for a new apartment."

"This is exciting." I raise my brows and grin at him. "Should we start packing now? What do you want to take with you?" I look around his room for anything worth bringing to a new space, mentally calculating how much square footage we will need for the two of us.

Ash says nothing, only laughs and brings a hand to my chin. "I think we have time to figure that out."

I have to appreciate his ability not to let anything sidetrack him. His gaze is unmistakable, unwavering. My throat tightens as I meet his eyes.

I kiss him, pulling our bodies together again. Together, we can figure anything out. After all, he's my best friend and with us it's friendship first, always.

ACKNOWLEDGMENTS

✿ ✿ ✿ ✿ ✿

*T*hank you to my husband, Mark Wenger, for helping me talk through ideas as I drafted. And then again as I tried desperately to fix plot holes. You're the best and you're stuck forever as my official idea man.

Thank you to my incredible critique partners and friends who helped me turn the first starts of this book into something readable.

Jessica Hall—you listened to so many unhinged Marco Polo ramblings about these characters, and this is why you're one of my best friends, not to mention one of the readers I trust the most. Thank you for loving Ash and Kell.

A huge thank you to Brielle Porter for reading a pitiful early draft of this book and still cheering me on and finding the good in this story. Your feedback, as always, is invaluable. I can't wait to see where your publishing journey takes you next!

Sarah Barkoff Palma, thank goodness for Write Mentor for letting us meet. Thank you for always being there to talk about books and publishing and for your feedback on early chapters of this book.

Audrey Lancho, thank you for your amazing notes and encouragement.

Thank you to my wonderful agent, Colleen Ofelein, for taking a chance on me and this book. Your support means the world to me. I can't wait to sell more books together and continue this partnership!

To the team at CamCat Books, I can't say enough good things about this publishing experience. It has been a dream, and I'm so grateful to Sue Arroyo for taking on my book and welcoming me to the CamCat family.

Helga Schier, your editing expertise has helped me turn this book into what I always hoped it would be. Thank you for your insight on LA and the industry as well as your guidance on richer worldbuilding. I've loved our time working together.

Thank you so much, Kayla Webb for editing this book and for championing and swooning over Kell and Ash the whole way through. Your notes on relationship development helped make them stronger, and I'm so thankful for the push to make them better. I feel so lucky to have worked with you.

Thank you to Penni Askew for your attention to detail and insight in copyediting. I so appreciate your work.

I would be remiss to not mention the wonderful artist who worked on my cover, Laura Duffy. Thank you for bringing Kell to life and making her look so good!

Lastly, a big hug of gratitude for my readers. I had so much fun writing this book, and I'm thrilled to have the chance to share it with you.

ABOUT THE AUTHOR

❀ ❀ ❀ ❀ ❀

*H*aleigh Wenger is an avid romance reader. Her debut young adult novel, *The Art of Falling in Love*, was published in 2019. Her most recent novel, *A Feeling Like Home*, released in 2021. It is the recipient of the Texas Author Project award for the same year. *Managing the Matthews* is her adult romance debut. When not writing or reading, Haleigh is chasing around her five young kids or baking cookies, sometimes both at the same time.

If you liked
Haleigh Wenger's *Managing the Matthews*,
we hope you will consider leaving
a review to help our authors.

Also check out
Roma Cordon's *Bewitching a Highlander*.

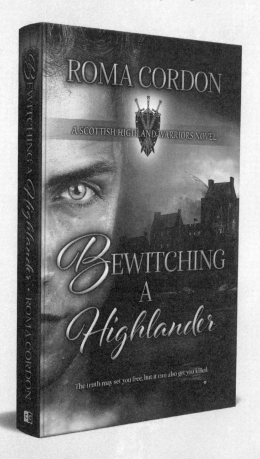

CHAPTER
1

"You have witchcraft in your lips . . ."
—William Shakespeare, *Henry V.*

October 28, 1747—Isle of Coll, Scotland

*B*reena MacRae's heart beat out of tune from the cacophony of their wagon's rattling. Sixteen horse hooves trampled the knurled road, pulling them southwest toward the Campbells' keep, a clan she blamed for most of her childhood miseries.

Three weeks ago, she'd awoken from nineteen years of delusions, yet it was no less painful living the truth. Her parents had neither died in some horrific accident nor left because of her. Breena was after all the most deplorable witch the MacRaes and Maxwells ever had the lamentable fortune to beget.

Uncle Craig leaned over and gave her shoulder a gentle squeeze. The clumsy yet affectionate gesture grounded her. It rid her of her punishing thoughts.

"We aught to go over the plan again."

She would always be obliged to him and Aunt Madeline. They'd been her guardians since she was six, although many times since then, despite the fact that she loved them both with all her heart, they'd made her want to either scream or blaspheme.

Sometimes both.

His familiar features reminded her of her mother's, his little sister.

"All right, but understanding the need to lie doesn't make it any less difficult," she said.

"Difficult it may be, but it will keep us alive."

She huffed. He was too cautious. Or was she not cautious enough?

Breena blinked up as the afternoon sun reconsidered slipping past horizontal puffs of clouds.

Mayhap she herself should reconsider her decision to come here.

No. Even if there was a remote possibility her father was alive, she had to attempt to find him. She had to free him. Her heart ached for all he must have endured. She'd believed him dead for the past nineteen years, until three weeks ago, when lovable yet scatterbrained Aunt Madeline had let slip the truth.

After suffering from dysentery and a bout of guilt, her aunt had blurted out that Ian might still be alive. Had Aunt Madeline known she wasn't at death's door, she might have been more steadfast in her secrecy. Craig and Madeline had insisted her parents wanted the truth kept from her all this time. The secrecy and deception might have been the stimulant for her childhood misery, but it hadn't been the cause. Nonetheless, it had resulted in long, wasted years.

Her dream from the previous night replayed in her mind. Beloved Grandmother Sorcha, their majestic matriarch, had told her Ian had something to reveal. If Breena believed dreams were a sign of things to come, then it was a sign her father was indeed alive. But she didn't know if she believed in dreams. After all, she lacked the gift of second sight.

The revered Sorcha on the other hand wielded her own gift of sight like a true proficient, when she was alive.

A chilled hollowness speared her innards, causing a shiver to run up her spine. It had been her tormentor since she was six. Often she paused and wondered what had slipped her mind, what she had forgotten—perhaps she'd missed something.

Then it would hit her. She hadn't missed anything, hadn't forgotten anything, nothing had slipped her mind. It was only that her parents had vanished, without a word, leaving an acute aching void. She pulled her woolen arisaid tighter around her shoulders and prayed not only that their scheme would work on the Campbells but that she could rid herself of this ache in the pit of her belly, once and for all.

She gazed out the wagon as the panoply that was the Isle of Coll rolled by. The crisp October breeze swept her cheeks as she eyed the chestnut-feathered corncrakes scavenging the beachgrass-infested sand dunes. Nature's russets, umbers, and olives, always vibrant at home on the Isle of Skye, were starved for luster here on Coll.

A lone angler in the distance slumped his shoulders in a small skiff, then gazed up at the sky as if beseeching heavenly bodies for a boon before casting a net onto the surface of the ocean. The earthiness of the damp ground below mingling with the briny sea air and the pungency of kelps filled her nostrils as she inhaled a cleansing breath. She was well acquainted with the pain of unanswered pleas. Well, mayhap the tide was changing for them both.

When she caught the incessant tapping of her fingers on the side of the wagon, she pulled her hand back into her lap.

"I'll wager they don't even remember the name Beth MacRae after nineteen years." Breena fought against the agonizing emotions that flooded her every time she said her mother's name.

Craig's brown eyes looked back at her from beneath shaggy brows, the slight impatience that twitched his cheek muscles highlighting his wrinkles. "That's a wager I'll not be taking, for the price of losing is finding our necks at the wrong end of a noose."

George, her uncle's worker, flipped the reins up ahead with a sharp, practiced snap. A throaty intake of breath escaped his mouth. "Holy Saints. It looks haunted."

Breena's head snapped up to follow his gaze. The back of her neck prickled. Castle Carragh loomed grim on the horizon. George was as strong as a feral goat but simpleminded.

"There are no such things as ghosts," she said. But from her sudden inability to swallow, she wasn't sure she believed her own attempt to assuage his fears.

If the builders of this castle had meant to strike terror into its visitors, they'd carried out their goal to perfection. The shadows cast by Carragh against the backdrop of the setting sun stretched out toward them like crooked talons, warning them to keep away.

She ignored the warning and said a silent plea that they were not too late, that her father was still alive.

As they approached the castle's outer gates, Breena made out two menacing sentries dressed in threadbare tartan trews of blue and green, the colors of the Campbell clan. They were each outfitted with a sword, mace, and a flintlock rifle; were they preparing for war?

George pulled their wagon up closer to the gate, reined in the horses, and lowered his head, awaiting instructions. It always caused Breena such disquiet to see such a large man lower his head like that. She had known George for close to a decade, since he'd come to work for Craig, and despite his broad, hulking body he was the gentlest person Breena had ever met.

When one of the sentries at the gate brandished his sword, Breena's dry gulp refused to be suppressed. His flared nostrils and squinting eyes made his pugnacious expression more acute. Did he wish to intimidate them? If so, he'd gotten his wish. The other sentry snarled, exposing crooked incisors, as he scratched his crotch. Breena eased the tension in her face into what she hoped was a pleasant smile, even as her fingers curled against her damp palms. The squinty-eyed sentry scowled. "What's your business here?"

"I'm Craig Maxwell. I'm a healer and spice merchant. May we be of service to your clan?"

Neither Squinty Eyes nor Crooked Incisors was impressed by her uncle's request. Squinty Eyes spat on the ground, his scowl deepening. He sauntered to the back of their wagon and started sifting through their supplies. All of a sudden he lifted his sword high in the air and brought it down in an echoing crash on the lock of a trunk. Breena gasped out loud in surprise.

Craig jumped down from the wagon and stumbled toward Squinty Eyes. "I'll show you whatever you wish, but there's no cause to break our trunks."

Squinty Eyes raised his hand, still gripping the sword, and slammed the hilt down, with a dull thud, into Craig's jaw. Breena's body froze with horror. Her uncle teetered backward and fell to the ground, landing on his rump.

"Unc—Father!"

Dread rose up her gullet as she jumped down from the wagon, almost buckling at the knees, landing with more force than anticipated. She ignored the approaching thunder of hooves and rushed toward Craig. She couldn't lose him too. She just couldn't. She took hold of Craig's arms and helped him from the ground.

"Are you hurt?"

Her uncle's mouth was open, his gaze flat. She took some of his weight as he leaned against her. He was in shock. There was blood at the side of his mouth, at the end of an ugly cut, where he'd been struck. A sharp pang of fear speared her midriff as she reached into her pocket for a clean square of linen and, with a gentle touch, dabbed the blood away.

Her uncle's worker approached them with hesitant steps.

Breena sent him a cursory glance, noting the fear in his bulging eyes when he saw Squinty Eyes.

"George, why don't you remain with the horses?" Breena said.

His head bobbed. "Yes, mistress."

George understood horses, but he had difficulty with people.

She returned her attention to Craig. She took hold of her uncle's chin, avoiding the darkening bruise that was now a stark contrast to his pale skin. She inspected the wound as she gently followed his jaw line with her fingers all the way to his neck. Nothing broken. She closed her eyes and exhaled a breath of relief.

Craig was a graying man of eight and fifty with a slim build, whereas Squinty Eyes was younger and more than twice the size of her uncle. Breena ground her teeth when another drop of blood fell from Craig's mouth. Her pulse raced with heated indignation. How dare this barbaric bully strike Craig? How dare he block them from entering this atrocious castle? It's not as if there were endless visitors clamoring for entrance. Losing her parents and years of this aching void pushed her to retaliate. But she couldn't.

They were at the utter mercy of this insolent sentry to gain entrance to the Campbells' keep. He held their fate and her father's life in his hands, a fact he was utterly unaware of.

As she tended to Craig, a loud snigger pierced the air. She swung around to see Squinty Eyes dangling a gossamer shift off the tip of his sword, right above the now-broken trunk. He jutted his flaccid chin in Breena's direction as he addressed Craig.

"You let me have a roll in the hay with the lass and I'll let you in."

Breena's eyes narrowed at the crude proposition. The insult dug in. Her heart rate quickened as self-preservation and a survival instinct unfurled inside her. The heat of it spread throughout her entire body like a wave of sickness, making her shake. "You bastard."

Rationality went out the window as she took two steps forward and dealt a resounding slap across the sniggering face of Squinty Eyes. He was caught off guard, judging by the way his mouth fell open and his head jerked back. His odious stench made Breena want to pinch the tip of her nose shut and breathe through her mouth.

But then, coldness sank into her stomach. Oh no. No. What had she done? She blinked, trying to swallow against the rising bile, and stepped back.

She would never forgive herself if they were barred entrance because of her foolhardy actions. She'd never done anything like that before. What was the matter with her? The earlier mention of a noose burned her ears.

Squinty Eyes recovered. He grunted and swore as he grabbed her. His grip, like cold steel, dug into her soft flesh. He wrenched her right arm forward. Her mouth tightened with defiance as she glared at him. Even as her right shoulder was at risk of dislocating under his granite hold, she held her chin high. She would not give this bully the satisfaction of seeing her cower.

"You brazen wench, how dare you strike me?"

His eyes bulged, and spittle escaped from his mouth. She tugged and pulled to no avail as the pounding of horses' hooves reverberated in the air around them. Out of the corner of her eye, she glimpsed a towering, broad-shouldered Highland warrior dismounting from the blackest stallion she'd ever seen.

He stormed Squinty Eyes from behind.

CHAPTER
2

*E*gan Dunbar, future chief of the Dunbar clan, had always prided himself on his restraint of temper. This was crucial when commanding the most lethal retainers in the Highlands, men he trusted with his life and who now dismounted behind him in a sea of swirling tartan kilts and glinting weapons. It was a shock to Egan, however, that he now experienced difficulty with said vaunted control. Abhorrent behavior by the ornery Campbells shouldn't come as a surprise to him, but somehow it did.

His lips curled, and heat surged through his veins as he grabbed the wrist of the Campbell guard. With deft skill, cultivated while fostering under the warlord Angus MacDonell, he twisted it back toward the man's shoulders. He utilized the guard's natural mobility as leverage.

The man was gutless; why else would he manhandle a lass?

And not just any lass, but the MacIntyres' bonny healer.

Egan had met her several months ago on the Isle of Skye. The meeting was brief but had ignited an esteem within Egan. If it hadn't been for the battle and his subsequent trip to negotiate prisoner releases from the Tower of London, he might have pursued her. But it was just as well he'd been needed elsewhere, for his father would have forbidden him from consorting with a lowborn healer. Although Egan himself never quite understood the need for such division among the classes. Egan fortified his grip on the guard as his seconds-in-command Dougray and Keith advanced.

He gestured with his free hand. "Stand down." He wanted to enjoy a bit of practice after straddling his stallion Heimdall all day.

The guard bellowed as Egan raised the pressure. The man lowered his head and whimpered, still maintaining a grip on the lass's arm with his other hand. But he discovered if he moved even an iota, the grip Egan held him under hurt like the devil. Egan himself had made such a discovery years ago. His foster brothers, Daegan MacDonell in particular, had taken great pleasure in restraining him in similar grapples during endless training sessions.

Was it just a few days ago he'd been surrounded by the Highlands, with their abundance of light, fresh, clean air and snow-peaked bens that towered against the backdrop of bluish white skies? Truth be told, squelching through a smelly peat bog would be preferable to this macabre isle. The stench was unbearable, the scenery dull, and the people less trustworthy than masked highwaymen. But he had orders to follow, despite his reservations.

The Campbell guard ceased his squirms and bellowed, "Let go! Who are you? What the hell do you want from me?"

"I don't want anything from you. But I do wish to greet the lass you are in the process of mauling."

The guard shoved Breena away. She stumbled forward, then righted her step.

"Good man. How thoughtful of you to allow me to have a word with the lass."

Egan eased his grip on the guard then released. He eyed the man, who grunted and cradled his wrist. The guard's contorted expression eased. The pulsating rush of blood through Egan's own veins slowed. But he maintained sharp eye contact with the guard. From his peripheral vision he noted the second guard holding position at the gate. Excellent. He was more intelligent than his appearance suggested.

A crooked scowl stretched across on the spineless guard's face, which somehow managed to make his bulbous nose even rounder. "What's your business with the Campbells?"

The guard had relented, but he didn't like it.

Egan drew back his lips in a smirk. He ignored the guard's question, and he swung around to face the fair Breena. While she'd faced down the guard in spectacular fashion, like a Valkyrie, she could have been injured. She didn't appear asinine or reckless. Several months ago, she'd facilitated their taking on the redcoats at Duntulm. She had also nursed Daegan's then betrothed, now wife, Eva Drummond, back to health. Had it not been for Breena's potent sleeping concoction, administered to the redcoats' food, they would never have had the advantage that garnered their victory. He owed her.

He let his features ease into a smile as the memory of their first meeting sauntered into his head. He'd seen her flouncing in the woods, outside Castle Duntulm, at point-blank range of a rifle-wielding redcoat. Chivalry had been called for: he'd rescued her from the blackguard by knocking the man out with a cudgel-sized branch.

Now, what in Hades was a skillful healer like Breena doing on Coll?

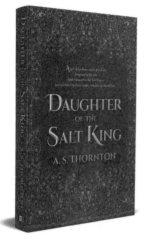
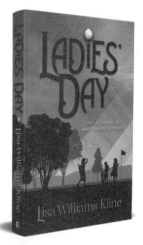
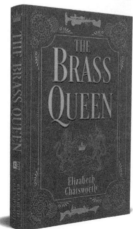

CamCat
Books

VISIT US ONLINE FOR MORE BOOKS TO LIVE IN:
CAMCATBOOKS.COM

SIGN UP FOR CAMCAT'S FICTION NEWSLETTER FOR
COVER REVEALS, EBOOK DEALS, AND MORE EXCLUSIVE CONTENT.

CamCatBooks   @CamCatBooks   @CamCat_Books   @CamCatBooks